2022

12/22

The Cross of Gallantry

A story about Marines in Vietnam who sacrificed, fought and died during combat operations along the DMZ in 1967-68.

Patrick M. Blake

Patrick M. Blake

AKNOWLEDGEMENTS

The Book Cover Photograph and Poem

The powerful image of "The Boots at the Wall" was discovered on the Vietnam Memorial website. Unfortunately, there is no information on the photographer who took this heart-wrenching picture. A sincere thanks to whoever took the photo and shared it on the Internet.

While looking for the creator of the photograph, I found the poem, "The Boots at the Wall" by Richard "Boon" Preston, another Marine Vietnam Vet – 3rd Battalion, 4th Marines 1966-67. Boon's poem is very moving and relevant to both the photo and *The Cross of Gallantry*. Many thanks to Boon for his beautiful poem and permission to use at the conclusion of the book.

Thanks to my editors

I am grateful for the expert editing provided by my friend, and fellow Vietnam Veteran, Bob Koehler. For over a year, Bob provided constructive and frequently humorous criticism, many recommendations for smoothing transitions in the story, and suggested re-writes for sections of the book. Bob's generous commitment of his time, comments, and advice has been invaluable.

Ken Forbes, a Marine buddy who served with me in 2nd Platoon in 1967-68, read the manuscript for accuracy and asked, "How do you remember the details after so many years?" I answered, "How do you forget?" Thanks Ken.

My Commanding Officer at my last Marine Corps duty station, now retired Brigadier General Pat McMillan, was kind enough to review the story, and correct details about the Marine Corps. I believe I am now "squared away." Thank you Sir.

I also appreciate the recommendations and edits provided by another Marine Vietnam veteran, Marshall N. Carter. His suggestions were very valuable and improved the overall story greatly.

I am fortunate to have the support of Nancy Navin, who always provides encouragement, feedback and detailed edits on the many iterations of the manuscript. Thank you Nancy for your patience and attention to details.

My marketing expert, Rich Navin, provided creative and innovative support in the preparation of the final manuscript for publication. Not a simple task, but Rich diligently worked through the final details to produce both the Kindle and paperback version of the book. Thank you Rich.

Research Source
Several more Marine buddies, friends and family read the manuscript and provided valuable feedback,

recommendations and suggestions. If I try to name each of you, I will certainly leave someone out. You know who you are, so I'd like to say many thanks to each of you for your help and encouragement.

The 3rd Marine Division and the 1st Battalion, 3rd Marine Regiment websites, helped provide details on dates and places. While in Vietnam, your world is limited to your buddies in your squad. You are not aware of, and you really don't care about, anything outside of your limited world. So details about operations, strategy, intelligence, etc., escape the typical grunt.

Author's Note

The Cross of Gallantry is a work of fiction, based on facts. I have tried to recreate events, locales and conversations from my memories and, in order to maintain anonymity in some instances; I have changed the names of individuals, identifying characteristics, and details such as physical properties. If there are mistakes in my account about military details, operations or battles, they are mine alone.

Dedicated to all the Fallen Heroes on the Wall

For Mike and the Marines of 2nd Platoon and Charlie Company
who died on January 19, 1968 in the battle on the DMZ,
Northeast Quang Tri Province, South Vietnam.

Their names are inscribed on Panel 34E on the Vietnam Memorial.

Visit the wall, touch them and say a prayer.

They will know you are there.

Patrick M. Blake

TABLE OF CONTENTS

Patrick M. Blake

FORWARD

Run to the sound of gunfire.

A Marine axiom

Over 14,000 Marines died in Vietnam, more than 51,000 were wounded, and about 230 are still missing in action. Most were between the ages of 17 to 22, and the vast majority of the Vietnam-era Marines were from modest or poor families. Growing up, they had been taught traditional American values like patriotism, duty, honor and courage. Most couldn't afford to go to college, and they didn't want to get married to avoid the draft. So they volunteered to join the Marine Corps and fight in Vietnam.

Vietnam combat veterans are part of a long line of American warriors who, throughout history, shared the experience of the horror of combat in their hearts and minds. Their achievements in the face of staggering adversity are comparable to battles fought and victories won by earlier generations of Marines at Belleau Wood,

Iwo Jima, Tarawa and the Chosen Reservoir. Often the very personal life and death struggles in Vietnam involved close combat. Marines were close enough to smell the fear, taste the adrenalin, hear the screams, and see the intensity in the eyes of their enemy.

Like many Vietnam combat veterans, I have been inextricably drawn to movies about the war. In 1979, I found myself sitting in a dark theater in Atlanta watching *The Boys from Company C*, a movie that was supposed to be about Charlie Company, 1st Battalion, 3rd Marines. It turns out that the movie was about my unit, and it supposedly portrayed actual events that took place during my tour in Vietnam. Watching *The Boys from Company C* was both surreal and infuriating to see how Hollywood twisted our proud and honorable service.

While Americans fought courageously and achieved victory on the battlefield, the war was lost in the streets of America and across the government of the United States. In 1968, even after the devastating defeat of the North Vietnamese and Viet Cong in the Tết Offensive, the tide of American support turned against the war and sadly, against the warriors. It is ironic that at the same time, the South Vietnamese government expressed its appreciation for the sacrifices, courage and victories of the III Marine Amphibious Force by presenting the Marines with the "Vietnamese Cross of Gallantry" unit commendation.

As the war was winding down and Americans began returning home, there were no parades to welcome home the returning warriors. After all, Vietnam was the first war America ever lost. The Vietnam combat veterans took the blame, endured the shame, and came home to a cold and isolated place we called "the world". The reality of our personal sacrifices and victories in battle were ignored. For most, returning home to anti-war marches, demonstrations, and protests was more painful than fighting in Vietnam.

The sharp pain of war experiences, and the antiwar sentiment and hostile reception received upon returning home has subsided over the years. Today, lingering images of wounded and dead Brothers return in the middle of the night. Sometimes the demons suddenly return even during the middle of the day. The nagging mystery of survival, of being alive, when so many others died, tears at your soul and breaks your heart. In quiet moments when alone, many warriors admit that they are grateful to be alive and confess, at least to ourselves, that I would rather be alive than to have been wasted like my Brothers. Quietly we carry our personal "cross of gallantry" in our hearts, souls and minds.

I am so grateful that today our country and America's citizens seem to have learned a lesson from Vietnam. We treat today's warriors with the respect, consideration and dignity that they so richly deserve. Thank God they are welcomed home and honored.

More needs to be done for them since they too suffer the scars of battle. I suspect many are dealing with the same haunting questions about survival and wondering why God spared them when their Brothers died. Like too many Vietnam veterans, sometimes the demons, the memories, nightmares, pain and guilt becomes too much, and today's young warriors commit suicide. An average of twenty-two American warriors die at their own hand each day. Sad, but I understand.

Those combat veterans who are overwhelmed and think of suicide should always remember why we fought the way we did. We wanted to live and we would die before letting our buddies down. So we, the survivors, owe it to our fallen Brothers to live and make the best of each day to honor their memory and the life they lost. We will all be back together soon enough.

My intent here is to provide an honest description of our experiences that took place in late 1967 and early 1968. The reader should remember that *The Cross of Gallantry* is a fact-based story about Marines in training and at war, so the language is authentic and often crude and coarse. I minimized the vulgarities, but the reality is that Marines have their own special vocabulary that can be offensive to the uninitiated.

The young Marines described in this book lived, struggled, suffered, fought and died together as Brothers in Vietnam. I want the reader to feel the unforgiving conditions, see the desolate places, experience the brutal battles, and gain some understanding of the lifelong impact of close combat. This is my recollection of how the Marines of 2nd Platoon, Charlie Company and the III Marine Amphibious Force earned their "Cross of Gallantry."

**The Vietnamese Cross of Gallantry
Unit Commendation Ribbon
Awarded to the III Marine Amphibious Force**

Patrick M. Blake

CHAPTER I – THE WALL

Memories, respect, sorrow, prayers and love.

Reflections of a combat veteran standing at the Wall

It was just after 6 o'clock in the morning when Frank walked through the hotel lobby and exited the door leading to 16th & K Street NW. It was miserable out – cold, windy and a slight drizzle. As he walked down the street, Frank buttoned his fleece-lined leather jacket up to cover his neck, pulled down the black knit watch cap over his ears, and set out into the morning's darkness. Frank would be celebrating his seventy-first birthday in February, and his pace was steady but a little slow -- unlike his early years when he was a conditioned, well-built strapping six-foot Marine grunt. After a few blocks, he turned right on Constitution Avenue, passed the Washington Monument and World War II Memorial, heading to his destination, the Vietnam Veterans Memorial.

The old habit of marching at the Marine regulation 30-inch steps at 120 steps per minute was still there. Frank remembered drilling troops, barking out almost unintelligible singsong sounds of a Marine cadence he had mastered when he returned home from Vietnam. He made the growling, staccato noise under his breath that sounded like "Laoo-riii-lao! Step yo lao, riii, lao, rii, leff!" Frank smiled and strained just a little to pick-up his pace to mirror his cadence. He made his boots pound the wet sidewalk with an old Marine's steady left-right-left marching cadence.

Every year, beginning January 19, 1969, Frank awoke before dawn to say his prayers, thanking God for sparing his life, honoring the sacrifices of his buddies, remembering his experiences, and meditating on his life since returning home from Vietnam. He always asked God why he had survived, and why God allowed him to live, when he should have been killed with his buddies during the firefight against the NVA on the DMZ that day in January, 1968. The events of that day haunted Frank – a sad mystery of his survival and a feeling of guilt for still being alive. God never answered Frank, so he kept praying and kept asking God why.

This year, business brought him to Washington, D.C. on January 19, and Frank was determined to go to the Vietnam Memorial Wall to visit his fallen buddies. The two-acre memorial was only about a 30 minute walk from his hotel, and the dark streets were mostly empty except for a few hard working cabbies looking for their first fare. Frank was enjoying the walk so he waved off the cabs. The old habit of scanning the dark around him and watching where he stepped was still with him.

As Frank approached the Vietnam Memorial, he

saw a homeless man sitting on a bench at the entrance to the sidewalk that leads to the Wall. A grocery store shopping cart was parked at the end of the bench with paper bags of empty cans, dirty bedding and assorted ragged cloths. Two broomsticks were tied to the front of the cart, standing straight up, one with the American flag and the other with the Marine Corps colors at the top of the improvised flagpoles.

The streets of Washington, like most major cities, have a large and growing population of homeless veterans, most from Vietnam. But too many were young vets scarred by their experiences fighting in Iraq and Afghanistan. Most suffered from post-traumatic stress and simply couldn't manage to separate the horrors of close combat and a return home to a normal life. After surviving battle, life is never the same.

The light from a street lamp shone down on the bench, and Frank could see that the homeless man wore a faded Vietnam era jungle utility jacket with metal Marine Sergeant stripes pinned on his lapels. He sipped steaming coffee from a regulation military canteen cup and stared straight ahead into the dark. Frank stopped, the vet looked up and their eyes met. "How's it going Sarge?" Frank asked.

"Couldn't be better," replied the old Marine. "Every day's a holiday and every meal is a banquet." They both laughed at the standard answer Marines have been giving for generations about living conditions in the Corps.

"What's your name?" Frank asked as he sat down next to him on the bench.

"Sergeant," said the Vet. Then he laughed and said, "Sam. Sam Johnson. From Houston."

"Frank O'Brian. From next door in Louisiana." They shook hands.

"I was with Charlie, 1/3, in 1967-68 on the DMZ," Frank said. It is important to pass inspection and confirm to other veterans that you are also one of them. Frank identified his infantry unit as C Company and 1st Battalion, 3rd Marine Regiment, a storied, highly decorated combat unit.

"Golf, 2/4," Sam replied. "I got dinged during Starlight in 1965. Forgot to duck." This meant that Sam was likely just a few years older than Frank. He had been in D Company, 2nd Battalion, 4th Marine Regiment during Operation Starlight, the first major search and destroy operation in Vietnam where Marines engaged hardcore VC battalions. The 2nd Battalion, 4th Marines were nicknamed "the Magnificent Bastards." Starlight was brutal. The operation cost the Marines over 50 dead and 200 wounded, while the VC lost over 600 dead and over 40 were taken prisoner.

They were quiet for a few moments. "Is there anything I can get you? Do you need anything?"

"Nah," said Sergeant Johnson. "I'm home here with them," gesturing toward the Wall. "Feels right to stand sentry. Me and the other homeless DC Marines take turns sitting on this bench, standing watch each month. Billy will take over in a few weeks."

Frank fully understood wanting to be near their buddies, and he appreciated having Marines watch over the fallen. He stood and turned to go. "Semper Fi" he said to the sentry.

"Semper Fi" said Sergeant Sam Johnson, "Semper Fi."

It was almost 7 o'clock when Frank walked down the sidewalk, past the stand holding the casualty book that contained the list of all 57,939 dead Americans. The index has their names, rank, branch of service, home of record, the date they died, and the panel where their names are etched in the wall. The book is protected from the weather in a plastic case with a light that allows evening visitors to look up the names of the fallen. Many vets prefer to visit the Wall after sundown when they have some privacy.

He turned and continued down the walk in front of the wall where night-lights shone up from the ground, illuminating the names of the fallen. He walked slowly, as the list of dead rose and grew from panel to panel starting with the first battlefield death in 1961. As the daily casualties grew through the 1960s the fallen peaked in May 1968 when 2,415 Americans died in a single month. The panels in the middle of the wall mark the highpoint in casualties.

On the other side of the peak, the wall angles off at 125 degrees and the list of names on each panel declines from May 1968 as casualties fell until the end of the war. The last American died in May 1975.

Frank stopped at Panel 34E where the names of his 2nd Platoon buddies were listed for January 1968. He found their names half way up the Wall. Seeing his reflection on the engraved panel, Frank whispered each of their names in reverence. He touched the cold stone, and could feel the letters of each name etched into the Wall. The tears flowed and his chest heaved. "Why," he wept softly. "Why them, and not me?"

The sickening memories rushed back, the deafening sounds, the rancid smells, and the vile taste in his mouth returned. He felt the hot burst of adrenaline that rose from the base of his spine and burst into the base of his brain as AK-47 bullets cracked past his head. He could still hear the explosions of grenades and the screams of fury and pain. The battle had lasted for an eternity.

Frank stepped back from the Wall and looked into the sky. Dawn was beginning to break through the clouds and cast a soft glow on the names on the Wall. Frank softy murmured a prayer, *thank you God for giving me all these years. I hope you have a good reason for saving my life.*

The rain started to fall in a slow, steady drizzle. The drops collected on the shiny face of the Wall and began to flow together forming small streams that ran to the ground. Frank thought the drops looked like tears that flowed from the face of the black wall. He was alone at the Wall that morning.

A police siren suddenly broke the silence. The rise and fall of the wailing siren brought back a tragic night in Vietnam.

"AhhHHHHHhhh. AAAAHHHHhhhhHHHH."

The siren sounded like the rise and pitch of a scream that Frank remembered had brought his battalion perimeter to full alert.

Frank's unit was providing perimeter security at

Alpha-3, one of the strong points being built on the DMZ. The only thing that separated the Marines' two man foxholes from the NVA was triple-strand concertina wire spread around their perimeter. The wailing in the middle of the night changed from "AhhhhHHHHHHaaaaa" to "NOOOOOOOOOO. NOOOOOOO!" And then it suddenly stopped.

Frank and Mike were best friends and foxhole buddies. They sat in the mud the following morning when "Frenchie", the veteran 2nd Platoon Sergeant made his rounds, checking on his Marines.

"What the fuck was that?" Frank asked. No need to be specific. Frenchie knew what Frank was asking about.

"The sin of sins," Frenchie spat. "Stupid shit in Delta Company fell asleep on watch while his buddy was asleep behind him in their foxhole. An NVA Sapper crawled through the wire and found that the guy on watch was asleep. So the Sapper crept by him, slipped into the foxhole and slit his buddy's throat."

"Damn. Damn," said Mike. Everyone who stands watch at night in the bush has to fight to stay awake. Physical exhaustion and the continuous lack of sleep take an unimaginable toll on Marines in combat.

"Yea," said Frenchie, with a weary sigh. "And his failure to stay awake and protect his buddy will haunt that poor bastard for the rest of his life."

Frank was relieved and grateful when the police siren stopped. He returned the image of Alpha-3 to that lock-box of memories where he stored his Vietnam experiences. Frank stood staring at the wall for a long time. He liked being close to his buddies. Frank thought back about how he got to Vietnam, almost 50 years earlier, smiled and shook his head.

CHAPTER II -- THE MAKING OF A MARINE

The Marine Corps is a family. At Parris Island we teach family values.

A Marine Drill Instructor in the mid-1960's.

Welcome to Parris Island

It was April 1967, and more than 400,000 Americans were fighting in Vietnam. Frank O'Brian sat on a crowded Greyhound bus as it rolled out of the Charleston Bus Station and began the short trip down the South Carolina coast to the Marine Corps Recruit Depot at Parris Island. He was like most other recruits: 17 or 18, just out of high school, and away from home for the first time. They were from all over the east coast, some from the north, but most like Frank were from the south. His blue jeans and short sleeve shirt were soaked with perspiration in the stifling heat, and Frank opened the window a crack to let in some fresh air before lighting another cigarette.

"Aw shit!" said the guy sitting next to him. He crushed an empty pack of Camels and dropped it on the floor. "Hey, buddy. I'm outta cigarettes," he drawled. "You got an extra smoke?"

Frank looked over at the dark haired, stocky kid and said, "Sure, here you go, I've got plenty."

"Thanks," he said, examining the cigarette. "Glad you smoke my brand. I'm Mike Morgan," he continued, lighting up his cigarette and extending his hand, "I live in Georgia but my folks live in Oklahoma."

"Frank O'Brian, from Louisiana."

"Wish we'd hurry up and get there."

"We'll get there soon enough."

"The sooner we get there, the quicker we get through," Mike offered, exhaling a cloud of smoke, flipping ashes on the floor.

"I know it's gonna be a real bitch," Frank said. "A friend of mine joined last year and came home tellin' all kinds of wild stories about basic training at Parris Island."

"Yeah I've heard some stuff, too."

The bus pulled up to a brightly lit gate where a boldly lettered red sign announced they had arrived at Parris Island. A Marine guard at the gate waved the bus through with a grin, and it continued down a narrow roadway, bordered on both sides by swampy waters that shone in the moonlight.

They stared out the window as they passed two-story wooden barracks that sat back from the road, and street lamps that lit an asphalt parade ground where a statue of the Marines raising the flag at Iwo Jima stood. The bus turned right and the white barracks gave way to three-story red brick buildings. They stopped in front of a sign that read *Receiving Barracks*, and the recruits could see row after row of yellow footprints painted on the sidewalk next to the bus. The driver swung open the door and everyone went quiet as a big black Sergeant wearing a broad-brimmed felt hat, called a "Smokey the Bear" hat, climbed aboard. They were now going to be introduced to a Marine Drill Instructor, or "DI", at the Receiving Barracks.

"You maggots got just thirty seconds to get off this goddamn bus and fall in on the footprints outside!" he bellowed. "The last man off better give his soul to God, because his ass is mine. Now Move! Move! Move!"

There was a mad scramble for the door as Frank and Mike pushed and shoved until they got off and found an empty set of footprints. Frank noticed the yellow footprints he was standing in were larger than his shoes so he shuffled his feet until they looked like they were centered. He thought the angry DI would like that and leave him alone.

They stood at rigid attention and looked straight ahead as the Sergeant caught the last guy off the bus and attacked him. "You think you are on vacation sweet pea?" The last man scrambled to escape the enraged DI and find an empty set of yellow footprints.

"You look like a momma's baby," the drill instructor screamed at an unfortunate slow moving, short, fat and trembling recruit. The "multicolored stinking mob of civilian scum" was herded inside the barracks where two angrier, bad-tempered sergeants ordered "the maggots" to sit at attention in schoolroom-like desks. The process of losing their identity began as each recruit was assigned a service number, told to "shut up" and to begin filling out what seemed like an endless number of forms.

"Hey Sarge, I got to take a piss," said a Spanish looking guy with a New York accent.

Big, big mistake! The DI attacked, shrieking at the unsuspecting kid from the Bronx in a sudden verbal assault that caused the Bronx kid to pee in his pants. The unlucky recruit finally got to go to the bathroom, or the "head" as the crazy man corrected, where the Spanish guy dried his jeans with paper towel as best he could.

Filling out endless paper work followed – once the Sergeants stopped screaming at the recruits.

> *Name:* O'Brian, Francis Mahoney, *Age:* 18
> *Height:* 6' *Weight:* 165 *Eyes:* brown *Hair:*
> black *Home of record:* Alexandria, Louisiana
> *Family:* Father deceased. Mother living.
> Two older brothers, *Education:* high school
> graduate, 1967.

At the end of one of the forms, they asked for "emergency contact" information and the Sergeants explained this is the person you want the Marine Corps to notify "when you get killed." Frank put down the contact details for his two older brothers, not his Mother.

Mike hated forms and was worried about misspelling some of the information.

> *Name:* Morgan, Michael, John, *Age:* 18
> *Height:* 5'10" *Weight:* 160 *Eyes:* brown *Home*

of record: Macon, Georgia   *Family*: Mother and Uncles.   No brothers or sisters *Education*: high school graduate, 1967.

They took a standard psychological test that the Sergeant said was designed to separate the sex perverts and deviates from the normal guys. Everyone was required to draw a picture of a man and woman. Frank sat for a few minutes trying to decide what he should draw. He wasn't an artist and didn't want to risk being accused of being a sex pervert. So he drew stick figures. Mike, sitting next to him, peered over, played it safe, and copied Frank's drawings.

One of the recruits from New Orleans decided to impress the DI with his gift for drawing. He made the mistake of drawing a voluptuous long hair, long legged beauty lying on her back. Her right arm was extended, and she was "giving the finger". Needless to say, the DI reviewing the drawing took it very personally.

"You one sick maggot, aren't you," bellowed the DI who seemed to like the drawing, but was officially offended by the figure. The drawing caused the New Orleans recruit to be separated and isolated from the "mob" because, as the DI announced to the other recruits, "this maggot needs a serious medical evaluation by a Navy shrink to determine his fitness to be a Marine."

After three hours of paper work, the mob was driven upstairs with screamed insults and threats to a squad bay area, lined with rows and rows of double bunk beds. One of the DIs stood at the door and screamed for them to "lay down and shut up!" Then the barrack lights were suddenly turned out. Frank just lay there, not moving a muscle, but listening to every strange sound and threatening noise in the building.

It was still dark outside when suddenly the lights were turned on and total bedlam followed. Under a constant barrage of yelling and screaming from the DIs, the recruits only had time to throw on clothes, make a quick "head call" to relieve bursting bladders, and run across the street to the mess hall. The breakfast chow included globs of steaming creamed beef, slopped on top of burned pieces of cold toast, universally known as Shit on a Shingle, or simply "SOS". In less than ten minutes, the DIs chased all of them outside to another set of yellow footprints.

Waiting near the mess hall, Frank saw three other DIs who looked different from the crazy DI in the Receiving Barracks. They were also wearing Smokey the Bear type hats, and they casually watched the commotion as the confused recruits were arranged in alphabetical order in what was referred to as a platoon formation. The DIs talked quietly among themselves, pointing out different recruits and shaking their heads, laughing occasionally. Their khaki uniforms were sharply creased, and all wore several rows of multi-colored ribbons on their chest, indicating they'd served in Vietnam. They were tall, lean and each wore a thick shiny black belt with a huge gold Marine Corps emblem on their belt buckle.

The Sergeant in charge of the Receiving Barracks checked all the names on a clipboard one final time before handing it over to one of the DIs. The three DIs swaggered over to the Platoon, and strolled through the formation, cocky and self-confident, inspecting each recruit carefully. No one moved as the DI with the clipboard stepped up in front of the group and put his hands on his hips. The expression on his face was complete disgust.

"My name is Staff Sergeant Brooks and I'm your Drill Instructor." He had a loud gravelly voice with a slight southern drawl. "When you were at home, your momma told you what to do and when to do it. Now that you are at Parris Island – I'm your Momma."

His penetrating stare went through the Platoon like a razor as the other two drill instructors took up positions on his left and right. "From now on," he growled, "you'd best do exactly what you're told to do, when you're told to do it, and you'd best do it right the first time! If you don't learn to do what you're told, I can promise you that you'll die in Vietnam." He paused and let his words sink in.

Holy shit! If he's trying to scare the hell out of us, he's doing a damn good job, Frank thought.

"I'll tell you when to eat, sleep, shit, shower, scratch your ass, pick your nose, go to church, write letters, and everything else," he snarled. "You're gonna learn discipline. You'll learn to do what you're told without question, without hesitation, and without mistakes." "Discipline," he bellowed, emphasizing each syllable, "is the only thing that will save your miserable life!"

He paused, and then began stalking back and forth in front of the group, his eyes constantly searching the ranks, never blinking.

"Every time you open your slimy mouth, the first

and last word out will be *Sir*. Do I make myself clear, ladies?" he hissed. And then slowly yelled each word, *Do...I...Make...Myself...Clear?*

There was a disorganized chorus of "Yes Sir, Sir and Sir, Sir Yes!" This less than enthusiastic response infuriated all three DIs.

"Damn, ladies! Let's try to do it right! Okay?" sneered one of the other DIs. "Try answering, *Sir, Yes Sir!*"

"Sir, Yes Sir," mumbled the scared shitless recruits.

"Louder and together, goddammit!" he screamed.

"Sir, Yes Sir!" they screamed in unison.

"This is Sergeant Gates." Brooks pointed to an especially mean looking Sergeant with bulging arms covered in tattoos. "And this is Sergeant Fritz," he said, pointing toward the other barrel-chested sergeant. "They are your Junior Drill Instructors, and in the next eleven weeks, we are supposed to turn you maggots into a platoon of Marines. Don't think for a second that just because you're here at Parris Island that you are Marines. You're not! Most of you will fall out, fail, quit, get an undesirable discharge and be sent home to your Momma. You're the lowest form of life in the universe! You're lower than whale shit on the bottom of the ocean!"

That seemed to be the signal for havoc to strike. In unison, all three DIs attacked the unsuspecting "mob." They ran through the formation, screaming, kicking, choking and punching everybody. Frank froze as Sergeant Gates ran past him, smacking everyone in the face. He stopped in front of Mike. Now only inches away from his face, Gates shrieked at the top of his lungs. "You! What's your name Sugar Tit?"

"Mike Morgan." But a sudden right jab in the stomach cut Mike off, causing him to bend over and gasp for air.

"What's the first and last word outa your stinkin' mouth you idiot?"

"Sir, my name is Mike Morgan, Sir," he gasped.

"Wrong dummy, the DI shouted. I'm not interested in being your friend, so I don't care about your fuckin' first name. I'm not your buddy so try, *Sir, the private's name is Private Morgan, Sir.*"

Frank stood at attention next to Mike, watching Gates out of the corner of his eye.

"What are you eye ballin' me for Sugar Tit? You think I'm cute? You queer for my gear or somethin?" Gates bellowed into Frank's face

"No Sir. I don't think you're cute." A kick in the shins cut off the rest of his answer.

"What's the first word out of your mouth, maggot?" Gates roared.

"Sir, no Sir. I don't think you're cute."

Gates jabbed a set of steel-like fingers into Frank's stomach, making him gasp. "You! You! Who you callin *you*? You called me *you*!"

Frank didn't understand what Gates was screaming about. He gagged when Gates grabbed him by the throat and began choking him. His eyes were wide and bulging.

"A ewe is a female sheep! Do I look like a goddamn female sheep! Do I smell like a sheep? Do I say *bah* like a sheep? Huh? Huh?" Gates screamed like a mad man, spittle flying from his mouth while shaking Frank like a rag doll.

"Sir, no sir! Sir, no sir!" Frank gasped over and over.

"What's your God damn name, shitbird?" Gates screamed at him again.

"Sir, the private's name is Private O'Brian, Sir," Frank croaked.

"Sergeant Brooks!" Gates bellowed.

Brooks reluctantly left the other side of the Platoon where other recruits were getting the same treatment. Brooks strolled up to Frank, and Gates began to explain. "I found him! I found him! This is the one! This is another one of those communist infiltrators sent down here to fuck up my Marine Corps."

"You a commie, puke?" Brooks screamed.

"Sir, no Sir. I'm not a communist, Sir!"

"You calling me a liar, asshole?" Gates growled.

"Sir, no Sir!"

Gates jabbed him in the stomach again with a sudden karate stab.

"You wet your bed, pinko?" Brooks snarled.

"Sir, no Sir!" Frank gasped.

"You a faggot, commie?" Brooks barked.

"Sir, no Sir!"

Brooks and Gates discussed Frank's answers and decided he was obviously lying. If he wasn't lying, that meant Sergeant Gates was lying, and that was impossible! Therefore, Private O'Brian was obviously a pinko, commie, bedwetting faggot, and the DIs discussed various ways to kill O'Brian right there on the spot. But the DIs announced that they would have to wait to kill him when they had more privacy. They said they didn't want anyone to see them when they choked O'Brian to death.

Oh my God, Frank thought, terrified, *They're gonna kill me! This is a mad house, an asylum! These guys hate me! My God! What have I done? What the hell am I doing here?*

Boot Camp – Day One

It was just barely dawn when the DIs finally stopped bashing, battering and belittling the recruits. They herded the shaken group with more screams, shoves and occasional kicks across a parade field, through several narrow streets, until they reached a barn-like aluminum warehouse.

"Getty up mob. Say *Moo* like multicolored cattle, you useless pukes," screamed Gates.

"Moo…Moooo…Moooooo," shouted the bewildered recruits.

"Hippity hop, mob stop!" Brooks barked in disgust. "Whoa herd! Stop walkin', goddammit!" The columns of staggering recruits stumbled to a stop.

Inside the warehouse, the "maggots" were issued laundry bags, soap, toothpaste, deodorant, shaving gear, writing material and other items essential to clean and comfortable living. They held each item up in the air so the Sergeants could check and make sure everybody got everything they might need, and then the items were stuffed into the laundry bag.

"The last thing that you may have, but will never

use are cigarettes!" barked the supply sergeant.

Brooks and the other DIs prowled around the ranks, laughing and making promises that anybody who chose to get cigarettes would never live to smoke one.

Frank stood across from Mike and exchanged a quick smile.

"Alright, now. Who wants cigarettes?" asked the supply sergeant.

Frank, Mike, and a few other guys raised their hands, which brought them immediate attention from the DIs.

"Hey Sergeant Brooks, the communist thinks he's going to live long enough to get a smoke!" Gates screamed into Frank's ear.

The Supply Sergeant walked around throwing cartons of Camels at the heads of the hand raisers. Frank and Mike stuffed their cigarettes into the laundry bags.

At the other end of the warehouse, Frank stood in line with the other recruits, worrying about being murdered, until it was his turn to get a haircut. In less than thirty seconds, the barber scalped Frank down to the bare skin, his dark brown hair falling into a growing pile on the floor, while the DIs watched, howling with laughter. Laughing, Sergeant Gates looked at all of the baldheads streaming out the door and yelled, "you're the ugliest, most pathetic bunch of maggots I ever saw. Your Momma wouldn't even recognize you!"

At the warehouse, they took quick showers to "wash off some of that civilian crud" before being issued a sea bag filled with green fatigues, skivvy shirts and shorts, combat boots and dress shoes. While Gates ran around screaming at the top of his lungs for everyone to hurry up, Frank quickly put on a green utility uniform that didn't fit, and struggled to lace his boots.

Frank had noticed the DIs, just like those Marines in the movies and on recruiting posters, had their trousers stuffed into the top of their boots. Frank thought they looked really sharp, so he bloused the cuffs of his trousers in the top of his boots. This was a huge mistake!

Just to let Sergeant Gates know there were no hard feelings about their earlier misunderstanding about Frank being a communist, Frank walked over to Sergeant Gates and said "Hey, Sarge, how's this look? Pretty good, Huh?"

Frank locked his heels and stiffened at the position of attention, as Gates began to rain down blows on him. When Gates started choking him, Frank realized that Gates didn't want to make up.

"Now, I'm gonna kill your worthless communist ass! You filthy faggot puke!" Gates screamed. His eyes were wild, filled with hate, as he jabbed, kicked, punched, and choked Frank until Frank's eyes began to water.

Frank's mind was a blur. *They are all crazy bastards!*, Frank thought. *I could take that Gates! No, I couldn't! He's sadistic* – gasping for breath in between blows – *Gates likes to hit on people. I wanna kill him! He'll kill me! Nah - any one of them could pound me into a pulp. If I swing, one of them will send me to the hospital. Shit! I've got to stand here and take this crap!*

Gates consulted Brooks and Fritz about Frank, and they decided to delay the "execution" until later. They kicked him in the butt, as he escaped into the bright sunlight outside, carrying his sea bag over his shoulder. He bumped into another totally confused looking private on his way out, but didn't recognize him until they were both standing at attention in formation. The grotesque looking recruit was Mike.

It had taken all morning for them to lose their identity as individuals and complete the initial transformation into becoming Marine recruits. The DIs shouted and yelled at a frantic pitch as the Platoon ran to a different mess hall for lunch. They marched into chow, but their misery continued as they ate in silence, at the position of attention, with hundreds of other new recruits. And they all had the same scared expression.

The DIs didn't stop to eat. They were busy roaming around from table to table, screaming and throwing food on the floor or at the recruits. Frank escaped their attention, but Mike sitting across from him was not as lucky.

Sergeant Fritz didn't like the way Mike was eating, and concluded Private Morgan was a hog, not a human being. He insisted that Mike eat like a real hog, so he poured milk all over Mike's mashed potatoes, peas, and sliced beef. After mixing it all into mush, the DI forced Mike to eat it all with his hands before leaving the table. Frank looked at Mike and thought, *My God, is it going to be like this every day?*

Early that afternoon, the Platoon stripped to their skivvy shorts and stood in neat rows, facing one another at a base dispensary, or "sick bay". A white-coated Navy corpsman marched down the alphabetically arranged rows, painting bold numbers on bare chests with a paintbrush soaked in mercurochrome. Frank had a red *35* painted on his chest and Mike, who was standing just down and across from him, sported a bright *28*. The DIs patrolled the rows and watched carefully for anyone who might want to eye ball the proceedings.

At the end of the row facing Frank, another corpsman came along with a tray filled with needles and syringes used for taking blood samples. Each recruit held out a stiff right arm as the corpsman found a vein and jabbed in the needle. After the blood began to flow into the vial, the corpsman waited impatiently for the vial to fill.

The next recruit would "eye ball" the flowing blood and anxiously wait for his turn. After finishing with each recruit, the corpsman wiped away the excess blood with a cold, alcohol-soaked cotton swab.

The third guy to get the treatment was skinny, scared, and his knees were visibly shaking. With the DIs watching closely, the corpsman smiled, jabbed the needle in and got the blood flowing. Both the corpsman and the DIs began to exchange looks and grin. Then the DIs began to laugh and jeer as the kid looked down at the blood flowing out of his arm into the clear vial. The recruit's eyeballs rolled back into his head and he fell backwards. No one tried to catch the recruit as he crashed against a radiator, with the blood from the syringe now running down his arm.

The DIs were on the half-conscious recruit instantly.

"Get up you sissy! Don't you die on me! Get up

you wasted maggot!" the DIs screamed at the semiconscious kid.

The skinny kid struggled to his feet as the DIs continued to scream into his ears. The corpsmen busied themselves with more jabbing of needles, laughing occasionally. Before the blood gathering was over, three other guys fainted. Frank was grateful he wasn't one of them.

After the visit to the sick bay, the recruits returned to the white wooden World War II-era barracks where earlier they had dropped off their bulging sea bags. They stowed their gear quickly in wooden locker boxes at the foot of their bunks, and rushed back outside, falling into formation again.

After another dehumanizing meal at the same mess hall, they returned to the barracks where they were given "instructions" on how to make a bed the "Marine Corps" way. There was a lot of screaming, hitting, ripping up of bunks, and endless push-ups for everyone. At nine o'clock, they were told to take ten minutes for showers and get ready for bed.

As Frank ran down the squad bay towards the bathroom, or "head", he read a boldly printed sign hanging over the doors leading to the DI's quarters.

Ask not what your Country can do for you,
Ask what you can do for your Country.

Dazed and utterly exhausted, he showered quickly and returned to his bunk. Mike was across from him, working frantically, trying to get his toilet gear put back in his locker box before the DIs ordered them all back in front of their bunks.

Standing at attention in front of their bunks, with sweat dripping down, they recited the *Lord's Prayer*, sang the *Marines' Hymn, From The Halls of Montezuma...To The Shores of Tripoli...,* and then said "good night" to a retired Marine hero named Chesty Puller. The lights were turned out, and they all crashed into squeaking bunks.

They had been ordered to sleep at the position of attention, and Frank lay ramrod stiff in his bunk thinking, *I gotta get outta this mad house. These guys are crazy. Communist? I'm no damn communist! Hittin', chokin', kickin' everybody. Ask not what you can do for your country. Fight for right and freedom. Our Father who art....Good night Chesty Puller, whoever and wherever you are.* Frank finally curled up on his side and fell into a deep sleep.

Forming

It seemed like only a few minutes passed when the silence of the pitch-black squad bay was shattered with the crash of heavy metal bouncing down the middle aisle of the bay, and raging howls as the lights came on.

"Get up! Get up! Get up ladies! Move! Move! Move!" the DIs screamed.

Frank threw himself out of his bunk and rushed to stand in front of it, where he found an empty garbage can resting against a post. Mike had obviously been too slow getting up, because Sergeant Fritz was in the process of yanking and dragging him out of his bunk. Other slow recruits were crawling out from under their overturned bunks as the DIs continued to yell and scream at them.

After endless push-ups for being too slow, there was another period of instruction on how to make your "rack" or bed. Everybody had his rack torn up at least twice before the DIs were satisfied. There was another ten-minute dash to the head, and Frank forgot about washing his face or brushing his teeth as he made a beeline for the commode. He was just pulling up his trousers as time ran out, and this extra few seconds cost Frank a few swift jabs in the stomach from Sergeant Fritz.

On command, the recruits burst out of the squad bay doors into the black morning and tried desperately to line up in formation. The DIs added to the chaos with screams and shoves.

"You ladies are supposed to fall-in at the position of attention!" roared Brooks. He stood dressed in utility trousers, a white skivvy shirt, Smokey the bear hat, and spit shined boots. He waited patiently as Gates and Fritz finished working over the last two guys who ran out of the barracks.

"Riiiiii Faaaa. Turn to the right you dumb ass!" he barked. "Fooooard Huh! Step off with your left foot, goddamn it!"

Gates and Fritz ran through the out-of-step, staggering mob, kicking and jerking the confused recruits into some semblance of order, as they headed for the parade field.

Marching as best he could next to Mike, Frank kept thinking, *Oh God! What'd he say? What'd he say? What'r they gonna do now? Oh God!*

Marine marching cadence is a sound totally unique to the Corps. Nowhere else can you hear the staccato, growling and intimidating sound of a non-commissioned officer, especially a Drill Instructor, barking and sometimes singing cadence. "Left face, right face, left face" is a garbled sound of "Le Faaaa", "Ri Faaaa", "Le Faaaa" that takes time to understand and respond to. Each command to turn right or left is often a snarl that communicates a threat to get it right. Frank could hear the chorus of other s in the darkness of the parade field marching and running as their DIs called their own personal and unmistakable sound of Marine cadence.

"Cooooolmmm Rii! Huh! Turn to the right for Christ Sake!" The Platoon moved toward the parade field in a disjoined, galloping movement.

"Lao-Ri-Lao-Ri-Left" sang Brooks. He blurred the words "left, right left" into his totally unique sound that was neither sung nor barked. Just trying to march in step at a walking pace was about to get worse.

"Duuuubltiii! Huh! Damn it. Move your asses! I said run! Duuubltii! Duuubltii!" Frank glanced over at Mike and they both shook their heads, totally confused. How could "Duuubltii" possibly mean "double time" or run? And how fast should they run?

Gates and Fritz were kicking recruits in the rear of the Platoon, so the recruits in the back got the message and picked up the cadence before the dumb-founded recruits in the front of the Platoon. This caused a chaotic stampede of bodies slamming into each other in the dark as they stumbled forward, trying to escape the DIs. Gates and Fritz continued to push, kick and shove the recruits in front of them. Brooks was approaching hysteria by the time all sixty plus recruits started running.

"Le. Ri. Le. Ri. Le. Le. Ri. Le. Ri. Le. Get in step you worthless maggots! Le. Ri. Le. Ri. Le. Oh shit! I can't believe this! Screw it! Getty up! Getty up, you goddamn mob," screamed Gates.

In the middle of the Platoon, Frank tried to run along with everybody else, but nobody was in step. Fritz kept slapping him on the back of the head every time his right foot hit the ground. The DI was screaming, "Le! Le! Le!" and eventually Frank changed step and skipped along until his left foot hit the ground when Fritz slapped him in the back of his head. Then Fritz stopped slapping him. He moved on to give "instructions" to the next out-of-step recruit in front of Frank.

The mob managed to run around the parade field, about a mile and a half, in the dark, stumbling and crashing into each other. The DIs continued to bark unintelligible cadence, kicking and screaming at the "maggots". Blessedly, they finally stopped on the "whoa" command like a herd of horses. They were in front of the mess hall where the smell of breakfast was in the air.

Breakfast, again "Shit on a Shingle", followed the morning run, but no one ate much. The "SOS" looked like vomit, and most of the recruits were about to throw-up anyway.

The rest of the morning hours were filled with clumsy attempts to march, taking aptitude tests, and then dental examinations. The DIs were constantly furious at the entire Platoon, as well as each individual recruit. It was impossible to do anything right, and the constant threat of punishment hung over everyone.

After lunch, the Platoon dressed in red shorts, gold T-shirts with *USMC* painted on the front, and red baseball caps. They ran across the parade field to the physical training area, where the DIs announced the Physical Training test, or "PT," would demonstrate how weak each pathetic maggot really was.

The PT test began with each recruit doing as many "pull-ups" on the overhead parallel bars as he could. As Brooks and Gates looked on, Frank was in good shape, and he did five quickly and correctly. Mike followed with six pull-ups that also seemed to get the approval of the DIs.

There were several guys in the Platoon who were overweight and in poor physical condition. They jumped up and grabbed the overhead bars to do their pull-ups. They could only hang there, unable to do even one pull-up.

When the DIs saw this, they pounced. "You fat-ass pussy! You can't do one damn pull-up! How in God's green earth do you think you'll ever be a Marine?" screamed Brooks.

Gates got a real kick out of the fat guys struggling and squirming on the parallel bars. He jeered, laughed, and tried to "help" them by grabbing their fat rolls around their waists and pushing them up. When it became obvious they weren't able to do one pull-up, Gates made them hang on the bar until they finally fell to the ground.

Frank and Mike quickly ran on to the other PT

events, and they both successfully completed the required number of sit-ups and push-ups. As the "fat bodies" struggled from event to event, the DIs continued abusing them, calling them every name in the book: *Pigs, Hogs, Cows,* and *Fat-Ass Pussies.* A thousand meter run ended the tests, and the platoon formed up to run back to the barracks. However, the seven unfortunate recruits who had failed their PT test, were forced to straggle along behind the formation in a dejected herd, mooing like cattle.

Back at the barracks, the DIs inflicted ingenious punishment on the entire Platoon because seven "fat-body" recruits had failed their first PT test. Brooks ordered everyone down into the push-up position. Frank's already worn out arm muscles trembled under the weight of his body, as Brooks, Gates and Fritz lashed out at the prone bodies with insults and kicks.

"We don't have seven fat bodies in this pathetic excuse for a Platoon! The whole wasted bunch of you are nothin' but a bunch of momma's babies!" bellowed Gates.

As the minutes ticked by, several guys fell to the floor in exhaustion, which earned them a shower of kicks. Frank looked across at Mike who remained steady. They exchanged pained grimaces. Each one was thinking, *I'm not going to quit! I'm not going to quit!*

"Alright! Everybody, back to the position of attention," Gates commanded. "Sergeant Brooks, I think we've been too hard on these ladies."

Frank closed his eyes as the sweat continued to pour down his face, and he thought, *I needed a big drink of water, and just a minute to lie down and recover.* But Frank had the feeling that Gates was about to go "one up" on Brooks.

"Maybe you're right." Brooks laughed as he and Fritz swaggered to opposite ends of the squad bay.

"Why don't we all just watch a little television?" Gates continued. "These girls just look all worn out."

Gates ordered everybody back down on their "gutless bellies", and for just a split second Frank enjoyed the relaxation of laying down.

"Now put your toes on the deck just like you were going to do push-ups. Put your thumbs behind your ears and your elbows under your head, just like you were watching television on the living room floor back home," Gates continued as Brooks and Fritz laughed.

Frank's arm muscles began to cramp as he put his thumbs behind his ears and his elbows dug into the wooden floor. He flexed and relaxed them, desperately trying to make the cramps go away.

"Oh, I almost forgot. To make you ladies nice and comfortable while you watch TV, push your bodies up in the air just like the push-up position, but this time, rest on your elbows and toes." Amidst groans and grunts, Brooks and Fritz began screaming, "Get em up! Get em up! Get your miserable dead asses up!"

Frank gritted his teeth and strained to contort his body into the proper position. The pain that shot up from his elbows was excruciating, and it almost buried the pain from his cramped back muscles. "Watching television", as the DIs laughing called it, caused all of his muscles to quiver under the stress. In an attempt to forget his own misery, Frank began to stare at Mike struggling across from him. It was almost like watching TV -- but not quite.

Frank knew that if he quit, and if he couldn't take the abuse from the DIs, he would end up being thrown in with the pathetic "fat bodies". He would be just another out of shape, weak, unfit recruit that needed to be weeded out and sent home to "Momma".

Time stood still for the recruits as the DIs ranted and raved about the failure of the seven "fat bodies". "Quitters get people killed in combat. This Platoon doesn't need any weak sisters!" Gates yelled.

Finally, after what seemed like hours, Gates ordered the Platoon back to their feet. Frank stood trembling at the position of attention while Gates called each of the seven fat bodies to assemble at the end of the squad bay. "These maggots are weak, like this one puke that was in my Platoon in Nam," Gates growled. His contorted face was almost touching the ear of one of the fat bodies. "And because he quit on us in the middle of a firefight, my best buddy was wasted. He got his head blown off."

Gates began to throw right jabs into the fat guy's stomach, and the third thump to the solar plexus sent the shaking recruit to the floor. "You're not fit! You don't belong here! You can never be a Marine! I'll kill you before I see you graduate from boot camp!" Gates roared.

While Gates started the same routine on the next "fat body", Brooks and Fritz fell on the kneeling, gasping recruits, screaming and kicking them.

Frank stared across the squad bay at a spot on the wall, unable to look at Mike, and not believing the ferocity of the attacks. With the DIs occupied, he cautiously shook his arms to help his muscles relax.

As Gates finished knocking the wind out of the last fat body, Brooks and Fritz made the seven recruits get down on their hands and knees, and crawl around the squad bay. On command, they mooed like cows. They were then ordered to scream at the top of their lungs, "we are fat bodies! We aren't fit! We are quitters! We aren't fit!"

After this procession had made several tours around the squad bay, Gates ordered the seven to pack their gear. They were leaving the Platoon, and being sent to the Special Training Battalion, or STB, which was equipped to deal with "unfit recruits".

Unbeknown to the Platoon, a few of the first training objectives had been achieved by the DIs. The recruits had been stripped of their individual identity. The entire group had been thrown into a state of shock and confusion by the constant stream of abuse. The weak and unfit recruits had been separated from the unit. The remaining recruits were now bound together as "survivors", who now collectively feared and hated the DIs.

The "survivors" also knew that they had to successfully complete boot camp because there was no escape from Parris Island. It was completely surrounded by swamps, where pools of quicksand, nests of poisonous snakes and alligators waited. The only way to get on or off the island was by Greyhound bus and the causeway leading to the gate. The only choice was to survive until graduation day.

During these first two weeks, what the DIs called

"forming", Frank and Mike adjusted, while several recruits failed. As the training pace intensified, Frank began to respond to screamed commands automatically, without thinking.

Ethos and Religion

The DIs taught indoctrination classes on the history and traditions of the Marine Corps. From the founding of the Corps in 1775, to battles fought and won in the World Wars, to Korea, and now, Vietnam. They emphasized the motto of the Marine Corps, *Semper Fidelis*, which they explained was Latin for "Always Faithful." The recruits were taught that a Marine's loyalty is to God, country and the Corps, in that order. By adopting these shared values, a bond began to grow between the individual recruits that is a critical step in becoming a member of the Corps.

The DIs were Vietnam combat veterans, and they knew that there was, in fact, no such thing as an atheist in a firefight. It was standard procedure for recruits to attend church, so on Sunday the DIs made sure that the recruits attended religious services. Every Sunday morning, the recruits went either to a Protestant or Catholic services conducted at the white wooden World War II era chapel at the far end of the parade field.

Frank and Mike were both Catholic so they went to Mass with about 20 other recruits from the Platoon. They were marched to the chapel without much screaming and cursing. It was Sunday, and the DIs didn't seem as angry as usual.

Frank, Mike and the other recruits filed into church

and sat shoulder to shoulder in pews packed with the other Catholic recruits from other platoons. The Navy Chaplin, Father Napoli, was a stocky, dark haired Italian with bright blue eyes and a strong Boston accent.

Father Napoli said he had served two tours in Vietnam where he had conducted Mass and ministered to the Marines fighting on the DMZ. His voice cracked when he described how too many of "his" Marines had been mortally wounded and he had given these young warriors their last rites.

"Love God, our country and the Corps. And always remember that in battle, it's each Marine's commitment to his buddy that makes us strong and gives us courage."

After the sermon and communion, the recruits stood and sang *God Bless America*. The 200 plus recruits were loud and passionate, and Frank noticed the DIs were singing along. He saw Gates and Brooks exchange a look that seemed to say, "These recruits are getting there." Frank, Mike and many other young men had tears in their eyes as Mass ended.

The Grinder

One morning, after physical training and breakfast, the "mob" was marched to the armory where they were each issued M-14 rifles. Frank had hunted with his friends back home, but he had never seen or felt a rifle like the M-14.

It had a wooden stock and a strange looking flash-suppressor at the end of the barrel. It weighed just a little under 10 pounds which, they would soon find out, would feel more like 50 pounds after hours of close order drill. He and Mike smiled at each other as they ran from the armory building and did their best to fall in and assume the position of *Order Arms*. The DIs gave specific instructions and then stormed through the Platoon giving "individual instructions" to any unfortunate recruit who was out of position.

All Marines are, first and foremost, riflemen, and the connection with their weapon is taught, drilled and pounded into each recruit. Everyone learned to recite the Rifleman's Creed:

> *This is my rifle. There are many like it, but this one is mine. It is my life. I must master it as I must master my life. Without me my rifle is useless. Without my rifle, I am useless. I must fire my rifle true. I must shoot straighter than the enemy who is trying to kill me. I must shoot him before he shoots me. I will. My rifle and I know that what counts in war are not the rounds we fire, the noise of our burst, or the smoke we make. We know that it is the hits that count. We will hit.*
>
> *My rifle is human, even as I am human, because it is my life. Thus, I will learn it as a brother. I will learn its weaknesses, its strengths, its parts, its accessories, its sights and its barrel. I will keep my rifle clean and ready, even as I am clean and ready. We will become part of each other.*
>
> *Before God I swear this creed. My rifle*

and I are the defenders of my country. We are the masters of our enemy. We are the saviors of my life. So be it, until victory is America's and there is no enemy.

There were endless classes where the DIs taught the recruits to disassemble and assemble their rifles in less than a minute. And then they had to do the same one-minute drill blindfolded. To reinforce the important bond, connection with their rifles, they frequently slept with their rifles.

As the early weeks of training passed, the DIs cadence changed from unintelligible garble to commands that Frank understood. The "mob" began to show signs of marching together, and they began to follow commands correctly. During the heat of the afternoons, the platoons would practice close order drill on the asphalt parade field the DIs called "the Grinder".

"Fooowrrd Huh!" Brooks shouted. The Platoon stepped off and marched along the street bordering the Grinder. Some guys, the slow learners, were out of step and Gates and Fritz screamed and shoved until they got into step.

"Cooolumm Ri! Huh!" They swung onto the parade field and headed toward the Iwo Jima Monument that stood at the center perimeter of the grinder. "Lao Ri Lao! Step Yo Lao Ri Lao! Dig in your heels! Lean back and strut! Strut! Strut! Strut! Make your own cadence! Lao Ri Lao!" shouted Brooks. Frank stared at the back of the head of the guy marching in front of him and concentrated on the commands, while his M-14 rested comfortably and naturally on his right shoulder.

Endless marching in formation, or "close-order drills", and intense classroom training, provided the recruits with intimate knowledge of their weapon. From the flash suppressor at the end of the barrel, to the butt plate on the end of the stock, the M-14 felt deadly, and handling it gave Frank great confidence. His rifle was fast becoming a part of his being, and Frank started to wonder what life had been like before he had his rifle.

"Platoon Halt! Lao Fa! Ooordrr Hrms!" Brooks commanded. The forty-nine rifles fell clumsily to the position of *Order Arms*, and the DIs shook their heads in disgust. Frank had executed the movement properly and was surprised to find that he was also disgusted with the few guys who still couldn't do it right.

For the next three hours, the Platoon learned and repeated the "manual of arms" in the scorching heat. "Right Shoulder! Left Shoulder! Port Arms! Order Arms! Inspection Arms! Trail Arms!" ordered Brooks.

Sore Arms! Aching Arm! Frank thought.

Brooks gave instructions and commands while Gates and Fritz concentrated on giving special attention to the screw-ups.

By the fourth week of training, Frank and his Platoon had drastically changed. Several more "non-hackers" were sent to STB or home with General Discharges. The arms, chest, stomach and leg muscles of the surviving recruits had hardened from the constant and jarring physical training. The long, endless runs had become exhilarating, with everyone running in unison, clapping hands, and chanting cadence with the endless crunch of forty-nine pairs of combat boots simultaneously slapping the grinder.

Extraordinary coordination and agility developed in the Platoon's ability to handle the rifle with precision and ease. Latent aggressiveness burst to the surface in hand-to-hand combat and bayonet training. They began to anticipate the rush of adrenalin that swept over them when a sheathed bayonet was slapped into their sweating palm, and they were told to kill their opponent in mock bayonet fights.

Frank became conditioned to pay for any mistakes he or his Platoon made. No longer confused or frightened by the drill instructors, he began to view them with a growing respect. The DI's job was to separate the fit from the unfit, the strong from the weak. They would ensure each member of the Platoon would learn the Marine Corps "family" values. They would be a disciplined, hardened, integral part of a combat unit. The brutal fact that a mistake in combat, or a lack of discipline, could cost Marines their lives was pounded into the recruits.

As the sun began to set on the sixth Sunday of their basic training, Gates marched the Platoon across the Grinder to the Iwo Jima Monument to conduct *Retreat*, a ceremony signifying the end of the duty day and the lowering of the colors.

The Parris Island Iwo Jima Monument is a smaller replica of the National Memorial that sits on the banks of the Potomac River in Arlington, Virginia. The six stone figures depict the six Marines who raised the American flag at the top of Mt. Suribachi during the 1945 battle for Iwo Jima. One of the first things all recruits learn is that the monument is a patriotic icon and source of great pride to Marines.

The recruits swung smartly through a column right, and started across the parade field, with the scarlet and gold platoon flag, flying from the guidon, blowing in the evening breeze. The sun was low in the sky, and there were no other platoons on the parade field.

"Lao! Ri! La!" sang Gates, as the Platoon picked up the cadence.

"Crunch! Crunch! Crunch!" answered the 49 pairs of boots in perfect harmony. Rifles stood at exact right angles and every set of eyes were locked straight ahead.

"Count Cadence, Count!", barked Gates.

"One, two, three, four! We love the Marine Corps!", answered the Platoon. Their chant boomed across the field and echoed off the surrounding buildings.

"La sholdr hrms!"

"Crack! Crack!", swung the M-14s in absolute unison.

Frank's hands stung from slapping the wooden rifle stock, as he snapped his weapon over to his left shoulder. He dug in his heels, threw his shoulders back, and breathed in deeply the cool evening air. He felt good and imagined the thousands of Marines who had passed this way before him. Frank was part of a new generation being trained to fight in Vietnam, and he was filled with a sense of belonging that he had never known before.

The shadow of the Iwo Jima Monument fell across the Platoon as they turned half left and drew abreast of the monument. The recruits stood in perfectly aligned ranks, and they could see the granite fingers that clutched the brass pole, holding high the American flag.

Gates dispatched four young recruits to relieve the World War II Marines of their standard. Frank's chest tightened at the site, and he stood ramrod straight as the lanyard was untied. A lone Marine bugler took his position next to the monument.

"That flag is ours", Gates said in a quiet voice. "It's worth fighting for. Never forget it."

The shrill blast of a whistle shattered the silence and alerted the platoon to stand-by to lower the colors. Gates took his position at the head of the formation and faced the stone Warriors who stood at the top of Mount Suribachi.

As the next whistle blast pierced the air, Gates barked, "Present Arms". Frank snapped his rifle up in front of his eyes in the ancient salute. The bugler began playing *Retreat* and *The Colors* as the flag was slowly lowered.

With the bugle sounds echoing across the grinder, the reverberation of each note sank into Frank's heart and soul. The last notes drifted away. The bearers folded the flag, and the star-studded triangle was marched away from the six stone Heroes.

The Rifle Range

Discipline, the first critical lesson, had been pounded into each recruit. Now they were ready to begin marksmanship training. At last, the Platoon was going to the rifle range where they would get to fire the weapon they all had come to know so well.

They were excited as the Platoon fell into formation with light marching packs and canteens hanging from their cartridge belts. For the first time they were ordered to loosen their rifle slings so they could be carried over their shoulders.

As the Platoon moved down the road, Frank and Mike marched side by side, as they had from the beginning, enjoying the steady, parade field pace.   Smiles crept cautiously across their tanned, hardened young faces as the platoon guide reached an intersection with another road running to the left.

Brooks barked them into the turn, and headed for the front of the formation. As he caught up with the guide, he shouted over his shoulder "Route Step, March!", a command neither Frank nor Mike had ever heard before or understood.

They continued their normal pace until they realized the guys marching in front of them were no longer in step, and that they were practically running trying to keep up with Brooks. Frank looked at Mike in confusion as they each fell out of step and lengthened their stride.

Fritz was marching on the side of the Platoon growling, "Come on people! Move out! Move out!" as the pace increased.

Sweat began to pour, their breathing became deep and hard, and pack straps cut into their shoulder muscles. The formation began to spread out like an accordion with Gates bringing up the rear bellowing, "any of you ladies fall out, and your ass is mine!"

What had begun as a normal march and new adventure suddenly turned into a nightmare for all of the recruits. Each step brought deep gasps for air, and the weight of their equipment grew heavier. Leg muscles carefully conditioned to pound out hours of the short, choppy double-time cadence were stretched and torn by the long strides demanded by the quick "Route Step March" cadence. Cautious smiles were replaced by grim, sweat-soaked looks of despair.

After 30 grueling minutes, Brooks turned to face the Platoon. With a big smile on his face, he raised his right fist in the air and began pumping it up and down.

Fritz and Gates began screaming, "Double-time! Double-time! Run! Run! Run!" as Brooks picked up his pace and began running.

"Oh Jesus, no!" Frank gasped, his mouth parched and lungs seared.

"I ain't believing this shit!" groaned Mike.

The Route Step March had been particularly hard on him because his legs were short, but he too picked up the cadence and began to run.

Each of them plunged into a very personal type of hell where they had to decide whether to quit or keep going. Frank, at the limits of his endurance, waited with each step for Mike to fall so he could drop out. Mike's short legs waited impatiently for Frank to stop running, so that he too, could quit.

"Lerilerilerile! Lerilerilerile!" called out Brooks.

The double-time pace kept up, and Gates began to

gather a group of stragglers in the rear of the Platoon. Listening and occasionally looking over their shoulders, the two recruits could see the kicking and hitting, and easily hear the shrieked abuse that Gates had promised earlier for those who couldn't make it.

Each waited for the other to fall, knowing they could not endure the pace much longer. Just two hundred yards down the road Frank could see red brick barracks, each with asphalt parade fields in front.

We gotta stop there! We gotta stop there! He repeated over and over to himself, keeping time with his boots hitting the pavement.

"Not much further! Not much further" Frank gasped, just loud enough for Mike to hear. Mike could neither speak nor shake his head, but he flashed his glazed eyes toward Frank, indicating he understood.

As they reached the first entrance to the barracks parade field, Brooks looked over his shoulder, smiled, and continued to run. Several guys crashed to the ground, rifles, helmets and packs clattering across the pavement. Less than thirty continued to the second entrance where Brooks turned and ran parallel to the barracks. He stopped the shattered remnants of the Platoon, faced them to the right, and ordered them to the position of Attention.

Frank and Mike stood next to each other, eyes closed, breathing deep, huge gulps of air into blistered lungs. Their legs shook, but they stood fast as Gates and Fritz kicked and shoved the stragglers across the parade field toward the Platoon.

The stragglers fell in at the end of the formation

and the Platoon assumed a semblance of order. Brooks paced back and forth for a few minutes and then faced the group.

"Well, ladies, welcome to the rifle range!"

During the first week at the range, they spent hours in outdoor classrooms learning safety procedures, basic marksmanship, sight alignment, how a sight picture should look, sight adjustments and time-tested, proven habits that make a disciplined shooter and an accurate one.

They learned the *BRASS* system which controls the breathing, commands the body to relax, aims the rifle, takes up the slack in the trigger and the art of gently, ever so gently, squeezing the trigger until the unexpected blast of the round exploding in the chamber tells you that you've just fired your weapon.

Frank and Mike had no trouble learning the classroom principles but, like everyone else, they suffered when attention was focused on actually learning the various firing positions. They believed a Drill instructor, probably Gates, had invented the excruciatingly painful shooting positions.

They worked, suffered, strained, and waited impatiently for the following week when they would fire their rifles, while the DIs pushed, twisted and jerked resisting bodies into the regulation firing positions. The kneeling position required the shooter to extend his left leg straight out front, sit on the ankle of the bent and tucked right leg, while bending and reaching with his left elbow until it rested securely on the outstretched ankle of the left leg. Frank believed it was easy only for an accomplished contortionist.

The DIs were driven to ensure each recruit learned how to shoot his weapon properly. In the evenings, back at the barracks, they spent hours talking about the importance of accurate shooting in order to survive in combat.

"The gooks are good in the bush," Brooks growled. "But Marines are better. Charlie is fightin' in his own backyard and he knows the countryside, but he's no match for a Marine that can shoot. All it takes is one clean shot right between the runnin' lights and Charlie is a dead son of a bitch! If ya can't hit Charlie first and bring him down, he'll blow your ass away!"

Frank listened attentively. He and Mike exchanged glances as Brooks continued his lecture. They both knew they would probably be going straight to Vietnam to a line company after completing the Infantry Training Regiment (ITR), which followed boot camp.

Monday morning, their second week at the range, brought clear skies and good shooting weather as the Platoon marched down to the 200-yard line for their first day of live firing. Frank and Mike managed to get on the same shooting relay.

"Jesus, I can't wait to shoot," Mike whispered as they waited to go to the firing line.

"Me neither," Frank answered. "I hope I don't screw it up." His stomach was tied in knots and his mouth was dry.

"You better not screw it up or Gates will not be happy," Mike warned.

They both snickered while the DIs paced back and

forth behind them.

"First relay of shooters, move to the firing line!" barked the range officer over the microphone.

They walked forward to instructors who sat on ammunition boxes at each firing position where they drew ammo. Using the 200-yard firing line, they slow fired in the off-hand (standing) position, and Frank had trouble holding the rifle steady. He fired several shots into the butts, missing the target completely and he felt sick when the men in the target pits waved *Maggie's Drawers,* a complete miss, at him.

Mike had better luck, or he had just worked harder on the off-hand position, because he hit the target each time, and several rounds hit the black bull's eye.

Frank and Mike compared scorecards after each relay, and it was apparent Mike was the better shot. He would easily reach the necessary 190 points needed to qualify, but Frank would have to do a lot better in the final relay, if he was going to make the score.

At the 500-yard line, Brooks walked over to take a look at their scorecards. "You ain't doing bad Morgan. You might luck out and qualify the first day."

Mike took back his scorecard and smiled.

"Damn O'Brian. You ain't got a chance in hell of qualifying. You best get to work if you expect to make it on record day."

He had fired a miserable 159 after four relays with only one remaining. "Sir, I think I might be able to do it today. All I need is 40 more points."

"Aw shit, Private," spat Brooks. "You ain't goin'

shoot no 40 at 500 yards. Experienced shooters have trouble doin' that."

"Yes Sir, but that's what I'm gonna try for."

Brooks laughed and gave Frank a good-natured slap on the head. "Okay, go ahead. I'll be watchin'."

Brooks continued to laugh and Frank heard him call Gates over as they moved up to the 500-yard firing line.

"Relax. You can do it," Mike said as they split up at the firing positions.

The instructor gave Frank his ten rounds as he lay down, assumed the prone position, retightened his sling and checked his sights. He threw his left elbow out in front, cradled his rifle gently, locked, loaded, and tucked the rifle stock snugly into his shoulder.

Looking down the rear peep sight, the target seemed to be a mile away from him and the bull's eye looked like a tiny pea-size saucer. The black circle was only twenty inches in diameter and Frank wished he hadn't told Brooks he was going to score the 40 points. He knew Brooks and Gates were standing behind him, watching.

They got the command to fire at will and Frank breathed deeply as other rifles on either side of him burst with the first volley. He closed everything out of his mind and prepared to take the first shot. He relaxed and aimed carefully down the barrel until the black circle sat neatly on top of the front sight blade. He took up the slack in the trigger and squeezed it further back, holding the black dot at the center of his sights. The rifle slammed back into his shoulder and a loud "bang" rang in his ears. He lowered the weapon and watched as his target was pulled down, marked and raised back into sight. A white disc sat almost dead center in the middle of the bull's eye.

"Good shot! Keep it up!" called the instructor.

Concentrating on the target, Frank relaxed and took another deep breath. He reloaded and fired another round in the black. His next two shots were wild and they fell in the three ring. He cursed, doubled his efforts, and one more fell in the bull's-eye, scoring five points each, bringing his five shot total to 21. His last five shots hit three bullseye and two in the four ring, bringing his total score at 500 yards to 44. He'd reached the 190 score, and passed it with four points to spare. After he fired the tenth round, he allowed himself to relax, laugh, and he was bursting with pride.

The week reached a climax on Friday, when they shot for "record scores" that would earn them their shooting badges, and appropriate entries into their service books. Mike, who had continued to improve throughout the week, fired 226 out of a possible 250 points. Frank finished with 212 points. On Saturday morning, the series commander pinned silver crossed rifles on Mike's chest, designating him a "Rifle Expert", and Frank received the silver Maltese cross of a "Rifle Sharpshooter". The Platoon had only three guys who didn't qualify.

Another grueling march brought them back to the main side barracks they had left two weeks earlier. Frank and Mike were sure they could make it through the last three weeks of boot camp.

Winning the "Boot"

During the Final Phases of training, the days were filed with inspections, more physical training, and the last minute dress uniform fittings. The Battalion Drill Competition was just a week away, and Brooks made it clear he intended his Platoon would win the prized *Battalion Boot Trophy*, which symbolized excellence in close order drill.

On a hot Tuesday afternoon, Gates put the Platoon through its paces, calling out, "To the Rear, March! Right flank! Left flank! Right oblique! Left oblique! Right Shoulder Arms! Left Shoulder Arms!" This close order drilling went on hour after hour.

Marching in front of Frank was a guy from Wisconsin named DeVoto. DeVoto had trouble with drilling, and Mike and Frank had laughed more than a few times when DeVoto messed up.

"Leoo sholdr hrms! Huh!" barked Gates.

DeVoto moved his head to the left, when he brought his rifle off his right shoulder, and he moved to the right again, when he positioned the rifle back on his left shoulder. Frank snickered to himself, knowing DeVoto was afraid of hitting himself in the head with the rifle every time he went from one shoulder to the other. It would be an understatement to say that marching and going through the manual of arms was something that DeVoto had a lot of trouble doing right!

"Goddamn it, DeVoto! I'd best not see you move your fuckin' empty head again," screamed Gates. He never missed anything.

"Crunch! Crunch! Crunch!" Cracked the boots.

"Lao! Ri! Lao! Steyo! Leo! Ri! Leo!" barked Gates.

"Crunch! Crunch! Crunch!" The boots continued.

"Ri sholdr Hrms! Huh!" Ordered Gates.

"Crack! Crack!" Smacked the rifles.

DeVoto moved his head again.

"Hippity Hop! Mob stop!" commanded Gates in disgust. "Well Miss DeVoto, I guess you think I'm out here talking just to hear the wind blow through your empty, fuckin' head, huh sweat pea?" growled Gates as he swaggered through the ranks.

"Sir, no sir!" screamed DeVoto in self-defense.

Gates stood right in front of Frank, bellowing into DeVoto's ear. "Well, maybe I'll just have to give you some special instructions on the manual of arms so you don't move your God damn head anymore!"

"Sir, no sir! The private does not need special instructions, Sir!" pleaded DeVoto.

"Like hell you don't!" Gates roared.

Frank struggled to control his laughter and with Gates occupied, Frank looked out of the corner of his eye at Mike, who was choking back a snicker.

Gates snatched Private DeVoto's silver painted pith helmet from his head, raised the barrel of his M-14 until it was level with DeVoto's skull and began to bang him in the side of the head with the rifle. With each bang, Gates screamed, "Now you still scared of hitting your empty, fuckin' head? Huh! Huh!"

On the fourth bang, Frank lost control of himself

and an unmistakable chuckle came out. Gates, the head banger, whirled around to face the laughter.

"Oooooh, Miss O'Brian. You think it's funny when Private DeVoto gets hit in the head, do you?"

Frank stopped laughing. "Sir, no sir! I don't think it's funny."

"Well, what are you laughin' at Miss O'Brian?"

"Sir, nothing Sir!"

Gates wasn't buying that for a second. He marched around Frank and removed the chrome dome from Frank's shaved, vulnerable head. Frank closed his eyes, gritted his teeth, and waited. He didn't have long to wait, because Gates raised the M-14 until it was level with the side of Frank's head and began to bang away.

"Still think it's funny, Miss O'Brian?" Gates growled.

"Sir, no sir!"

Frank felt a golf ball size lump growing on the side of his head. But as the Platoon resumed the march, he saw a similar lump sprouting on the side of DeVoto's head.

On the following Saturday, the platoons participating in Battalion Drill Competition met on the grinder. Spectators filled the bleachers next to the Iwo Jima Monument as Brooks marched the Platoon into position. Everyone was keyed up and nervous. But they had worked hard, and Gates had said, in a moment of weakness, that they were probably as good as he had seen.

They stood at parade rest while the other platoons went through the required movements. They didn't dare move their eyes to get a better look at what was going on, but they could see pretty well with their expanded peripheral vision. Everybody in the Platoon was hoping for one of the privates in the competing platoons to drop his rifle or fall on his face.

Then it was their turn. Brooks snapped the Platoon to attention and marched them out to center stage. Staff NCOs, judging the competition, circled them as they crunched to a halt, with Gates and Fritz watching from the sidelines. Brooks barked the commands and the Platoon responded in unison. Heels dug into the asphalt. Everyone hit their pivot points making column movements, flanking movements were executed with precision, rifles were held at exact angles, and toughened hands came close to breaking rifle stocks when the weapons were slapped from position to position.

When it was over, they waited at parade rest while the judges tallied their scores. Frank could see Gates and Fritz standing next to each other, hands on their hips, tense expressions on their faces. Brooks stood in front of the Platoon motionless.

The Battalion Commander stepped up to a microphone with the results, and announced Brooks' Platoon had won the *Bronze Boot*. They cracked to attention as the colonel approached Brooks and presented him with the Boot Trophy, a long-standing tradition at Parris Island that was reserved for the winner of the Battalion Close Order Drill Competition. Frank saw the expression on Brooks' face change from the usual nasty glower to a slight smile as he walked back to the Platoon with the *Boot* in hand.

The sight of a Marine Recruit platoon in their final days of boot camp marching across the grinder is an impressive site. They make their own cadence, and they move as one: rifles held at port arms, boots digging into the asphalt in a pounding, rhythmic *crunch, crunch, crunch*, shoulders held high, and all eyes locked straightforward. The commands of the DI are executed with precision.

Graduation

After eleven weeks, seventy-seven grueling days, the unfit recruits had been weeded out, discharged and sent home. What remained were young men who had earned the right to wear the *Eagle, Globe, and Anchor*, the official emblem of the U.S. Marine Corps.

Graduation day came in the middle of June. The Platoon fell into formation that morning, and the seventy-one "survivors" moved as one, following the sounds of the drum and bugle corps out to the familiar parade field for the last time. Frank and Mike marched shoulder to shoulder, beaming with pride and satisfaction. The day had finally arrived when they would be called Marine.

The ceremony moved along in crisp Marine Corps fashion, and Frank was proud, relieved and thankful the ordeal was over and he had survived.

Frank studied Brooks, Gates, and Fritz as they stood at rigid attention in front of the Platoon. Frank saw them for the first time as fellow Marines. Frank, Mike and sixty-nine of the original eighty recruits had survived the crucible of Marine Corps boot camp. If the training had been cruel, it was not because the DIs were sadists. Each

Private had to be able to deal with hardship and adversity. Each Private had to be an excellent marksman. Each Private had to survive in combat. Each Private would not.

Brooks' voice barked the commands, and they stepped off marching behind the band. They made two column lefts and marched abreast toward the reviewing stand as the band struck up the *Marine's Hymn*. Shoulders were drawn further back and chests almost burst from their uniforms as the music echoed through their ranks. Frank knew that if his Father had been alive, he would have been very proud of his youngest son.

The cadence on graduation day was the heartbeat of boys who believed they were men. Their lives would never be the same. They were now Marines.

CHAPTER III - PROJECT *DYE MARKER*

The war in Vietnam is going well and will succeed.
There are many ways to make the death rate increase.

Secretary of Defense Robert McNamara, mid-1960

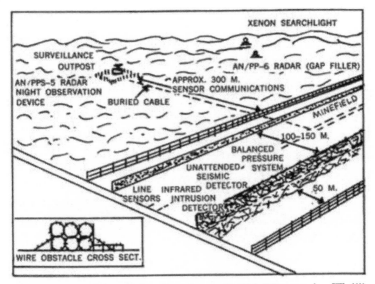

A Pentagon Planner's drawing of "McNamara's Wall" across the DMZ.

When Frank, Mike and thousands of other recruits graduated from Marine Corps boot camp and entered the Vietnam replacement pipeline in the spring and summer of 1967, they all believed they were going to fight and win the war in Vietnam. But what they didn't know was that President Johnson and Defense Secretary McNamara's Pentagon experts were developing a defensive strategy, a war of attrition, in Vietnam. The politicians had concluded that there was no need to go on the offense and invade North Vietnam because, they believed, U.S. casualties would be too high. Congress and the American civilians would object. Their reasoning was straightforward: an invasion of the North would cost too much, take too long, and there was a real risk that the Russians and Chinese would come into the war. They settled on a "face saving" plan designed to achieve a stalemate instead of an outright victory over North Vietnam.

The Pentagon experts used computer programs to generate tables and tables of statistics that showed a kill ratio of 10 NVA dead to 1 dead American would force the NVA to give up and stop their efforts to invade South Vietnam. To that end, the Pentagon ordered all American combat units in Vietnam to carefully report the body count of dead enemy soldiers as well as the number of dead or wounded Americans.

To further the stalemate, a major tactical Pentagon innovation was to build an "impregnable" wall across the 62 mile wide DMZ dividing North and South Vietnam. *Project Dye Marker* was a plan conceived by a well-respected Harvard professor who was a consultant hired to advise

Secretary McNamara and his Pentagon staff. The professor's analytical, logical, intellectual approach to the war appealed to Secretary McNamara, a successful business executive who, along with his team of "whiz kids", used systems analysis, statistics, and modern operations research methods to solve problems and improve productivity at Ford Motors.

When the *Project Dye Marker* was implemented, it was assumed McNamara's Wall would stop the infiltration of North Vietnamese Army units crossing into South Vietnam. The design included a 600-meter wide field of fire that would be bulldozed by Marine Engineers, and then the Air Force would spray Agent Orange chemicals to kill the foliage in order to deny the enemy camouflaged hiding places. After the defoliating, Marine grunts would string triple concertina wire around the strong points, and plant thousands of sophisticated electronic sensors and land mines across the DMZ. *Project Dye Marker* obstacles would increase NVA body count and convince the leadership in Hanoi that they couldn't win the war. The cost in American lives would be much less and, so the planners believed, America would prevail.

The III Marine Amphibious Force Generals, Lew Walt and Robert Cushman, both decorated World War II and Korean War veterans, pushed back hard on a defensive strategy, especially *Project Dye Marker*. Defensive strategies violated the basic concepts of fighting and winning a war, and it reversed the traditional mission of Marine combat units. The Generals loathed the idea of ordering their Marines to hunker down in fixed, defensive positions.

Filling sand bags, stringing concertina wire, and building bunkers would make the Marines sitting ducks for heavy NVA artillery, mortar and rocket fire. In effect, the *Dye Marker* bunkers would provide perfect target locations for the NVA gunners. In the end, the Marine Generals lost the argument, and the Marines did what they always do. The 3rd Marine Division officers and men followed orders.

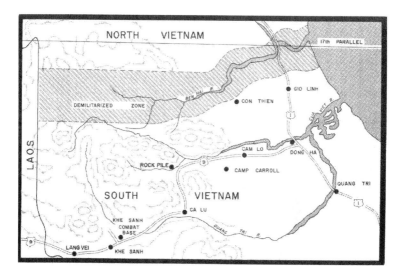

Throughout 1967, the number of dead and wounded Marines increased week after week. The III Marine Amphibious Force Headquarters at Danang held a daily press conference where reporters were briefed on current operations that included enemy body counts and Marine casualties. The Pentagon experts considered the kill ratio statistics proof that the Americans were winning.

As the Pentagon experts entered the tallies into their computers, the 3rd Marine Division grunts used their entrenching tools to fill thousands of sandbags that were stacked several layers deep on top of bunkers. The reinforced structures were designed to survive all but direct hits by NVA artillery. But the Marines knew that the NVA gunners were experts at firing barrage after barrage of 122 and 130-millimeter howitzer rounds with great accuracy.

Work on *Project Dye Marker* slowly and painfully progressed through 1967, but the DMZ body count and kill ratios reported by the Marines to the experts in the Pentagon didn't meet the brass' expected tallies. The Pentagon sent word back to the Marines that they needed to kill more of the enemy because the "kill ratios" processed in their computers didn't show the right outcome. Frank and the other replacements would be faced with improving those Pentagon "kill ratios".

CHAPTER IV – WARRIOR TRAINING

The more you sweat in peacetime,
The less you bleed in war.

A Marine Corps axiom on training

Infantry Training Regiment

It was a hot, sunny day in the middle of June when Frank, Mike and two hundred other boot camp graduates were bused to the Marine Corps Infantry Training Regiment (ITR) at Camp Geiger, North Carolina. ITR is the Corps' basic infantry training school.

It was early afternoon when the buses pulled into Camp Geiger where tough NCOs, most Vietnam Veterans, greeted the green troops. They piled off the buses in a parking lot surrounded by white, one story, brick barracks. Frank could see hundreds of combat-equipped Marines crowded in the maze of streets that crisscrossed the area around the parking lot. Frank and Mike jumped off the bus and quickly lined up in platoon formation, listening to the familiar sounds of screamed commands and crunching boots.

A Gunnery Sergeant, or "Gunny", in starched utilities paced back and forth in front of the formation of four platoons with a clipboard in his hand while other NCOs prowled through the ranks, scowling and barking orders until everyone was in place.

"Christ, don't tell me it's another boot camp," Mike mumbled.

"I don't see any Smokey the Bear hats," laughed Frank.

"Yeah, but the way these guys are actin', they think they're DIs," Mike whispered without moving his lips.

"Just as long as they only think it and don't try thumpin' on us, everything will be okay," Frank concluded.

"Listen up!" barked Gunny. "When I call out your name, line up behind me in new platoon formations."

"Well, shit!" Mike snapped. "I thought we'd stay in the same platoons for this crap."

"That's what you get for thinkin."

Gunny ran quickly through the two hundred names listed in alphabetical order until four new platoons were formed. O'Brian and Morgan were fairly close in the alphabet so they ended up in the same platoon again.

"During the next three weeks," growled the Gunny, "you people will learn the finer points of being a Marine rifleman. During your stay here, the troop handlers will expect the same cooperation and respect you gave your DIs. If there are any problems, I'll take care of them," he threatened.

The troop handlers swaggered back and forth, cocky and belligerent, and were poor imitations of Brooks,

Gates and Fritz. Gunny, however, was a different story.

"Your training will be conducted under tactical conditions, simulating combat conditions in Vietnam," he continued, "and that means you'll spend all of your time in the field, force marching with full combat gear. You'll learn to eat, sleep, live and survive in the bush."

"More fun," Mike whispered.

"Classes will cover small unit tactical operations concentrating on fire team maneuvers. The fire team is the smallest and most important combat unit in the Marine Corps. It consists of a fire team leader, an automatic rifleman, an assistant automatic rifleman, and one riflemen. A squad has 13 Marines, consisting of three fire teams and the squad leader. Practical application exercises will involve running patrols, ambushes, making assaults, using camouflage, building defensive positions and communications, using a field radio. You'll each learn how to handle and defend against land mines, booby traps and high explosives."

"Peachy. Just great," Frank mumbled. "I wonder how many people get killed each year learning this crap."

"You'll learn to fire, clean and maintain a complete line of weapons used at the company level, including the M-60 machinegun, M-79 grenade launcher, a light anti-tank weapon, a rocket launcher called the LAW, and you'll learn to throw grenades without blowing your head off. Hours will be spent learning land navigation, map reading and using a compass."

"Jesus, all I want to do is learn to find my way home," Mike snickered.

Gunny paused and tried to find the laughing private in the ranks, but wasn't sure who the offender was, so he continued. "You people best pay close attention to what's being taught here, because what you learn will save your ass in Nam. Your troop handlers will take over now and get you settled in the barracks. Later, you'll go to supply to draw your "782" field gear, as well as your packs, helmets, flak jackets and cartridge belts. You'll also draw rifles at the armory because tomorrow morning, training begins."

He turned on his heels and marched away as the Platoon Sergeant, a guy named Maze, called them to attention, faced them to the right and marched them off. The solemn atmosphere established by the Gunny was shattered.

"Left. Right. Left. Right," Maze sang out in a singsong monotone.

Everyone was expecting the crisp bark of a Parris Island cadence, but Maze's attempt produced uncontrolled laughter in the ranks.

"You people might laugh now, but you won't have anything to laugh about when we go to the field," he threatened.

"Hey, Sergeant, where's the field anyway?" Mike said with a chuckle.

"Shut your damn mouth wise ass. No talking in the ranks! You'll find out soon enough," barked Maze.

That night, they settled into their new homes, ate chow at the mess hall, and before they hit the sack, assembled a field marching pack for the first day of training.

The Racetrack

Before sunrise, they were in platoon formation in front of the barracks, decked out in full combat gear. They smiled, told jokes, laughed until the Gunny appeared with the troop handlers in tow.

"I guess now we'll find out where the field is," Frank said, standing next to Mike.

They both snuffed out their cigarettes and quickly stripped the butts, as Sergeant Maze called the troop to attention and began roll call.

"Yo!" answered the troops as Maze ran down the list of fifty names.

"All present or accounted for," reported the sergeants.

Facing to the right, they slung their rifles over their right shoulders and moved out. The Gunny called cadence like a DI, and the entire company began to march down the streets leading to the field.

The sky began to change from pitch black to dark blue and eventually the pale blue as the sun crept closer to the horizon. The morning air was cool and fresh as they marched at a steady pace to the outskirts of the base. The sound of their boots pounding the asphalt streets mingled with the crunch of other boots from other units, marching in various directions

"Hell, this ain't bad. Wonder what Maze was talkin' about yesterday," Mike whispered.

"Oh, I'd be willin' to bet we won't march all the way to the field like this," Frank answered.

"Wherever the hell the field is," he added.

They marched through the dawn without noticing the weight of their helmets, flak jackets, packs and rifles. The lead platoon rounded a corner and began to march off the road, down a dirt trail in columns of twos. The other platoons marked time until it was their turn to head off into the woods. One of the troop handlers stood at the beginning of the trail, repeating over and over again, "Welcome to the Racetrack. Route Step! Route Step!"

Frank and Mike plunged into the bushes and ran, in order to catch up with the guys ahead of them. The four platoons in the company spread out and contracted as the fast pace of the Route Step march moved through the woods. Up and down hills, across uneven ground, some stumbled and fell. There was a lot of cursing amid barked orders to "close it up…close it up."

Two brutal hours later, they understood what Sergeant Maze meant about going to the field. It was the first of many forced marches they would take during their training at Camp Geiger. Each march was longer and harder than the comparatively short hikes they'd taken back at Parris Island.

The Field

As the first week of training at ITR moved along, Frank came to believe that boot camp had been the introduction to endless days and nights filled with new and special trials. Physically, ITR was tougher than boot camp because of the forced marches, field exercises and most of all, the lack of sleep. They averaged three or four hours sleep each night, and the strain was brutal. They staggered in from the field late each night, took ice cold showers because there was never enough hot water, cleaned their rifles and equipment for the next day's training, and then hit the sack.

In the field, at mealtime they learned to cook and eat C-Rations, the military's individual canned, pre-cooked meal for one person. Frank became a whiz at opening the G.I. green cans of food with his "John Wayne" C-Ration can opener, but he could never force himself to eat all of the foul tasting food. The worst meal was ham and lima beans, a green, lumpy, slimy mixture that most Marines threw into the bushes.

On Friday, they attended the last class on land navigation, map reading and using the compass. The practical application exercise included a night compass march through the snake-infested North Carolina woods.

"Okay. Each fire team will have a compass, a map and a set of coordinates that will mark your objectives," explained the instructor. "Each checkpoint," he continued, "will be manned by an NCO who will note that you've reached that objective, and send you on to the next one."

Frank was designated fire team leader for the exercises, and Mike and three other guys made up the rest of the fire team. They all gathered around Frank as he examined the map, using an instructor's flashlight, planning the march.

They reached the first objective and continued on to the others with Frank guiding the patrol. They were one of the first fire teams to finish the exercise and get back in to the staging area.

Class and Gas

In the second week, the troops sat in one of the outdoor classrooms listening to an instructor talk about germ warfare and gas. He explained the Geneva Convention outlawed these two methods of waging war, but that didn't mean a potential enemy would not use these weapons. Gas and chemical warfare training didn't make a lot of sense for troops headed to Nam. The North Vietnamese were not known to use these weapons, but the training was a requirement during ITR.

"When there's a gas attack" he explained, "it's imperative you get your gas mask on immediately. Any delay may cause serious injury including burned lungs, blindness, shortage of breath and eventually death. It could be mustard gas, nerve gas or tear gas."

He went on to describe the parts of a gas mask in detail and then demonstrated how to use the contraption. When he put the mask on, he looked like an insect and the troops laughed. They stopped when he told them they would get a taste of gas during the exercise following the class.

"Jesus, these crazy sons of bitches aren't going to gas us, are they?" Mike asked.

They marched through the woods, away from the classroom, to a long wooden shed with doors on either end. A metal, stovepipe smoke stack stuck out from the roof. The troops became nervous when one of the instructors put on a mask and went inside. In a few minutes, smoke began to drift from the top of the smoke stack and when the wind blew in their direction, the troops began to cough and choke.

"Damn, my eyes are stingin'," Mike complained.

"Jesus it smells awful," Frank choked

They were ordered to put on their gas masks and march into the shed, one squad at a time. Inside, an instructor wearing a mask, made sure the tear gas canisters were burning strong enough, to give everybody a healthy whiff. When the door closed, he ordered the troops to remove their masks and sing the Marine's Hymn. The men coughed, choked, gagged, and several threw up before they were told to run out the other door. Their eyes burned like fire, and tears streamed down their faces as they ran coughing and choking into the wood.

"Rotten dumb asses," Frank gagged and spit globs of phlegm on the ground. But he had "survived" another day!

Liberty

During ITR, no one was allowed to go off base into Jacksonville on liberty. They could go to the enlisted club, affectionately referred to by the troops as the Slop Chute, a name derived from the chute toward the aft of a ship where its slop, or garbage, is dumped overboard into the sea.

The club was a converted warehouse, with unpainted aluminum walls, high ceiling, and a bar made of unfinished wood planks that ran the length of the building. Tables were bolted to the cement floor and the chairs were light, cheap plastic. The troops could get hotdogs, precooked hamburgers, pizzas on paper plates, and warm draft beer in plastic cups.

There was no place else to go on the weekends, so every Friday and Saturday night, Frank and Mike went to the Slop Chute for a few beers.

"Jesus, I want out of this pit," Frank said over the Saturday night din as the old jukebox blared *Hang on Sloopy*, a song that had been popular years ago.

"Yeah, me too," Mike answered, helping himself to one of Frank's Camels, as he always did.

"When are you gonna start buyin' your own damn smokes?" Frank laughed.

"When you stop buyin' them for me."

"What are you gonna do when you go home on leave, Mike?"

"Get caught up on my sleep, eat a lot, get drunk and get laid – but not necessarily in that order," he said smiling. "I'll be glad to see my mom and dad again. They were kind of disappointed when I joined the Corps, since I'm the only kid, but I didn't want to go to college and the draft was hot on my ass. Maybe when I get out, I'll go back and feel like goin' to school. But, in the meantime, mom says dad feels real good about me bein' in the Marines. In her last letter, she wrote that all he does is brag about me down at the plant."

"My dad would be proud of me, too," Frank said thoughtfully, "if he was still alive. He always thought the Marines were hot shit." He took a few swallows of beer before continuing. My mother didn't like me joinin' either, but I wasn't ready for college or maybe college wasn't ready for me," he laughed. "Anyway, the one semester I went, I had to work and go to school. Ended up flunkin' out."

It was Mike's turn to push and shove his way to the bar where he bought four more cups of warm beer. He struggled back to the table, balancing the cups in an effort to keep too much from spilling on the floor. They sat drinking, watching the Military Police, or MPs, break up a fight between two drunk Marines.

"Stupid bastards got nothin' better to do except beat up on each other," Mike commented.

"Can't handle a few beers."

"Bet we get orders for Nam," Mike said, changing the subject.

"That's a safe bet."

"Well, that ain't so bad," Mike continued. "That's one of the main reasons I joined."

"Yeah, me too," Frank agreed. "Damn communists been sayin' for years how they're goin' to conquer the world. And ya know somethin', that's exactly what they'll do if we don't stop them. Besides, Americans been fightin' and dyin' in Asia for years. It's time we kicked their asses and put an end to the damn war."

They drank and talked for another hour before leaving the club. It was almost closing time as they made their way through the maze of identical streets, heading for the company area.

"You kinda scared about goin' to Nam?" Mike asked in a strained voice as they walked alone.

"Yeah, about some things, I guess." He thought for a moment before he said, "I think what worries me most is not knowing, not knowing for sure what I'll do in combat. I'm scared I'll chicken out – be a coward. That and getting' captured or bein' shot up real bad. Especially in the legs. I've got a real bad fear of not being able to stand up and walk around."

"Yeah. Not sure how I could live with myself if I broke and ran under fire. I can't imagine being captured either. Locked up in cages by those little yellow bastards. And I'd rather be dead than have to live in a wheelchair for the rest of my life. An dyin'," he concluded, "is somethin' that's goin' to happen anyway. When your number's up, it's time to go."

Grenades

Forced marches, classes, and "live fire" exercises continued at an exhausting pace. One Friday morning, they went to the hand grenade range.

"Men. This is one of the deadliest weapons available to the infantryman. It's an M-26 fragmentation grenade and if you use it right, you can screw up Charlie's day forever," droned the Sergeant. "But, if you don't use it right, you'll blow you and your buddy to hell and back so fast, you'll never know what hit you."

Frank and Mike sat near the front of a group of 200 Marines and listened carefully as the instructor continued his lecture. He held up an unarmed M-26 hand grenade and described the various parts and how they worked. The grenade was oblong, almost pear shaped and it fit neatly into the hand of the instructor. He said it weighed less than half-a-pound, had an explosive charge called composition B that was at the center of a serrated coil of metal. When the grenade exploded, the metal coil became deadly fragmentation that killed.

"Grenades are like hand-held artillery for an infantryman and is used in close combat," said the instructor. "The blast range for the M-26 is about 5 meters so it's a good idea to be well away from the grenade when it explodes." The instructor demonstrated how to take the safety off the grenade by sticking your index finger into the metal "O" ring attached to a cotter pin key that ran through the top of the firing mechanism. By twisting the cotter pin key and pulling hard, you extract the pin and take the safety off. As he demonstrated pulling out the pin, the instructor added, "and unlike the heroes in the movies, don't try to pull the pin with your teeth. All you will do is pull your teeth out." The 200 Marines laughed.

"As long as you hold this spoon in place," he pointed to the thin metal lever that ran down the side of the grenade. "The grenade is harmless," he said. "When your take your hand off the spoon, it will fly off the grenade making an unmistakable "ping" sound. After the safety lever (or "spoon") flies off, the timer is running and you only have 4-5 seconds before the grenade explodes.

He cocked his arm back like a baseball pitcher and said, "Throw the grenade as hard as you can, like a fastball, directly at the enemy. Be careful trying to lob it in an arc, especially in a forest," he cautioned. "It could bounce back and end up at your feet." No one laughed.

After the class, they lined up and got ready to throw live grenades. Ten sandbag-lined pits provided the Marines and instructors protection from the explosions. Frank and Mike watched as ten privates ran into the pits, threw their grenades as far as they could, ducked in the pits as the grenades exploded, and then ran back out.

Just before their turn to throw, one of the recruits ahead of them started to freak out about holding a live grenade. He unceremoniously pulled the pin on his grenade, but then accidentally dropped it into the pit at his feet. The instructor standing next to him dove for the grenade and heaved it out of the pit just as it exploded.

"You stupid son of a bitch! Shit! You're trying to kill both of us!" raged the instructor.

The private was trembling as the range officer sent him and his instructor back to the base. They were shaken by the near fatal accident, and neither one was fit to stay in the field for the rest of the day.

"Jesus! That guy almost blew himself and the instructor away!" Mike said.

"Yeah, no shit! You gotta be careful with the hand-held artillery," Frank answered.

It was then their turn in the pit. Frank jumped into the hole, and the instructor handed him a grenade.

"Don't screw it up Private!" snapped the Sergeant. "I don't want to die today. Just do exactly what I tell you to do."

Frank's guts were in a knot as he gripped the smooth, green, pear shaped grenade in his sweating hand. The pin was still in place, but he squeezed the spoon like it was ready to fly off.

"Okay. Do it just like we showed you in class," the instructor said in a calm, controlled voice.

Facing down range, Frank stood with his feet

slightly spread, with the grenade held against his chest, ready to pull the pin.

"Ready to pull pin!" ordered the sergeant.

Frank hooked his left index finger through the ring attached to the pin and made sure he had a good grip on it.

"Pull pin!" commanded the instructor.

Frank pulled the pin out smoothly, arming the firing mechanism. "Ready to throw!" warned the instructor.

Frank drew his right arm back, squeezed his hand around the grenade's spoon as hard as he could, and looked down range.

"Throw!" shouted the instructor.

Frank felt as if he had thrown his arm out of its socket as the grenade flew through the air, while he and the instructor dove for the bottom of the hole.

One! Two! Three! Four! He silently counted to himself. There was a cracking, ear splitting explosion, and bits of shrapnel sliced through the air. "Okay, get up and move out! Move! Move!" shouted the instructor. Frank's legs shook convulsively as he ran.

Three-Day War

That weekend, they celebrated the Fourth of July by marching in the training battalion parade, together with a Marine Corps band, dressed in full combat gear. After the ceremony, Frank and Mike went down to the Slop Chute and proceeded to get drunk. Later that night, Frank and Mike stumbled over to the outdoor theater, sat down on wooden benches, and watched John Wayne in *The Sands of*

Iwo Jima. They crashed in their bunks and slept all day Sunday.

The three weeks of training ended with a "three day war," a tactical exercise that kept them in the field for three days and two nights. They fought running battles with instructors, who were posing as the enemy. The instructors got a kick out of ambushing the green troops at all hours of the day and night. The troops operated in fire teams, squads and platoons, force-marching through the bush, attacking the enemy and then moving on. They were completely exhausted after going without sleep for the better part of three days, marching mile after mile in full combat gear.

The last exercise ended on a Thursday afternoon. And as the sun began to dip, the weary company began the long march back to the base. The pace was brutal as they half ran through the woods, and it seemed the troop handlers were more anxious to get back than the troops. They cleared the woods after an hour and marched to a paved road leading to the barracks. The platoons automatically fell into standard formations and they began the last leg of their hike.

Frank and Mike marched shoulder to shoulder in 3rd Platoon, exhausted and winded. They were relieved the last day of training was over, and they had survived another test. Finally, it was time to go home.

At the head of the column, somebody in 1st Platoon began to sing a Marine Corps marching song that had been around for years. The tune had been borrowed from the song, *Sink the Bismarck*, but the words were original. The singing spread from platoon to platoon until everyone was singing at the top of his lungs.

> *You can have your Army khaki ...you can keep your Navy blue. For here's another fightin' man, I'll introduce to you...His uniform is spotless...the best you've ever seen...the Germans called him Devil Dog...but his real name is Marine...*

Frank, Mike and all the troops naturally fell into step, threw back their shoulders and dug in their heels. They belted out the last lines of the final stanza as the sun fell below the horizon.

> *His rifle is his best friend...it never leaves his side...he shoots it with the deadliest eye that no one can deny...and in the midst of battle... you can hear his warlike cry... screaming come on Leathernecks ...we'll fight until we die...So listen to me ladies...here's a tip for you...get yourself a good Marine...there's nothin' he can't do...and when he gets to heaven ....Saint Peter he will tell... another Marine reporting, Sir... I've served my time in hell.*

CHAPTER V – *OPERATION RANCH HAND*

There aren't any birds in Quang Tri Provence.

A Marine's observation in 1967

At the same time Frank and Mike were finishing ITR and heading home on leave, Pentagon planners were ordering the implementation of a new operation that they thought would make the North Vietnamese realize that they couldn't win: U.S. troops would use chemical dioxins to defoliate the terrain across the DMZ.

Earlier in 1965, the Pentagon analysts and planners embraced the idea of defoliating the countryside and crops in Vietnam with chemical herbicides. They determined that removing leaves from bushes and killing trees would make it harder for the NVA and VC to conceal and camouflage their troops from the Americans. The Pentagon was certain that this would give the Americans a significant advantage by making it easier for the Marines to detect NVA soldiers trying to infiltrate across the barriers and obstacles of McNamara's Wall along the DMZ (*Project Dye Marker*).

The Pentagon "whiz kids" logically concluded that massive defoliation would allow the Marines to kill more NVA and VC, thereby improving the kill ratios that were so carefully calculated on their computers. The charts, diagrams and tables of data they used to present their plans to the Secretary and his academic advisors proved, at least on paper, that their defoliation plan would produce the desired results. Cleared fields of fire would expose the enemy to American artillery fire and air strikes, -- but only if enemy units were stupid enough to get caught in the open.

Beginning in 1965, the Military Assistance Command, Vietnam (MACV), America's Headquarters in Saigon, ordered the Air Force to use C-123 aircraft to spray defoliants across several areas throughout Vietnam. The code name was *Operation Ranch Hand*.

The Army designated specific target areas that included most of Quang Tri Provence, and they specifically targeted the entire 62 mile long DMZ as high priority areas. The MACV Commander, General Westmoreland, told the Marine Generals that *Operation Ranch Hand* would help their grunts defend the DMZ and kill more enemy soldiers.

Various types of herbicides had been tested in Vietnam on limited areas since 1961. They were referred to as "Rainbow Herbicides" because the 55-gallon drums containing the various mixtures of defoliants were marked with White, Purple, Pink, Green, Blue and Orange stripes. After observing the effects of the spraying on limited target areas, it became obvious that a herbicide, designated as "Agent Orange", was the most effective defoliant in killing everything from crops to underbrush and trees.

Aerial herbicide spray missions in southern Viet Nam, 1965 to 1971
(Source: U.S. Dept. of the Army).

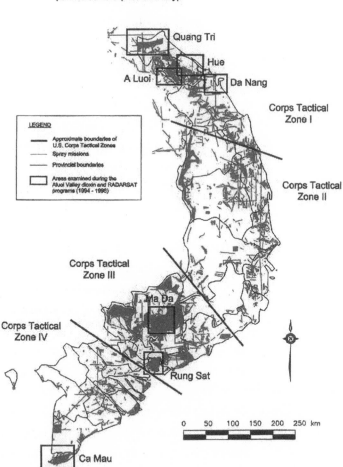

In the early 1960s, the original goal was to ruin crops, especially rice, which would deny the Viet Cong with a valuable source of food. The South Vietnamese farmers would be compensated for the loss of their crops and farm animals. In addition, their families, especially the children, would be monitored and observed to assess any long term effects of the dioxins.

Because there were so many areas of dense jungle foliage in Vietnam, the plan soon expanded to include large areas of the countryside that needed to be defoliated. The analysts at the Pentagon listened carefully to sales presentations made by representatives from Dow Chemical, Monsanto, and Diamond Shamrock. Each company had the capability and capacity to manufacture Agent Orange, and they emphasized the cost of manufacturing Agent Orange was inexpensive compared to other herbicides.

The Pentagon planners wanted to make sure that the Air Force had sufficient supplies of Agent Orange to accomplish its mission. So between 1962 and 1971, the Pentagon issued blanket purchase orders with all three companies to manufacture and deliver over 20 million gallons of Agent Orange. The peak deployment of *Operation Ranch Hand* occurred from 1967 through 1969. Corporate executives and researchers knew that the highly toxic polychlorinated herbicides they were manufacturing for the military would kill plants and harm humans and animals. A single Agent Orange 55-gallon drum contained mitochondrial toxins, immunotoxins, hormone disrupters, genotoxins, mutagens, teratogens, diabetogens and carcinogens which were implicated in a range of diseases. Exposure to the chemicals would likely cause several kinds of cancer, diabetes, Parkinson's and heart disease.

Operation Ranch Hand was fully implemented in 1967 while the 3rd Marine Division grunts filled sand bags, built bunkers, and dove for cover from enemy bombardments. The powerful chemicals killed every green plant and tree, soaked the earth, polluted water, got into C-Rations, stung the men's eyes, soaked every crevice of their body, and smelled and tasted like shit.

The terrain on the DMZ looked like a black and white photo of "no-man's land" during the trench warfare of World War I. There were the same foxholes, barbed wire, shell holes, and deadly open areas. It seemed that the Marines had stepped back into a deadly and dumb way to fight a war. Birds were lucky. They could fly away to escape the explosions, filth and poison that saturated the DMZ. So they did.

Back in Washington, D.C., the U.S. was winning the war in Vietnam – according to the Pentagon.

But casualties were mounting. As the Marines loaded their dead and wounded onto medevac helicopters along the DMZ, the Pentagon analysts insisted that combat units report larger numbers of enemy dead. Their attrition strategy required kill ratios to go up to "prove" the Pentagon plans were successful. But at what price to those Marines?

CHAPTER VI – HOME

Leaving on a jet plane,
don't know when I'll be back again.

Lyrics to *Leaving On a Jet Plane*, by John Denver

Orders to WESTPAC

It was mid-August when the platoons completed ITR, and the new Marines began receiving orders for their next "Permanent Duty Station". They waited impatiently outside the company office in a torrential downpour, until the Gunny came out and began to read off their names announcing their next assignment. Frank and Mike were not surprised when they were included with most of the others who were going as replacements to WESTPAC, or Fleet Marine Force, Western Pacific, Vietnam. Only a handful, five out of the two hundred men in the company, were assigned some place other than Vietnam.

The platoon was quiet, not having much to talk about as they went back to the barracks, changed their wet clothes, and packed their sea bags. Each would have ten days leave, a short time at home, before reporting to the

Staging Battalion at Camp Pendleton, California. There, they would go through a few more weeks of training before going to Nam.

In the summer of 1967, thousands of replacements were flowing through the troop pipeline headed for combat units in Vietnam. Men in the war zone were serving a thirteen-month tour of duty, casualties were high, and the numbers of wounded and KIAs, or killed in action, were increasing each week. New men had to take their place in the line units. With so many men going overseas and others coming home, Frank and Mike believed they would never see each other again.

They dressed in their neatly pressed tropical service uniforms, put on their dark green raincoats, and boarded a bus that took them to the airport in Jacksonville. They flew to Atlanta together, and there they said goodbye. Each wished the other good luck, exchanged home addresses, and promised to look each other up after the war. Frank flew on to New Orleans where he would make connections with a flight to Alexandria, and Mike went on a direct flight to Oklahoma City.

Frank was flying "military standby", and in New Orleans his luck ran out. A civilian passenger who had a full-fare ticket bumped Frank off the last flight to Alexandria. He called his mother and told her that he would take a bus for the last leg of the trip and gave her his arrival time.

Frank got comfortable in his seat as the bus pulled out of the terminal. He was going home, and he thought about his father and how much he missed him. Frank was

13 when his dad had a massive stroke that paralyzed his left side and caused the side of his face to sag. The head of the family, the strong, active always-positive role model was down on his back and never to recover. His father died two years later after a third stroke. The family was devastated by the loss and nothing was ever the same.

At nine o'clock, the Trailways bus pulled into the station and Frank, cramped, wrinkled and tired, looked out of the window and saw the family car parked in the lot. Passengers began to get off, and Frank saw his mother waiting near the station door. Her silver gray hair looked like she had been to the beauty parlor that day, and she wore a big smile.

"Oh son...I'm so glad you're home. You look so handsome in your uniform."

He hugged her tightly, kissed her cheek and hoped that she would not break down and cry. People stopped and stared, embarrassing Frank.

"Come on Mother. Let's go pick up my gear."

He put his arm around her and she fit snugly under his shoulder as they walked through the station to the baggage claim area.

"I'm sure glad to be home, Mother!"

Frank noticed that people were staring at him in his uniform, and that made him uncomfortable. He was relieved when a baggage handler pulled a cart filled with luggage into the room and began to unload. Frank pushed closer, so he could get his sea bag and get out of the station. He hoisted the green canvas bag up to his right shoulder and they headed for the car.

Frank hadn't heard from his two brothers for several months, so he asked, "what do you hear from Sean and Kevin?"

"Oh, they're fine," his mother answered, walking as fast as she could, trying to keep up with him. "Sean's got one more year at L.S.U., and he's working so hard trying to get his degree, bless his heart. Kevin's doing real well in Los Angeles. He got a promotion, and now he's responsible for supervising the unloading of the ships at the steamship line." Frank took the car keys, fumbled around until he found the trunk key, and dropped his sea bag in. Automatically, he opened the passenger door for his mother and as she got in she said, "are you sure you want to drive Frank, it's been so long since you've been behind the wheel of a car."

"Sure, Mother. I think I can manage."

As they pulled out of the parking lot onto Lee Street to head home, Frank could see that nothing had changed in Alexandria. It was Friday night, the streets were nearly deserted, and there was little or nothing going on.

Alexandria was a small town, about 65,000, and most people stayed home on the weekdays. It was hot and muggy with the high humidity Frank remembered.

They talked about mostly nothing on the way home. His mother chattered nervously about the neighbors and her friends.

"How's Tammy?" he finally interrupted.

Frank's pet collie and companion during his early years, Spotty, had died just before he finished junior high school, and he had bought Tammy, a beautiful, honey and white collie to fill the void.

"Oh, she's fine. She's really become quite a watchdog since you've been away. No one can come near the house without her raising the roof."

They passed Kroger's in the brightly lit shopping center where Frank had spent so many hours working after school, unloading trucks, stocking shelves and bagging groceries. He thought about his friends who probably still worked there, and made a mental note to be sure and stop in to see them while he was at home.

They pulled into Plantation Acres, the sub-division where they lived, and wound their way through the darkened streets, until Frank saw the family home. All the outside lights were on, and most of the lights in the front part of the house burned brightly.

"What are you doing, trying to support the power company?"

"No, Frank, I just wanted the house to look warm and lived in, when you got home."

When he got out of the car, he heard Tammy barking viciously from the fenced backyard. "Tammy! Tammy!" he called as he approached the gate. She kept barking and snarling, and Frank suspected she didn't recognize him in his uniform.

"I don't think she knows it's you, Frank."

He opened the gate and Tammy came charging out, still growling until she sniffed his outstretched hand. She began to cry, whining and pawing at the feet of the boy who had raised her.

"It's okay girl. It's okay Tammy. I'm home now."

He knelt, hugged and petted his dog for a while until she began to quiet down. He opened the back door, and she followed him down the hall to his bedroom where Tammy sat and watched while Frank unpacked his sea bag.

"Honey, are you hungry? I have your favorite, spaghetti and meat balls," his mother called from the kitchen.

"Yeah, that sounds great. How about a cold beer?"

"I bought you some today."

"I'm going to Vietnam."

His mother and Tammy sat watching him eat, and they listened while he talked about boot camp and infantry training. He made light of how tough it had been, and he changed the subject to Mike, his new best buddy. Frank told his mother what a great guy Mike was, and described some of their experiences during training.

"He sounds like such a nice boy, Frank."

"He's not a boy, Mother," he corrected with a smile.

"Oh, I know son," she sputtered. "He's a man and so are you."

He took his cleaned plate to the sink, rinsed it, dropped it in the hot water, went to the refrigerator for another beer and sat back down. He decided that now was as good a time as any to tell his mother where he was going.

"I guess you know I'll be home for ten days before I have to leave, huh, Mother?"

"Why, yes. I know. And then you go to your first duty station." His mother's deep, brown eyes were slightly glassy.

"Mother, I've got orders to Vietnam," he announced bluntly, knowing no other way to break the news.

"Oh, God, no! Not you! Not my son! Please, God, no!"

A flood of tears streamed down her face and she shook convulsively with deep sobs. Frank knelt and held her while she cried, trying to comfort her, hoping she would stop before she made herself sick. He went to the bathroom, wet a washcloth while she lay down on the couch in the living room, and with the cloth on her forehead, she calmed down.

"Frank, your Father's been dead for more than five years now, and both of your brothers live away from home. I won't be able to stand it if you go to Vietnam."

She began to ramble, trying to build a case for him not to go when there was nothing on earth that could change things. He was only one of the hundreds of thousands caught up in the age-old machinery of war. Besides, he believed it was his responsibility and his duty to fight.

"Daddy would agree with me Mother, he'd understand. He would be proud of me for doing the right thing. Anyway, if I hadn't joined the Corps, the Army would have drafted me. Remember, I lost my student deferment when I flunked out of college my first semester."

"Oh you haven't been reading the newspapers and watching the news on television like I have!" she cried. "Our boys are getting killed and maimed over there every week by the hundreds, and you're going...."

"Wait a minute, just hold on for a minute and listen to what I've got to say," he interrupted. "What makes me any different from those guys you're talking about? I'm no better than they are. I'm not too good to fight for this country, and I don't intend to die either. If you think the Marine Corps taught me how to die, you're wrong! I've been taught how to fight and live and how to make the other guy die for his country." He smiled at the old Marine joke. "I've learned how to do whatever it takes to win and survive. I'm going to have to take my chances, just like everybody else, and nothing can change the fact that I'm going."

Frank stood and held his mother in his arms until she stopped sobbing. "I'll be OK. I'll be fine," he promised.

"Oh no. No! No! No!"

Skippy's

He had a restless night and at dawn, out of habit, he went on a three-mile run with Tammy through the neighborhood. He was feeling better after his shower when he sat down for breakfast.

"Look, Mother," he said, as he buttered his toast, "I know this isn't easy for you, and I can promise you it's not easy for me. But while I'm home, I don't want to talk about the war or me going to Vietnam. I'd like my leave to be as normal as possible. Okay?"

His mother poured two cups of coffee and sat down at the table. "Alright, Frank. But I want to have you and your brothers together again. I called them while you were out this morning, and they plan to come home your last weekend here."

After his mother went to work, Frank spent the morning cutting the grass, trimming the driveway and sidewalk, and by late afternoon, he sat with Tammy in the flowerbeds, pulling weeds. It was a typical hot Louisiana afternoon and his T-shirt was soaked with sweat.

Frank's family home was a modest, but nice house and he remembered the years of financial struggle to keep it. His Father had left little money in the bank and one very small life insurance policy. Maintaining the home had been a long and hard fight, especially for Frank, the youngest and the last to leave home. At boot camp he'd taken out an allotment to be sent to his mother each month. Not much money but ever little bit helped cover her expenses.

That night, he dressed in civilian clothes and went to Skippy's, his old high school hangout, to meet some friends from work and school. The drive-in hadn't changed much, the same orange neon sign flashed in the window of the joint, announcing they served cold bud. Annie, the middle aged woman who ran the place, still sloshed mug after frosted mug of beer across the counter to boys with false IDs who claimed to be eighteen.

The big busted girls riding elephants and swinging from circus trapezes that was painted on the plate glass front of the pinball machines, smiled down at the guys who constantly poured roll after roll of nickels into them. Skippy's was one of the few places in town that paid off on the pinball machines, and Frank remembered bitterly the night he'd decided to gamble on them. He had gotten loaded on beer and lost his entire paycheck, dumping nickels into the machines.

"Well, I'll be damn! Look who's here!" Horrible Rusty roared above the din when Frank walked in. "Where'd you get that goofy haircut, O'Brian?"

"Hey, Frank! Welcome home," Annie shouted from behind the bar.

"How's it goin' Annie," he waved, ignoring Rusty momentarily. "How 'bout a cold one, Sweetheart?"

Annie poured Frank his usual draft, insisted it was on the house, and kissed him on the cheek. Frank walked to the end of the bar where his three buddies waited, slopping down beer after beer.

Frank had known Rusty, Fred and Will almost his whole life. Rusty was a big, thick chested blond who loved his '56 Chevy, and he drove it like a mad man. Rusty quit high school in his senior year and joined the Marine Corps, but unfortunately, he was injured in boot camp and he was forced out of the Corps with a medical discharge. Now, Rusty sold life insurance and Frank suspected that Rusty was envious of him becoming a Marine.

"Go to hell, Rusty," he laughed good-naturedly. "Glad to see you three useless pricks are still where I left you." They all laughed and shook hands.

Fred was the slim, scholarly type. He held down two jobs to pay for college and he played a wicked alto sax in a Dixie land band that also earned him a few dollars. He knew Fred was planning to get an advanced degree in English and teach college.

Will and Frank had been friends since the first grade. The played together, dug foxholes and fought Japs together, they teased Will's big sister and they built a tree house in a pecan tree in Will's back yard. They spent so much time together Will's mother considered Frank a member of the family. She had cried when Frank said goodbye and left for boot camp. Frank wasn't looking forward to telling her he was going to Vietnam. Will and Fred were both taking classes at the LSU extension campus in Alexandria.

"Yep. We're all just the way you left us, Frank," Will announced. "Drunk or getting drunk."

"Gotten laid since ya left?" Rusty asked.

"Nah, hadn't had time. I been so busy getting screwed by the Corps," Frank laughed, chugging down half his beer.

"I can believe that," Fred replied without smiling.

"Must not be too bad, Frank," Rusty said. "You lookin' all fit and trim. That Marine shit must be agreein' with ya."

"Ah, it ain't too bad. You guys makin' your grades or are ya gonna screw up, flunk out and get drafted?"

"Christ, I hope not," Will shook his head. "I'm barely maintainin' a *C* average and this semester I'm sweatin' my Econ final. Makes me vomit to think of bein' drafted and I got this hard ass Prof who's a World War II vet. Thinks everybody should be in the Army when there's some fightin and dyin' to be done."

"Hope he gives you an *F*," Frank chuckled, while Will blanched.

He didn't really mean it, knowing that Will would never make it in the military. He'd just get in the way.

"Come on, man. Don't say that," he whined. "I ain't goin' in the Army and get my ass shot off."

"How you doin' Fred?"

"Got a strong *B* goin' right now, and with a little luck, I'll have an *A minus* at the end of the year."

"Still humpin' the books, huh?"

"Better than humpin' an Army pack and rifle through some miserable ass jungle." Rusty gulped his beer and looked Frank in the eye. "By the time you get outta the Marines, I'll be on my way to bein' the president of an insurance company."

"You're serious about this stupid war aren't you, Frank?" Fred asked.

"Yep. It's never gonna end, unless we finally decide to kick ass and take names." Frank paused and looked at his old friend, who was obviously serious. "Why? You think we oughta' do somethin' else?"

"I think we oughta' let the Vietnamese people fight their own civil war, by themselves. It's none of our business."

"Give me a break, Fred! Hey, Annie!" Frank shouted, over the racket, "How 'bout another round? You don't believe that propaganda do ya?" Frank continued. "You want to just sit back while the communists take over all of Southeast Asia?"

"That's a little exaggerated, Frank. The North Vietnamese want to unite their country. They're not interested in Cambodia or Laos."

"Who told ya that crap? Ho Chi Minh? I guess you believe it, too." Frank took a swig of beer and tried to calm his temper. "Vietnam is no different than Korea. The north wants to conquer the south, and if they're not stopped, they just keep on goin'."

"I don't believe that crap!" Fred answered.

"Well, I do, ya goddamn liberal pansy!" Frank growled. He hadn't expected the conversation to take this direction, and now he was mad.

"Here ya go boys,'" Annie interrupted as she put four dripping mugs on the bar, clearing away the empties.

"Frank, you're sure lookin' good," she laughed, patting him on the cheek. "Sandy was in the other night askin' about ya!"

Frank had never gone steady in high school, but Sandy had been one of the best looking girls he'd ever dated. They had gone to the graduation dance together and now, she was going to college with Will and Fred.

"No shit, Annie? I'm gonna look her up while I'm home," Frank answered, still a little hot over the exchange with Fred.

Sandy

They sat for a few hours just shooting the shit, telling jokes, drinking beer, but carefully avoided discussing the Marine Corps or Vietnam. Then about 10:30, Frank's old girlfriend, Sandy, walked in, waved, and walked over to join the group. As she walked toward them, Frank thought, holy shit, she looks terrific!

Sandy had beautiful blond hair that fell down below

her shoulders, and she had a terrific figure that everyone admired. She wasn't very tall, about five foot three, with beautiful legs. As she approached, Frank laughed himself, remembering on several occasions when Rusty had observed, "Sandy had a perfect pair of legs that went all the way up to her butt."

Frank also remembered that when they were dating, they had made out passionately on a number of occasions, but had never made love. None of the guys ever claimed to have scored with Sandy, and Frank had often dreamed of being the first. She was obviously glad to see him, and she gave Frank a big hug and kissed him warmly. Warming to the occasion, the crowd at Skippy's stood and clapped their approval. A little embarrassed, Frank reacted by giving her his bar stool, putting his arm around her tiny waist, and giving her a gentle squeeze.

After Annie served them another round of beers, Frank whispered to Sandy that he thought they should go someplace where they could be alone. Sandy smiled, finished her beer in one swallow and whispered back, "my parents are out of town for the weekend, so let's go to my home." They got up, said their goodbyes to the guys, and headed out the door. All the while, Frank thinking, *oh, man, I can't believe this is happening! I can't believe it!*

They drove quickly across town to Sandy's neighborhood where they found her house dark and unlit. They parked in the garage and Sandy fumbled with the keys to the back door in the dark. Inside, she grabbed his hand and led him quickly through the kitchen, the den and finally to the stairs leading to the bedrooms upstairs. They took the stairs two at a time and half ran down the hall to her corner room. There, Sandy turned on a small desk lamp, quickly closed the curtains, and turned with open arms to embrace Frank as they moved toward her bed.

About an hour later, they lay exhausted in sweat soaked sheets. They talked in low voices, almost a whisper.

"How long will you be gone this time?" Sandy asked.

"A year. Maybe a little longer."

"Are you scared?"

Frank paused, and then quietly said, "a little, I guess, but I'm excited and anxious to get going, more than anything." He reached over and took a cigarette from the pack sitting on top of the nightstand.

"I always knew, even when I was a little kid, that someday I'd join the Marines. I've always thought that going to war would be the ultimate adventure, a real test for any man. And it'll be great to come home after the war with my Unit. It'll be like it was after World War II, when all of our soldiers returned. I can see my Unit in a parade, marching down the street in some big city, maybe New York, while crowds wave and cheered our return." Frank paused, then added thoughtfully, "there'll be plenty of time afterward for me to go back and finish school, get a good job, and settle down somewhere."

Time flies

During Frank's leave, he and Sandy were almost inseparable. But although they were constantly together, both were careful not to voice or express any type of long term commitment to the other. They knew this was only for the "here and now" because he was going to Vietnam and Sandy was going off to college. Neither wanted the stress of a relationship that would complicate the very different lives they were going to be living in the days to come.

Frank's days quickly fell into a routine. He ran each morning, worked around the house, played with Tammy, took his mother to lunch, visited with his buddies at Kroger's in the afternoon, and picked Sandy up at school after her classes.

Frank and Sandy regularly ate dinner with his mother, and Sandy made an effort to make Frank's mother like her, but with little success. His mother thought Sandy was "loose" and "too fast", but she seemed to understand their relationship, and didn't interfere. Each night after the dishes were washed and stacked, Frank and Sandy disappeared for the remainder of the evening. And more often than not, Frank didn't come back home until the next day.

His brothers made it home on the last weekend of his leave for the family reunion, and Frank was glad to see them. They were still the same. Sean was tall and skinny, and he was concentrating on finishing college, while Kevin was still overweight and worked as a supervisor at a Los Angeles steamship line. They both thought Frank looked great, "all lean and mean," as Sean said.

On Frank's last night home, Sandy joined the family for a backyard barbeque. They were all gathered around, drinking beers, with his brothers telling "secrets" – pranks and practical jokes that the three of them had done but had kept hidden from their mother. But as they reminisced about the "good old days", Frank became worried that the stories were going to lead to a very emotional "farewell" scene. He just wanted to be with his family, to enjoy drinking beer and eating good food. As the conversations became separated by long periods of silence, Frank opened more beers and encouraged everyone to "chug up". They all knew – this was no time to get emotional.

Later that evening, Frank said goodbye to Sandy. They didn't make any promises or commitment to a relationship. They were going in separate directions, and there was no way to know if Frank would return from Vietnam.

His mother insisted they go to Mass on Sunday morning, his last day at home, even though it had been years since they'd gone to church as a family. Frank put on his uniform, and they took pictures of Frank and his brothers in the front yard. His mother beamed with joy and shed a few tears, knowing that this might be the last time she would have all three of her sons together with her.

His mother held his arm tightly, lifted her head high and marched down the middle aisle of the church with her three sons. They sat in the second pew on the right, just as they always had in the old days, before Frank's father died. The parish priest, an old friend of the family, nodded his recognition from the pulpit as the choir began to sing, *Holy, Holy, Holy. Lord God Almighty....*

Frank wasn't listening to the priest's sermon. His thoughts roamed from memories of the past to trying to imagine the future. If boot camp and infantry training was only a taste of the real thing as his DIs said, Vietnam would be much worse. He sat motionless and prayed that God would give him strength and courage. Like any untested, uninitiated warrior, the nagging fear of being a coward and letting his Brother Marines down in battle was overpowering. *God, please give me the courage to stand and fight.* He couldn't stand the thought of running in a firefight. He recalled the saying that "brave men die once, cowards die a thousand times."

If I'm wounded, please don't let it be my legs. Please God. I couldn't stand not being able to stand and walk. Frank remembered that after his father had his stroke, he was paralyzed and bound to a wheelchair. Being crippled broke his father's heart.

Frank believed in God and life after death, but wondered what it's like to die. Will it hurt? Will it be quick? Will I suffer? *Please God. Let me survive and come home.*

Frank remembered the Marine Rifleman's Prayer he learned in boot camp and sitting safely in the church pew, he pleaded with God:

> *Dear God, my Father, through Thy Son, hear the prayer of a warrior son. Give my eyes a vision keen to see the thing that must be seen. A steady hand I ask of Thee. The feel of wind on land or sea. Let me not ever careless be of life or limb or liberty.*
> *For Justice sake, a quiet heart and grace, and strength to do my part. To God and Country,*

Home and Corps, let me be faithful evermore.
Amen.

Frank was jolted back to the church service when everyone stood up for the final hymn, *Onward Christian Soldier.* He looked at his mother and saw tears running down her cheeks.

It was August 30, 1967, and Frank's two-week leave was over. They drove to the airport, and his mother and brothers hugged him, and they all tried unsuccessfully not to cry. His mother pressed a miniature bible in his hand and Frank promised to carry it with him wherever he went.

"I love you brother," his brothers said. "Take care of yourself."

"I love you son. God speed."

Frank walked across the tarmac, climbed the stairs to the door of the Eastern Airlines jet. He stopped at the door, turned and waved goodbye to his family, wondering to himself, *will I ever see them again?*

CHAPTER VII – WAR OF ATTRITION

The military strategy of attrition consists of belligerent attempts to win a war by wearing down the enemy to the point of collapse through continuous losses in personnel and materiel.

Attrition Warfare - Wikipedia

The Defense of South Vietnam

As the Eastern Airline stewardess concluded her pre-flight announcements and dimmed the cabin lights, Frank buckled his seat belt, turned on his reading light, and picked up a magazine that had been discarded by a passenger in the seat pocket in front of him. It was going to be a long, lonely flight to San Diego, then on to Camp Pendleton where Frank would join other Marines on orders to Vietnam.

As he thumbed through the magazine, he turned to an article on the U.S. involvement in Vietnam, and the heading grabbed his attention:

SEARCH & DESTROY

In 1954, Vietnam was partitioned along the 17th
Parallel, with North Vietnam led by Ho Chi
Minh, and South Vietnam headed by Ngo Dinh
Diem. In the same year, President Eisenhower
committed the United States to defend South
Vietnam from the conquest and takeover by the
Communist North. The foreign and military
policies of Presidents Eisenhower, Kennedy and
Johnson, operated under the "domino theory", an
assumption that, if not checked, Russia and China
would spread communist control across South East
Asia, beginning with Vietnam, then followed by
Laos, Cambodia, Burma, the Philippines and
eventually Australia. The United States couldn't
allow this spread of Communism to happen, so the
U.S. military was committed to defend South
Vietnam against any attempt by North Vietnam
to invade the South.

In the 50s and 60s, the Cold War required the
United States to stop the spread of communism.
From the beginning, the military strategy was
defensive in nature; that is, a war of attrition that
would have U.S. and allied troops inflict massive
casualties on the Viet Cong (the Communist
insurgents located in the South) and North
Vietnamese Army, forcing their leaders, General
Vo Nguyen Giap and Ho Chi Minh, to cease
aggressions against the South Vietnam government.
It has been reported that President Johnson,

Secretary of Defense McNamara, and a conference room filled with academic consultants, have chosen to ignore the advice of the generals on the Joint Chiefs of Staff. Instead, the President and his advisors determined that they couldn't "win" the war without committing thousands of more ground troops to secure the entire South Vietnam border and protect the Vietnamese population

The Generals wanted to pursue an offensive strategy for winning the war and defeating the North Vietnamese. The Generals were veterans of World War II and they knew that you won wars by attacking the enemy. Offense won battles and wars and defense led to casualties and stalemate.

The Generals were too aggressive. McNamara and his "whiz kids" considered their experience, ideas and advice as being "old and out of date". The Generals, they concluded, didn't understand modern operations research tools, analysis techniques, and innovative programs that would stop the North Vietnamese aggression by inflicting heavy casualties. That was why accurate body count was so important.

Frank was stunned that the military – especially the Marines – were not there to win the war against the Viet Cong and the North Vietnamese Army. He couldn't believe it. But as Frank read on, the article did make it sound as if he would be involved in a war of attrition:

In response to this directive, General William Westmoreland, Commander of US Military Assistance Command (MACV) has called for "search and destroy" missions, where U.S. troops would seek out and engage enemy strongholds and positions in the jungles, then return to their base camps. It has been confirmed that to measure the success of these missions, General Westmoreland has ordered that all combat units are to provide MAVC Headquarters a "body count" of the enemy killed on those missions. The goal was to have a body count ratio of 10 to 1 against the enemy.

Based on the most recent information reported by, MACV Headquarters, between 1961 and 1966, 159,500 Viet Cong (VC) and North Vietnamese Army (NVA) troops have been killed, compared to the deaths of 8,671 US force and 40,958 South Vietnamese (SVN) forces.

Frank closed the magazine, stuffed it back in the seat pocket, and thought, what type of bullshit policy is this? We've been trained to kick ass and win. And now we are expected to engage in combat to make the VC and NVA stand up and wave a white flag at us! He put his head back, closed his eyes, and said to himself, *what a crock of crap!*

General Giap and the NVA Offense

In 1967, General Vo Nguyen Giap, the Commander of the North Vietnamese Army, sent three seasoned North Vietnamese Army Divisions with over 40,000 hard core troops south, across the DMZ to attack the Marines. While the NVA ignored the "prohibition" against hostile forces crossing the DMZ located along the 17th parallel, President Johnson directed MACV to order the Marines to observe the integrity of the DMZ and remain south of the Bến Hải River that divided South and North Vietnam.

Giap deployed hundreds of artillery and rocket batteries buried in caves that fired support for the NVA infantry attacking the Dye Marker bunkers. They had Forward Artillery Observers (FAOs) hidden all around the strongpoints, and the spotters directed deadly accurate fire on the Marines. When the Marines heard the report of incoming fire, they ran for cover, ducked and dove into foxholes. They prayed they wouldn't be hit with the deadly explosions and jagged flying shrapnel.

In May of that year, the 812th NVA Regiment launched a night attack on Con Thien, one of the Dye Marker strong points, manned by a company from 1st Battalion, 4th Marines. NVA Sappers blew holes in the concertina wire and attacked the Marine bunkers with flamethrowers. The NVA closed with the Marines and there was vicious hand-to-hand combat. The battle went on for six hours and by dawn, the Marines had killed almost 200 NVA, captured 8 and the Marines suffered 44 killed and 110 wounded.

In September, the NVA tried to destroy Con Thien again. A company from 3rd Battalion, 9th Marines took their turn in "the meat grinder" when the NVA began to pound the small hill daily with 152 howitzers, 120mm and 82mm mortars and 122mm rockets. The record for incoming rounds was set on September 25th when 1,500 rounds hit Con Thien.

The Marines had held, and General Giap could not have his American "Bien Dien Phu" at Con Thien.

Body Bags, Caskets and Flags

The Pentagon "whiz kids" created tables with their computer programs that showed the carefully calculated progression of the kill ratios: *20 dead NVA only cost 2 dead Marines. 100 dead NVA only cost 10 dead Marines.* Page after page of tables -- all estimates carefully calculated so the "actual body count" could be compared and measured against their estimates.

The Pentagon sent a strongly worded message to General Westmoreland, the MACV Commander in Saigon, which emphasized that body count reports must be accurate, and they should be sent each day to the Pentagon so as to arrive no later than 7:30AM EST. The Pentagon was certain that the kill ratios would certainly break the will of the NVA. But the Pentagon didn't know the resolve of General Giap, or the Viet Cong, or the North Vietnamese Army soldiers. The Vietnamese had decades of "attrition" experience, and they would continue to be a determined and aggressive adversary.

As U.S. combat losses began to dramatically increase in 1966 and into 1967, the Pentagon planners told purchasing to order more body bags, caskets and flags. No one knew how many Americans would have to die before the attrition of North Vietnamese killed and wounded would cause them to give up.

CHAPTER VIII --THROUGH THE PIPELINE

I do not find it easy to send the flower of our youth,
our finest young men, into battle.

Lyndon B. Johnson, *News Conference,* 1965

Camp Las Pulgas

In 1967, the number of Americans in Vietnam grew
to over 480,000, and by September the monthly "killed in
action" (KIA) was over 460 and growing. Another 3,800
were wounded each month, hospitalized, treated and sent
back to combat but many wounds were too severe and the
warriors were sent home. The Americans who were lucky
enough to survive their 13-month tour in Nam were
rotated back to the United States and many were discharged
from the service. The pipeline to provide replacements for
casualties and troops returning home was increasing to a
flood of young men from all across America.

Frank arrived on September 1, 1967 at Camp Las
Pulgas, the Staging Battalion and training area for Marines
headed to Vietnam. Las Pulgas means "the fleas" in
Spanish, and Frank thought that it was a very fitting name

for a Marine training area! The valleys and mountains several miles inland from the Pacific Ocean were infested with fleas and all types of insects. These pests made climbing up the hills and down into the valleys in the California heat a real challenge!

The Marine bus from the San Diego airport was loaded with other young Marines headed to Staging where they were to begin the final three weeks of training before being shipped overseas. Thousands of men were being trained and processed every month, and Frank wasn't surprised to find he didn't know any of the guys in his unit.

On the first day of training, he was issued an M-16, the type of rifle that was then being used in Nam. It was shorter and lighter than the M-14, but the stock was plastic instead of hard wood. It seemed fragile to Frank, and he didn't like or trust the weapon. Instructors taught them how to clean and maintain the rifle, insisting that it was the fastest firing, most deadly rifle in the world.

He fired it during exercises and had to admit that it did fire faster than the M-14, and it was easy to carry. But a lot of the men's M-16s experienced jamming during training on the firing range. Particles of dirt or sand would get into the magazines and on the ammo, so when a "dirty" round was chambered, it fired but it wouldn't eject, blocking the remaining cartridges in the magazine. Frank thought it would be a great weapon to use -- if you could limit your fighting to a nice, clean, dirt-free battlefield.

During the following weeks, they force marched all over the Base, twenty miles each day, and spent endless hours learning small unit tactics in jungle operations. They were introduced to mines, booby traps, bamboo stakes, called punji sticks, and other surprises the NVA and VC, or "gooks," might have in store for them.

During patrol exercises, instructors constantly ambushed the units, firing blanks and screamed their heads off, which scared most of the troops. Frank learned to attack when ambushed, and never dive in the opposite direction, looking for cover. "Gooks," the instructors said, "usually planted punji sticks in the ground around ambush sites. Diving for cover would earn an undisciplined Marine a chest full of bamboo spikes. The only defense for an ambush was to charge and kill the attackers."

All during training, indoctrination lectures stressed the savagery of the NVA and VC. They also were warned never to trust any civilians -- men, women or children -- and that the VC and NVA would even use the bodies of their own corpses and those of villagers to kill Americans. The enemy had been known to booby trap them so that an explosive charge would go off when the body was moved. Horror stories were told about the enemy torturing and mutilating Marines who were captured. It was common for the enemy to castrate an American, and then stuff his genitals down his throat before they shot him. They then would leave the body in the open so that other Marines would discover him.

Flight to Okinawa

The last week in September 1967 they finished training and boarded buses for the ride to the Los Angeles Airport. As Frank and the other Marines rode along the

California freeways in rush hour traffic, people returning from work looked inquisitively at the green buses packed with troops. The commuters were going home to have supper, watch the news, and probably see the latest reports on the fighting in Vietnam. And just three week later, on October 21, nearly 100,000 people would march to the Pentagon to protest against the U.S. involvement in the war in Vietnam. Americans support for the war was rapidly falling.

A Continental Airlines DC-8 Stretch waited on a remote runway for the troops. As the sun began to set over the ocean they were about to cross, Frank and other Marines climbed the stairs leading to the cabin. Smiling, polite and good-looking stewardesses helped them get settled in their seats as the jet taxied out on to the runway. The *Fasten Seatbelts* and *No Smoking* signs looked down at the two hundred plus men as the engines roared.

Everyone was quiet as the plane cleared the runway and headed for the open sea. Frank looked out the window, watched the coastline disappear, and retreated further into his thoughts, as did everyone else on the plane.

He lit a cigarette and tried to stretch, but there was little or no room on the packed airplane. He had been lucky to be assigned a window seat, which would allow him to rest his head against the bulkhead and sleep. But he was having trouble finding space for him to stretch out his legs. Two other Marines sat to his left, both of them as young as or younger than Frank. And like everyone else going to Vietnam, they had freshly skinned heads, "complements" of Marine Corps barbers!

"Hey, buddy, where you from anyway?" drawled the guy sitting next to him. "Louisiana. What about you?"

"Hell, I'm from Mississippi. I guess that makes us neighbors or somethin," he nudged Frank in the ribs and laughed at the weak joke. "Jim Thompson's my name."

"Glad to meet ya, Jim. I'm Frank O'Brian."

All of the men began to loosen up and talk as the stewardesses moved up and down the aisle preparing to serve dinner, and it wasn't long before the girls were joking and cutting up with the troops as they passed through the cabin.

"What's your MOS (Military Occupational Specialty)? You a grunt or what?" Jim asked.

"Yeah, *0311 Infantryman*, what else. What about you?"

"Yep. Me, too. A basic ground pounder," he laughed.

"I wonder what Division we'll be assigned to. I'd kinda like the 1st Marines."

"Yeah? How come?"

"Oh, I guess I've always heard a lot of good things about them. They fought at Guadalcanal and all the other islands during World War II, and then they fought their way out of the Chosin Reservoir in Korea. I guess they've got a lot of history and tradition, and I'd like to be a part of that."

"Yeah, but the 3rd Marines ain't no bunch of slouches! They've done pretty good, themselves, and they were the first to land in Nam."

They talked for a while about the pros and cons of

each division now fighting in Vietnam, and decided it wouldn't make much difference which unit they were assigned to.

The stewardesses came by and served their chopped steak dinners. "Hey, sweet pea, how about a couple of bourbons to wash this down with?" drawled Jim.

"I'm sorry, but there isn't any liquor on this flight," smiled the stew.

"Well, if I can't have anything to drink, how about sitting on my lap and helping me cut up my meat?"

Everyone laughed, including the stewardesses, but she shook her head. "Maybe if you clean your plate, I'll come back and help you with your dessert," she replied. The men laughed and cheered at her response. "But right now, I've got to finish serving all of these other hungry guys."

"Nice try, Jim," Frank laughed. They attacked their food.

"Ya know," Jim said, in between gulps, "I'd like to get to Nam just in time for a big operation. I mean all I hear about is how we're constantly fighting the VC and NVA in the south. Playing cowboys and gooks." Frank laughed at the joke as Jim continued. "What I can't understand is how come we don't land a division or two in North Vietnam and out flank the bastards the way we did in Korea."

"This makes sense to me. But the Chinese would probably come in, just like they did in Korea."

Their discussion of battles to be fought, broken by intermittent naps filled the many hours that it took for the

DC-8 to reach Okinawa. Engines were throttled back and flaps were extended as the plane began the descent. Those who were not awake opened their eyes as the stewardesses turned on the lights in the cabin in preparation for the landing. All of the stewardesses had been great with the troops, laughing, telling jokes and talking about hometowns across the country that they had visited. Frank and Jim looked out into the black night and they could see the lights shining from the cities on the island.

"I'll be glad to get off this plane. My legs and ass are numb, and I got a crick in my neck from sleeping crooked."

"Yeah, me, too," Frank answered, lighting one more cigarette that he probably wouldn't have time to finish before the *No Smoking* light came on.

The plane continued to slow, losing altitude, and it seemed to stop altogether and hang motionless in the ink, black sky.

"In preparation for our landing at Kadena Air Force Base in Okinawa, please fasten your seat belts and observe the *No Smoking* sign when it appears," announced the senior stewardess. She was a little blond from Chicago, and she waited patiently as guys returned from the bathroom, took their seats and strapped themselves in. The other four stewardesses assigned to the flight stood around and they talked quietly at the front of the cabin.

"Have all you guys had a good flight?" she asked over the intercom.

"YEAH!" shouted the troops in unison. Everyone laughed.

"Was the service okay?"

YEAH! they yelled amid cheers and whistles.

"Okay, we'd like to ask you guys to do something for us, if you wouldn't mind."

"Sure. You name it! What do ya want?" roared the men.

The five stewardesses looked at each other and then the blond switched the intercom on again. "How about singing the *Marines Hymn* for us."

Everyone began to struggle out of their seatbelts so that they could stand up and assume the position of attention as tradition required.

From the back of the plane, the hymn rolled forward until everyone was singing as best they could, blasting out their song.

From the halls of Montezuma to the shores of Tripoli...We'll fight our country's battles....

The plane began to make its' final bank...*First to fight for right and freedom...We are proud to claim the title of United States Marine!*

The stewardesses joined in, tears streaming down their faces. A deafening cheer ended the *Hymn*, and they all took their seats, buckled back up, and prepared for landing.

Schwab

Frank and Jim were able to stick together on Okinawa. They were processed at Camp Schwab, a Marine Base on the north end of the island where they waited for hours in line at the personnel offices of the 3rd Marine Amphibious Force. Clerks frantically pounded out reams of orders, assigning the replacements to specific units. In the late afternoon, after a long and boring day, Frank and Jim received their orders and found they'd been assigned to the same battalion.

With orders in hand, and not quite believing their good luck, they rushed to supply where they were issued their jungle utilities, or uniforms, and jungle boots. They had to hurry because they were scheduled to leave Okinawa on an Air Force transport the following morning. They spent that night in a troop transit barracks.

It was a cloudless, breezy morning and their spirits were high because finally, the waiting was over and they were on their way. They marched with other troops across the tarmac to the giant, green camouflage-painted C-130 where the rear cargo ramp was lowered to take on the Marines. They marched up into the bay area, which was lined with rows of shoulder-to-shoulder webbed seats that faced each other. They took their seats, tried to adjust their bodies, and strapped themselves in.

The ten-hour flight was a noisy, cold, miserable experience for the troops. The deafening roar of the engines, and the bone chilling cold in the unheated cabin, made it impossible to talk or sleep. They were relieved when the plane touched down at Da Nang, the rear-loading ramp was lowered, and the new arrivals were greeted with a blast of hot, humid Vietnam air.

Nam

They arrived in-country on October 1, 1967, the beginning of Vietnam's monsoon season. The air base at

Da Nang looked a lot like the one they had just left in Okinawa, with a few noticeable differences. Hangers and planes were spread all over the place, and the Phantom jet fighters, painted camouflage green, were parked in open pits surrounded by sandbags. There were mountains surrounding the base and every now and then, they could hear the pounding thud of big guns being fired. As soon as they arrived, the troops were rushed out of the heat and scorching sun into a hanger where clerks waited to process them in.

About forty of the new arrivals stood in a line designated for replacements for the 1st Battalion, 3rd Marine Regiment. They had been told to wait while the clerks marched past and pulled off one copy, the original, of their orders and returned to their desks. Hours later, the clerks passed the orders back to the new arrivals with their company assignments. As the clerks marched down the row, they handed back the assignment sheets saying, "Alpha, Alpha, Alpha, Alpha, Bravo, Bravo, Bravo, Bravo," and by the time they got to Frank and Jim, the clerks were call out, "Charlie, Charlie, Charlie" company.

A burly 1st Sergeant marched into the room and took control of the proceedings.

"Okay, shut up and listen up!" he growled. "You men assigned to 1st Battalion which is the Battalion Landing Team for the 3rd Marine Division and right now, they're in Da Nang Harbor onboard the U.S.S. *Iwo Jima* or the U.S.S. *Cleveland*. Men assigned to Alpha and Bravo companies will go to the *Cleveland*. It's an LSD, or Landing Ship Dock for those that don't know what LSD stands for.

Men in Charlie and Delta companies will go to the *Iwo*, an amphibious assault ship, LPH or Landing Platform for Helicopters. Buses will be here in a little while and they'll take you down to the docks. Landing craft will pick you up there, and take you out to your respective ships. Any questions?"

"Yeah, Top, I do," Jim raised his hand.

"What is it!" snapped the 1st Sergeant.

"Is the Battalion Landing Team gettin' ready to invade North Vietnam or what?"

"Holy shit, no!" barked the 1st Sergeant. "You'll find out about how they operate when you get to your unit." He turned on his heels and marched away, shaking his head.

"Kinda pissed him off, huh?" Jim chuckled.

"Yeah, I guess we aren't going to be kicking ass on their home ground anytime soon," Frank replied. "I wonder why he's so bent outa shape."

"All 1st Sergeants get pissed when you ask questions. Even if they told you to ask the question."

Da Nang

During the afternoon, buses and trucks came and went, taking the replacement troops to various units in the Da Nang area. Finally, the 1st Sergeant announced that transportation was waiting out front to take the 1st Battalion replacements to the docks. Tired of being cooped up in the hangar, they were glad to get outside to see a little bit of the country.

"Christ! Get a load of that bus, will ya!" Jim

gasped.

The windows of the bus were covered with heavy mesh, and the driver wore a flak jacket, helmet and carried an M-16. Patched bullet holes covered the sides of the bus near the driver's seat and along the right side.

"Excuse me driver, but isn't New Orleans the next stop?" Frank asked as he got to the door.

"Shit, Frank, you gettin' on the wrong bus! This one's going to Hattiesburg!"

"Wrong boots! This bus is going to the grinder, and you are fresh meat!" laughed the driver.

"Very damn funny," Frank replied. "What's with the wire mesh?"

"We don't want some VC throwing a grenade or satchel charge in the bus and blowing you cherries away," chuckled the driver. "Considerate. Very considerate."

When everyone was settled in their seats, the driver gunned the engine, popped the clutch and the bus roared down the street. They cleared the hangar area and pulled out onto a dusty main road that ran parallel to the runways. A group of Phantoms were taking off, two at a time, and the noise was deafening. Their wings were loaded with clusters of bombs and rockets of various sizes and shapes. Flames and smoke belched from their afterburners as they roared into the air, banked to the left, and headed north.

Flights of choppers, Hueys, CH-34s, and the big double rotor CH-46s, rose from various areas and skimmed off in different directions. Da Nang looked like the Grand Central Station of combat aircraft, and Frank and Jim sat in awe. As they neared the outskirts of the base, they passed bunkers and roll after roll of barbed wire, which was part of the perimeter security. Marines manning the positions shot the finger and cursed at the bus as the driver gunned the engine and kicked up more dust. They could see several guys lying around reading magazines, but they jumped up and ran into the bunkers to escape the dust as the bus passed.

When the busses cleared the gate, the road became packed with civilians. Small vendor stalls crammed with black market candy, cigarettes, booze and anything else you might want, lined the sides of the road. The merchants all looked alike with the round bamboo, conical hats, black pajamas and their teeth blackened from chewing betel nuts, a common habit among the Vietnamese. They were small and wiry. Each had black, greasy hair and they were constantly jabbering at one another. Half-naked kids ran along beside the bus shouting, "Chop-Chop" or "Cigarette, Cigarette!" Everyone was filthy. And as the buses passed, some looked up and shouted, "GI numba one! VC numba ten!"

Old women and young girls mingled with the men, and most were carrying loads of merchandise of one type or another. Most of the women were dressed in long flowing white skirt over black pajamas pants, call an Áo Dài. Some, obviously whores, dressed in American miniskirts and flashy blouses. Some were beautiful with their olive skin and long, shiny black hair. "GI want boom-boom? Tree dolla get ya plenty!" they yelled.

Squalid huts built with poles, grass and an occasional piece of corrugated sheet metal were spread in every direction. Mothers nursing babies sat near the huts where pedestrian, truck, motorbikes, and bus traffic constantly spread the dust in the scorching heat.

"Jesus! What kind of place is this?" Frank asked the bus driver, who was concentrating on driving as fast as he could without running over anybody.

"They call this Dog Patch. It's part of Da Nang, but it's not what you would call a secure area." He swerved around a corner and began to head down a hill that led to the harbor. "The Americans and VC share the neighborhood. The Americans control it by day, but the VC controls it by night. The place is jammed with whore houses that both sides use."

"Are you kidding?" Jim asked.

"Naw, I'm serious. This place is crawlin' with VC all the time. Why do you think we got wire on the bus, and if you think I like to drive like this, you're crazy?" He shifted into third and popped the clutch with the throttle wide open.

When they pulled into the naval facility surrounding the harbor, everyone, especially the driver, seemed to relax. They stopped near a dock where working parties were busy unloading cargo ships. The harbor was filled with all types of ships but the biggest were the *Iwo Jima* and the *Cleveland*, the two ships assigned to support the 3rd Marine Division Battalion Landing Team. Both huge ships sat peacefully in the blue water, with landing boats coming and going. A continuous stream of choppers landed, unloaded, and took off from the flat top.

A salty, bearded Navy boson's mate came over to

the troops as they got off the bus, and told them to get on a waiting landing craft that would take them to the ships.

"Good luck to you guys! You'll need it!" shouted the driver.

"Yeah. See ya later!" Frank called.

"If you're going to see me again, it'll be back in the world, Man! I've only got seven days and a 'wake-up' to do in this God forsaken place, and then I catch my bird home!"

"Cheerful son of a bitch," Jim mumbled as he picked up his gear. "Real encouraging."

The boat stopped at the *Cleveland* first, to drop off the guys assigned to Alpha and Bravo Companies. The water was not as calm as it looked, and some guys got sick before the landing craft pulled into the loading bay in the back of the ship.

The sun was beginning to set as they headed for the *Iwo Jima*. Getting troops on and off the *Cleveland* from a landing craft was not a very complicated or dangerous maneuver. The *Cleveland* was built to accommodate landing craft pulling in and out of the loading area in the back of the ship, but it was a real problem getting off the bobbing landing craft up the sides of the Iwo.

U.S.S. *Cleveland*

Copyright National Archives

The USS *Cleveland*, LSD-7, was a dual-purpose amphibious assault ship that carried two of the four Marine companies that made up the Battalion Landing Team. The *Cleveland* had a landing platform for helicopters at the stern or rear section of the ship. Below this aft deck, there were stern loading doors that opened to the sea that served as a dock for amphibious landing craft called amtracs.

Waves and swells made the ride to the *Iwo* choppy, and by the time they got to the *Iwo*, everyone was wondering how they would get aboard. The landing craft pulled around the stern of the assault ship and headed for an opening in the side, high above, near the hanger deck elevator. When they pulled up alongside, landing nets were thrown down from above.

"Holy shit! They expect us to climb those nets with all this gear," Jim moaned.

"Yeah, I guess they do, but I think they're crazy!"

The landing craft bobbed up and down like a cork next to the huge ship. It rose six feet or more on each swell, crashed into the side of the ship, and then slid down the sides, as the swell passed.

"Alright, pull that landing net out tight and try to steady the boat!" screamed the boatswain's mate.

"Steady the boats! You gotta be goddamn crazy? Somebody's goin' to get killed if we try to climb that damn thing!" Frank screamed back.

"It's the only way to get on the ship, asshole! Now move it! The ships gotta be out of the harbor by nightfall, so we don't have any time to screw around!"

Several of the Marines caught the net, pulled it tight, and tried to steady the boat, as others got ready to make a running dive at the highest part of the net when the boat was at the crest of a wave. Frank and Jim decided to give it a try with the first group. They slung their sea bags over their shoulders and waited.

"NOW!" screamed the boatswain's mate.

Five of them, including Frank and Jim, jumped as high as they could, grabbed the climbing net and frantically began to climb. The boatswain's mate gunned the boat and pulled it out from under them as the craft suddenly dropped and pitched back and forth.

"Oh, Shit! Don't look down! Don't look down! Climb! Climb!" Frank screamed. Jim was already two feet ahead of him. They pulled and strained as the net swayed and slammed into the side of the ship. The further up they went, the easier it was to climb because the net wasn't swaying at the top.

U.S.S. *Iwo Jima*

Copyright National Achieves

The USS *Iwo Jima,* LPH-2, had a landing platform for helicopters, and it provided two Marine companies with the ability to make vertical assaults on enemy positions. The deck of the *Iwo* was crammed with CH-34 Sikorsky choppers designed and built in the late 1950s, and still being used by Marine Aviation Squadrons.

They made the forty-foot climb without anybody falling into the sea or getting hung up in the net, but they were all exhausted when they got to the top. Several Marines stood around and watched as the newcomers dropped their sea bags and bent over, gasping for breath. "Jesus Christ! What a bitch!" moaned Frank.

"Jesus Christ! What a bitch!" mimicked one of the Marines watching. "Sounds like a first class candy ass to me!"

Frank and Jim exchanged glances and then looked up to see the smart ass smiling back at them was Mike.

"You son of a bitch!" Frank yelled as he jumped in Mike's direction. "How the hell are you, man?"

"I'm okay, Frank. How about you?"

Jim stood and watched as the two friends slapped each other on the back.

"You two know each other or somethin'?" Jim interrupted.

"Yeah, sure, yeah," Frank laughed. "We were in boot camp and ITR together. Mike this is Jim Thompson. Jim, Mike Morgan."

"How ya doin' Mike." They shook hands. "I thought you were some smart ass lookin' for trouble." They all laughed.

"Christ! I can't believe you're on the same ship, Mike. Which company are you assigned to?"

"Charlie Company."

"I can't believe it! We are too! When'd you get here, anyway?" Frank asked as he and Jim picked up their sea bags and the three of them walked across the hanger deck toward a stairwell. Marine mechanics were busy working on the Korean War vintage CH-34 helicopters as they passed.

"A week ago. I got here while the battalion was out on an operation and they decided to keep me on the ship until they got back. They're due back to the ship tomorrow."

"Where do we check in and find out where we go and all that crap?" Jim asked.

"Follow me. I'll take you to see the company 1st Sergeant," Mike answered, as they climbed down the ladder to the deck below. They passed sailors dressed in shipboard blue denim uniforms as they made their way to the compartments assigned to the Marines. The ship shuddered and began to pitch slightly as the engines drove them out of the harbor into the safety of the South China Sea.

They checked in with the 1st Sergeant, a typical gruff staff NCO, and were told that their assignment to individual platoons would wait until the units returned to the ship the next day. Their assignment would depend on which platoon suffered the most casualties during the operation.

Mike led them to their sleeping quarters further down in the bowels of the ship where they found five tiers of bunks jammed one on top of the other. The troop space could accommodate fifty or sixty men, but since no one was around, Frank and Jim helped themselves to lower bunks near Mike.

"Spacious quarters ya got here, Mike," Frank said as he began to unpack his sea bag.

"All the comforts of home," Jim sarcastically responded.

"It's really not that bad," Mike answered, reaching for one of Frank's cigarettes.

"Glad to see you haven't changed much, ya cheap skate! They got hot showers or what?" Frank asked, remembering the freezing water they'd had to use back at Camp Geiger.

"Yeah, they got hot showers and pretty good food, too. From what I hear, this place is like staying at the Hilton compared to being out in the bush."

They finished stowing their gear, drew linen from supply for their bunks, and headed for the mess hall. They stood in line with mostly sailors who seemed to make a conscious effort to steer clear of the Marines. "What's the matter with the 'squids' Mike? They don't like Marines? Or are they just scared?" The three of them laughed.

"Nah, it isn't that they're scared or don't like us. I guess they see the guys come back off operations all beat to hell, and they just kind of respect the combat troops or something. That's what another guy told me anyway."

Navy cooks served huge portions of beef stew over steaming rice with corn, asparagus, hot rolls with butter and chocolate cake. The three found an empty table and sat down to eat.

"So, how was leave, Mike?"

"Great. Really great, mom and dad are okay. Went down to the plant with dad in uniform so he could introduce me around. Mom cooked herself silly, and I ate until I almost got sick, but best of all, I got myself laid."

They laughed and kept eating, waiting for Mike to tell his story.

"Really a nice girl named Wanda. I'd known back in high school but never had much to do with. She's goin' to a junior college back home, and we ran into each other at a party one night."

"What'd she look like?" Jim asked.

"36 Cs with a set of buns you wouldn't believe,"

Mike bragged. "Brown hair, brown eyes, just five-one and a pretty decent face, too." They broke up over Mike's description of his honey.

"Anything serious, or what, Mike?"

"Nah. She just felt sorry for me because I was going to Nam, so I took advantage of it."

After they finished their meal, they sat and talked, drinking coffee and smoking.

"I guess the hardest part about going home was having to leave again," Mike said.

"Yeah, that's a real ball buster for sure." Frank agreed.

That night they all slept soundly with the ship gently rolling on a calm sea. The ship's loudspeaker woke them with reveille and they showered, shaved, dressed and headed back to the mess hall for a gigantic breakfast.

Warriors Return

The 1st Sergeant assigned them to a working party on the Iwo's flight deck, un-loading helicopters that flew in supplies and mail. It was dangerous on the flight deck with chopper blades whirling around and they had to be careful while they worked. The blue sea stretched as far as the eye could see, and the sun became hotter as it climbed in the sky. About noon, the loud speakers announced that choppers with returning troops would be arriving in two waves.

The three stood in the shade of the superstructure looking west, trying to see the incoming choppers.

"There they are," Frank said, pointing at a line of

pinheads dotting the horizon.

"Where? Where? I can't see anything," Jim squinted.

"Yeah, I see 'em!" Mike said.

"Okay, okay. Yeah, now I see 'em!"

As they flew closer, the green birds looked like a swarm of insects about to attack. The squadron's insignia, a four leaf clover, was painted on the nose of each chopper, and as they hovered, anxious troops looked out of the side doors at their floating home. Deck crews waved their arms, guiding the birds in, and as they neared the deck, the choppers pulled up sharply before landing.

Operation Medina was a combined Marine and Army of the Republic of Vietnam assault on a North Vietnamese base camp located in the Hải Lăng forest in southern Quang Tri Province. The Marines and ARVNs attacked the NVA from separate directions while the Battalion Landing Team was assigned to be the blocking force to prevent escape. During the middle of the night, waves of trapped NVA slammed into the Marine positions. Fighting was close, vicious, and sometimes hand-to-hand. Casualties were high: 34 killed in action and 134 wounded. The NVA losses were 53 killed and 3 captured.

Troops began to disembark and head for the *Iwo*'s hanger deck elevators on the other side of the ship.

"Jesus Christ! Look at those guys!" Frank said.

Mike and Jim couldn't say anything. They just stood and gawked as the Marines moved across the flight deck. Old, sunken cheeks, blood shot and glazed eyes, each man covered with filth, all wearing ragged beards, the troops moved slowly under the weight of their packs and weapons. In torn uniforms, mud caked boots, the worn out procession staggered toward the elevator that would take them to the deck below.

"I wonder where the dead and wounded are," Frank asked.

"They go straight to hospital ships or graves registration down at Da Nang," Mike answered thoughtfully.

The empty choppers lifted off and flew into a circular holding pattern near the ship as the next wave approached. The grisly scene was reenacted, as the rest of the two companies landed on the ship's deck.

The 1st Sergeant sent for the new men so that they could be assigned to platoons. "2nd Platoon almost got overrun two nights ago," explained the 1st Sergeant, "and took a lot of casualties." His eyes glazed slightly, but he continued. "They killed a lot of gooks too. Anyway, you three will report to Staff Sergeant LeBeaux, 2nd Platoon. He'll assign you to squads. Any questions?"

Frank had learned not to ask questions so he didn't say anything. "No 1st Sergeant. No questions."

"Good. Morgan, you'll find 2nd Platoon in the next troop compartment forward from where you've been staying. See to it that you and your buddies get down there right away."

"Yes, 1st Sergeant."

They turned to leave the admin office. "Men. Good luck!"

As they climbed down through the ship, Jim said, "I

don't mind tellin' ya that I'm goin' to feel pretty damn funny joinin' that bunch that just got off those hellos."

"Yeah. I know what you mean. Being a new guy with those guys is going to be something."

"I wonder how they treat replacements," Mike asked. "I wish my jungle boots and utilities didn't look so shiny and new."

2nd Platoon, Charlie Company

The replacements found the compartment where skinny, naked, wet men struggled through crowded passageways, coming and going to the showers. Their arms and faces were darkly tanned, contrasting sharply with their lily-white bodies. Many had scars -- long, jagged, deep purple rips in the flesh -- and others had multiple round holes gouged into their skin. They were whooping, hollering, laughing and joking as they pushed and shoved their way into the steaming, hot showers. Filthy uniforms and equipment were stacked knee deep on the deck between the rows of bunks.

"Excuse me, buddy, but can you tell me where I can find Sergeant LeBeaux?" Mike asked one of the men.

"Sure. He's right over there," the grunt pointed. "You guys new replacements?" He was drying his sandy brown hair with a clean white towel.

"Yeah, how could ya tell?" Frank answered, making several men nearby laugh.

"Welcome to 'Purple Heart Charlie'. I'm Ken Forman." He reached out, shook hands with each of them as they introduced themselves. He wrapped the towel around his waist and said, "come on, I'll introduce you guys to 'Frenchie' and the Lieutenant. They'll be as glad to see you as I am."

Replacements in Marine line companies were typically called "FNGs" or "fuckin' new guys". Statistically, new guys didn't last long and the old timers, or Salts, didn't want to go to the trouble of getting to know them. It made it harder to put them in body bags or load them on medevac choppers.

So Forman's welcome was a surprise, but then he explained the reasons. "Everyone's glad to get replacements since each unit's under strength. New guys can help us split up the gear we take to the field and that reduces the load everyone has to carry. For months, we've only had two fire teams per squad instead of three, and after the other night when we got overrun, we don't even have enough men for three squads. Damn right, we're glad to see ya."

Frank noticed a strange looking M-16 laying on Forman's bunk. "That's a night vision scope, called Starlight. Very new, and very secret technology. It allows you to see in the dark, and we can catch the gooks moving around when they think they are safe." He laughed. "And they don't know how they get shot in the head in the pitch dark."

Ken explained that he was also the company interpreter. After ITR, he had gone to the Defense Language Institute in Monterey, California, where he had learned to speak Vietnamese. "The school was a real bitch and I only learned enough Vietnamese to ask simple questions like 'which way did the VC go', and then Ken spoke in an unintelligible sing-song language that made no sense.

Forman led them to the other side of the compartment to meet the Platoon Sergeant. Staff Sergeant LeBeaux, or "Frenchie" as the men called him behind his back, proved to be the typical "don't screw around with me" staff NCO. He stood well over six feet tall with bulging arms that hung from broad shoulders. His short black hair clung tightly to his scalp, and he wore a "Fu Manchu" mustache that grew down the corners of his mouth.

They found the Platoon commander, a 1st Lieutenant named Mosley, looking at a report over Frenchie's shoulder. The Lieutenant, or "LT", was smaller than the staff sergeant, but he was muscular and wiry. His blue eyes were like the others, blood shot and sunken. He smiled as Forman introduced the replacements, but Frenchie never cracked a grin.

LT shook hands with the replacements and welcomed them to 2nd Platoon. "We are lucky," he said. "The Skipper is Capt. Olson and this is his second tour in Nam. He knows what he is doing and while we always achieve our objective, be assured your leadership will do everything we can to see to it you go home in one piece."

"Thank you Sir," Frank said. "Hope you are right." Then the rugged sergeant questioned the men quickly and efficiently, while LT listened.

"Where ya from? How old are you? How long you been in the Corps? Married? What'd ya do before ya joined? Got any problems? How's your health?"

"I'm healthy as you can get, except I'm color blind," Frank answered the last question, innocently.

"Really?" Frenchie asked with interest. "What colors?"

"Brown and green, green and red. Doesn't bother me, though. Hell, I guess I'd have never known if they hadn't found out when I had an eye exam at Parris Island."

"You three will be assigned to Sergeant Sims's squad," Frenchie said, pointing at Frank, Jim and Mike.

"Damn, that's great, French - I mean Staff Sergeant LeBeaux. That's super...." Frenchie glared back at Forman who stood awkwardly nearby, trying to correct himself.

"O'Brian, be sure to tell Sergeant Sims about your color blind problem. He'll know what to do with you."

Frank's guts tightened, and he wanted to ask what Frenchie meant but he didn't ask any questions. He knew he should have kept his mouth shut and was sure something was wrong. He'd find out soon enough.

Sergeant Sims was on the other side of the compartment. He wasn't much like Frenchie. Sims was pale, dark hair and slim build. He was small, about 5 feet 9 inches, and skinny like everybody else. He was unusually nervous, more nervous than the new guys.

Forman, still wrapped in his towel, stood around as the introductions were made. He really seemed happy to see the three new guys. Other men in the area looked on with curiosity, but didn't say anything.

"Welcome to 2nd Squad, men. Glad to have ya. We probably got the best Marines on the ship in this squad, and I intend to have the most squared away men in the Platoon." Sims had been writing a letter home and an open tablet with a pen sat on top of his gear. "You show me a squared away, disciplined Marine, and I'll show you a good combat Marine." He pulled himself up to his full height, threw out his chest and tried to look and act like Frenchie.

Ken stood to one side, slightly behind Sims, listening and occasionally rolling his eyes. "Glad to see you men have haircuts and clean uniforms. Good first impression. Be careful that you don't end up like Forman here. He always needs a haircut and his uniform always looks like shit."

"That's because we're always wading through rice paddies filled with buffalo shit so we get dirty," Ken growled.

Sims overlooked the wise crack and the three new guys tried not to smile. "What'd Staff Sergeant LeBeaux tell you men you'd be doing?"

Ken started to answer the question, "He's assigned O'Brian point and...." "I was talking to the new men, Forman. They can answer for themselves." Ken didn't answer Sims, he just stood back and glared at him.

"Staff Sergeant LeBeaux said he wanted me to walk point," Frank began. "Yeah, why's that?" Sims asked nervously.

"Says me bein' color blind will help me see camouflage in the bush."

They went through the same question and answer routine. When Sims got to health, Forman spoke-up before Frank could say anything.

"How bad is it?" Sims asked.

"I get brown, green and red screwed up, but it's like I told Fr...Sergeant LeBeaux, it's not a big deal. I can see just fine. It's not a problem. Matter of fact, I spotted the choppers bringin' you guys in before Morgan or Thompson. I'm tellin' ya, it's not a problem."

"Nobody said it was a problem, O'Brian. Calm down. It happens to be good. It'll probably end up savin' your ass and a lot of others in the bush."

Forman kept saying, "that's no shit! That's no shit!" Finally, Frank asked for an explanation.

"It's like this, O'Brian," Sims said. "The gooks use camouflage better than you can imagine and if you're not careful, you end up marching right into an ambush or a mine field. Most likely the gooks that camouflage these positions have normal vision, and when they finish, they fix up the foliage so that even they can't see their own position. But, for a guy that's color blind, the rearrangement of the foliage changes the normal pattern of the bush just enough for it to stand out. A color blind Marine can see the positions with his screwed up eyes when guys with normal vision can't see shit. It all has to do with the colors, green, brown and some red." That kind of made sense, but Frank really didn't understand.

"Yeah, well, I'm no doctor so I really don't understand either, but I can tell ya this much. After two and a half years in this damn place, I've seen a lot of shit I don't understand, and color blind guys pickin' out camouflage positions is just one."

"Well, I'll be sure to keep my eyes peeled for

anything that looks a little outa place...."

"That'd probably be a good idea since I'm going to have you walkin' point."

"Walkin' point? Damn, I just got here and you want me to walk point?"

"You got it!" Sims answered. "Best point man is a new guy who's obviously going to be real careful. And if he's color blind, it's just that much better."

Jim and Mike had stood quietly during the exchange, but their turn was coming. "You other two will be assigned to the same fire team, first fire team. Forman, go get your clothes on. It's almost time for chow."

The three followed Forman back to his bunk and waited while he dressed. "What the hell does all of this mean, Ken?" Mike asked. Frank was quiet and nervous, deep in thought and he didn't feel like talking.

"What it means is that you guys are now in my squad and this guy Sims, who's a first class dip shit, is our squad leader."

"Yeah, but what'd he mean about Frank walkin' point?" Jim asked.

"Look." Ken sat down and bent over to lace up his boots. "This battalion is the battalion landing team for the 3rd Marine Division. We normally go in and bail out some other outfit that's gettin' the shit kicked outa them, but other times we catch the gooks in a large unit concentration and go after them. We typically operate near the coast where Alpha and Bravo Companies can make an amphibious assault and can hit the beach in amtracks from the Cleveland. Charlie and Delta fly in on choppers and land behind the gooks and cut them off. Alpha and Bravo come charging inland, pushing the gooks back where we can get at them." He finished his explanation for the FNGs and leaned against the bunk.

"Charlie Company is almost always in the first wave that lands and, most of the time, 2nd Platoon is the first unit that hits the ground. When we've all landed and we move out, 2nd Platoon takes the point and second squad leads 2nd Platoon. When the Battalion moves all together, everything stays pretty much the same."

Ken stopped to think before continuing. "So walkin' point means that Frank will take the point for first squad. Second squad takes point for 2nd platoon, then 2nd Platoon is point for the Company, and the Company is point for the Battalion. The good news is the Skipper, LT, and Frenchie really know their shit and when we make contact, you don't have to look far to see them right up front with the point."

"Christ!" Frank mumbled.

"It's not that bad, if you stay on your toes. A lot of times, the gooks let the point unit move through an ambush site and go after the main force."

They were following Ken across the compartment as he talked over his shoulder. "Of course, the gooks typically assign a squad or platoon to get the point after it passes the kill zone, and you have to be careful about that, but," he paused and laughed, "the best thing to do is not walk into any ambushes."

"That makes sense. Forman will take the three of you down to the armory where you will draw M-16s."

FNGs – Salts – Short-timers

They went to chow and found that the mess hall was jammed with Marines gorging themselves. Ken introduced them around and most of the guys were glad to see them.

After chow, they wound their way through the ship to the lowest deck where they found the armory. Each filled out a "weapon check out" card that would be held on file by the NCO in charge of the armory until the equipment was returned. The M-14 that Frank had qualified with in boot camp and trained with in ITR was replaced with the M-16, a newly developed lighter Colt rifle officially called an AR-16A1.

Ken closely inspected the M-16s issued to the new guys and said, "be careful with these pieces of shit," he warned.

"What a ya mean?" Jim asked.

"I mean you gotta be sure to keep your weapon and ammo clean at all times. They're temperamental as hell, and they jam real easy. All you gotta do is chamber a round with sand or dirt on it, and they will jam real easy. Always clean it when you get a chance. Your ass will depend on it."

Ken was reinforcing rumors they had heard about the unreliability of the new M-16, and it scared them. The new men were worried.

From the armory, they continued to *Supply*, where they were issued their World War II packs, called "782 Gear" that included cartridge belts, ammo pouches, ponchos, etc. The Marines signed a government form 782 for each piece of antique equipment. Forman said the U.S. Army, and the South Vietnamese Army soldiers or "ARVNS", had brand new field equipment, and the Marines were famous for stealing Army equipment at every opportunity.

For the next few days, they rested, cleaned their equipment, stood inspections, went on working parties that the older guys referred to as "chicken shit harassment" and the new men got to know the other troops in the unit. It was a typical Marine outfit, with men from every part of the country and every walk of life. There were blacks from the Deep South and the ghettos of the big cities, Puerto Ricans from the northeast, Mexicans from the southwest, and Indians from reservations in the west and there was one Japanese guy from Los Angeles that everybody called "Tojo". The white guys came from all parts of the country too. Hicks and hillbillies from the south, street wise city kids from New York and New Jersey, burly Irishmen from Boston and Philly, blond- haired Swedish guys from Midwest farms, and even a few "California surfers."

Everyone talked about home, and mail call was the most important time in every day. On those days when mail didn't come in, everyone seemed to have a short temper. It was depressing for the new guys to sit around and listen to the other men talk about how short they were. "How many more days before ya catch your flight back to the world?" was the way they asked the question. "20 days and a wake-up" was the answer for Marines, meaning he had 3 weeks to do in-country.

Short-timers all laughed at the FNGs who had a

"life-time to do in country" before catching the silver bird home. Graffiti on the bathroom wall included a message to all remaining in Vietnam – "screw you short-timer, I went home yesterday!" Mike thought it might be a "get even" message from one of the FNGs.

No one talked much about the next operation. They just seemed to take one day at a time and didn't worry about the next. Frank, Mike and Jim heard the men talk about the last campaign, and the one before, and the stories of agonizing "walks in the sun", the tedium and boredom interrupted by enemy contact, firefights, ambushes, and being over-run in the black of night.

The veterans didn't talk to the FNGs about these things, just to each other. It wasn't that they didn't like the new men, or that they weren't glad to see them. It was because they were talking about a very private and personal part of their lives, and they didn't want to share it with anyone who hadn't lived the experience with them. Frank thought they were trying to get it all out of their systems, to make room for more.

Frank and Mike listened to the Salts talk and began to understand the new vocabulary they used to describe combat. The overall term for anything really bad was that it was a "bad bag." The "bag" included a series of terms that described the various levels of wounds up to death. "Dude got dinged," meant that someone suffered a superficial bullet wound that didn't hit a vital organ, break a bone or destroy a joint. "Dings" earned a Purple Heart and a short stay on a US Navy Hospital Ship or the Hospital in Da Nang. After treatment, the pleasure of sleeping in a clean bed with sheets and contact with "round-eye" nurses, the "Dinged" Marine returned to combat with his unit.

The serious injuries were called "being fucked up." These wounds included bullet and often multiple bullet wounds that struck and destroyed organs, bones, or both. The loss of limbs, serious burns, or mangled body parts earned a Purple Heart and a return to "the world" to a hospital near the Marine's home of record where they were treated and typically given disability retirement.

The most serious "bad bag" was getting "blown away", or "wasted", or KIA. No rhyme or reason, but more often than not, the KIAs were the FNGs or Short Timers. The term "blown away" typically meant that you were unlucky enough to be hit with a landmine, booby trap, mortar, artillery, or friendly fire. The effect of the blast literally blew away anything that resembled a whole body.

The term "wasted" was used to describe all types of death, and meant the Marines were coming to believe that their courage, suffering and sacrifice meant less and less to the American public. "Don't mean nothing" was often heard after a dead Marine was loaded on a helicopter to be flown to Graves Registration. It was painful to hear and depressing to think about. A really "bad bag."

Awards and Decorations

On the fifth day aboard the *Iwo*, Charlie and Delta Company lined up in formation on the hanger deck and Lieutenant Colonel Stark, the Battalion Commander, addressed the troops. Frank, Mike and Jim were tucked in the middle of Charlie Company's 2nd Platoon.

"Those to be decorated, forward, Huh!" barked a crusty battalion Sergeant Major.

Fifteen or more men from Charlie Company and about half dozen guys from Delta marched from around the end of the formation and came to attention in front of the colonel. They faced to the left, almost in unison, and everything on the hanger deck fell quiet.

Citations for five bronze stars were read by the Sergeant Major as each recipient stepped forward. A red ribbon with a pointed bronze star dangling from the bottom was pinned to their jungle utilities. Most of the other men were presented with Purple Hearts for wounds they had received in earlier operations. They had gone to the hospital, recovered, and returned to their units. For many, it was their second award. Frank understood why Ken referred to the unit as "Purple Heart Charlie." Three Purple Heart awards meant that at last, the third wound suffered by a Marine meant he was taken out of a line company and assigned to a rear area job.

After the medal awards ceremony concluded, Colonel Stark talked about how well they had fought in the last battle, *Operation Medina*. The 1st Battalion had been the blocking force for a 3rd Marine Regiment operation that had cornered a battalion of NVA regulars between a river and another Marine battalion that maneuvered like a swinging gate, closing off the escape route for the NVA. Charlie and Delta Company were on the right wing of the blocking force when the remnants of the NVA battalion charged through their perimeter and broke for freedom, escaping the trap. The NVA and Marines mingled together in the dark, firing and throwing grenades. Casualties were high on both sides and the effect on the Marines of being overrun, the close combat, and losing so many buddies, scarred the hardened veterans. The assembled Marines listened intently to the Colonel. They were restless and anxious to learn about the upcoming operation.

"As you all know, the 3rd Marine Division has been assigned to interdict and stop the infiltration of North Vietnamese Army units crossing the DMZ into South Vietnam," said the Colonel.

Robert McNamara, President Johnson's Secretary of Defense had developed a strategy, the *Dye Marker Program*, for closing the NVA infiltration routes by building fortified bunkers across the DMZ. These fire support bases ran from Khe Sanh, in the west near the Laotian border to Charlie-4 and Cau Viet in the east on the China Sea. The "strong points" would be equipped with electronic sensors, and the new "Starlight" night vision technology would allow Marines manning the fire bases to detect enemy ground troop movements. The Marines could call in airstrikes and artillery to destroy the enemy units.

Colonel Stark continued. "As the Battalion Landing Team for the Division, we have been the reactionary force assigned to support and bail out any of the other 3rd Marine battalions fighting along the DMZ. And we all know that we have landed in the middle of intense combat as a result of our mission. We will search and destroy NVA units in the eastern sector of Leatherneck Square." And the Salts in Charlie Company all knew that another "search and destroy" mission was going to be a "very bad bag."

CHAPTER IX –- LAND THE LANDING PARTY

On the one hand it was an extremely sophisticated war, with complex weapons unlike even World War II or Korea. On the other hand it was a return to medieval war, pitting man against man on a battleground where only the courageous could win.

Lt. Gen. Lew Walt, Commander of III Marine Amphibious Force Vietnam. New York Times interview, 1971

Preparing for the landing

The U.S. military divided Vietnam into four Corps tactical zones, each with its own military command. The most northern Corps, designated as "I Corps", was where the North Vietnamese soldiers of the 90th NVA Regiment were stationed. Theses were soldiers who were the sons and grandsons of the Vietnamese soldiers who had fought and defeated the Japanese in World War II, and the French colonial forces in the 1950s. The Regiment's battle flag included streamers marking their participation with 40,000 Viet Minh in the siege and the devastating defeat of the French at the Battle of Dien Bien Phu.

Unlike the American troops, the NVA soldiers didn't have a 13-month tour of duty in Vietnam. Vietnam was their home, and they would fight in northern Quang Tri Province, or anywhere else in Vietnam, for the duration of the war. They, like their Marine adversaries, were young, highly motivated, well trained, well led, and equipped with the latest weapons provided by their allies, Russia and China.

The 3rd Marines and the 90th NVA Regiment had met several times before during the previous year's fighting in I Corps. They had bloodied each other in operations *Hastings* and *Prairie* in 1966, and *Hickory* and bloody *Medina* in 1967. They had never engaged in a decisive battle where one side prevailed. The enemy stood and fought but when supporting airstrikes and artillery hit their forces, they always became elusive and avoided traps set by the Marines.

The next operation for 1st Battalion, 3rd Marines was *Ballistic Arch*, a combined amphibious and helicopter assault on suspected VC and NVA units operating near Mai Xa Thi, a village just west of the China Sea in Quang Tri Province. Vietnamese civilians, regarded as friendly, lived in villages near the coast and inland where the Marines would land. Because of these "friendlies", artillery and air bombardment that would normally precede a landing could not be used. The area was not a "free fire zone" and orders were to fire only if fired upon. The two exceptions were at night when curfews required the civilians to remain in their villages, or during the day when troops could clearly see an armed enemy soldier. Only then could the Marines shoot first.

The *Iwo Jima* and the *Cleveland* steamed north through the China Sea, their holds crammed with Marines who knew they were going to another fight. Escort ships circled constantly, their radar scanning the ocean, watching for North Vietnamese gunboats that might try a quick hit and run torpedo attack. It was a moonless night, with brilliant stars sparkling from horizon to horizon as the ships plowed smoothly across gentle swells on a calm sea. They were scheduled to arrive on station near the DMZ before dawn, where the landing force would jump off.

Planning and coordination with units supporting the operation had been thorough. Artillery batteries that would be called on to provide "tactical fire support missions" had been given map coordinates for depopulated areas between the villages, where enemy contact was most likely. Marine Phantom jet fighters and helicopter gunships were scheduled to fly above the Marines, providing close air support. Medical units and hospital ships had been alerted to expect incoming wounded.

On both ships, final preparations were being made as "H-Hour", the specific time to commence the operation, approached. Helicopter mechanics put the finishing touches on finely tuned engines, and they checked all helicopter weapons to make sure everything was ready. Navy working parties hauled cases of ammunition, grenades, rockets and flares from the ship's magazine to staging areas where the troops would be armed in the morning. Navy cooks began to prepare the traditional breakfast, steak and eggs, well before dawn. Many of the Marines slept soundly while others tried unsuccessfully to sleep. Many just lay awake thinking about previous operations what would happen the next day.

Frank lay awake in his bunk and felt the ship sway from side to side. When he finally fell asleep, the nightmares came:

> *He saw himself cowering in a hole while bullets ripped the air, explosions rocked the earth and his buddies fought and fell all around him. He got up, crying, trembling and crapped in his trousers. He dropped his rifle and screamed for everyone to stop shooting but no one would listen. All the Marines in his platoon saw him crumble and break. They sneered at him and shook their heads. A mortar shell exploded next to him and he saw his legs lay in front of him, partially attached to his body, broken, mangled, shredded, bloody and useless. He howled for help and prayed that it wasn't true, that he wasn't crippled and that he would be able to walk. Mike and the other Marines ran past him and each looked down and shook their head, saying "Wasted. Too bad Frank, too damn bad!" Frank could see about a dozen NVA soldiers surrounding him. They were small, ugly, yellow men with cruel smiles. They pointed their bayonets at him and jabbered in their strange language. Frank smashed one of the NVA in the face with his fist, but it had no effect. He hit him again and again but the enemy soldier just laughed. He screamed over and over, "I can beat you! I'm gonna hurt you! Let me go! Let*

me go! I've gotta go home!" But they just laughed
and dragged his broken body down a dark trail
deep into the jungle, which led anywhere but home.

When reveille sounded well before dawn on November 24, 1967, Frank was soaked in sweat and shaking. He was grateful to find that he was actually still on the *Iwo* and the ritual of preparing for combat was now going to begin.

The men were quiet and sullen as they showered, shaved, dressed in jungle fatigues, and none of them bothered putting on skivvy shorts because in the bush, underwear rotted and caused heat rash. Cigarettes and matches were put in water tight plastic cases, stuffed into front pockets for easy access and extras were wrapped in plastic bags and stowed in the tops of their packs. Some took writing material, tablets and pencils so they'd be able to write home during the operation, but most didn't bother. Equipment and weapons were checked, adjusted and stacked on bunks with great care before they went to breakfast.

It was warm and comfortable in the galley, the air heavy with the smell of steak, fresh eggs and hot coffee. Frank, Mike, Ken and Jim filled their trays and found an almost empty table near the coffee pots.

"Don't forget your bug juice," Ken said. "You won't believe the mosquitoes, flies, every kind of bug you can image. The bug juice helps but you still get eaten alive. The bug juice is great for getting rid of leeches." The rice paddies, streams, rivers and lakes in Vietnam were alive with blood sucking leeches that attached themselves to every part of a man's body.

Ken shifted his attention back to breakfast. He knew this would be their last hot meal for a while. "Damn, this looks good! Pass the sugar and cream will ya, Mike?"

They began to eat, Ken attacking his plate while the others ate slowly. "What's the matter, you guys lose your appetite or somethin'?"

"Nah, I'm just not very hungry," Jim answered.

"I didn't sleep much last night," Frank explained.

"Yeah, I know. I heard you rollin around in your bunk."

"You'll learn to sleep anytime you get a chance. After a couple of days in the bush, you'll be dead on your ass from lack of sleep." They sat quietly for a while until Ken had cleaned his plate. "Frank, if you're not goin' to eat that piece of steak and those biscuits, pass them down."

The three new guys sat drinking coffee and thinking. Frank didn't feel like eating. His head felt light and fuzzy, his legs were watery, his stomach queasy. With all the training and preparation behind him, and the final test a few short hours away, he thought about dying and fought to dispel the nightmares that haunted him.

His conscious thoughts told him to adopt the fatalistic attitude expressed by most men going into battle, *if it's your time to die, and your numbers up, there's nothing you can do about it.* But deep in his heart, he believed that it could never happen to him. Men would be shot or blown to bits and killed, but it could never happen to him. He'd never get killed. He wouldn't die in combat. It couldn't happen!

Operation Ballistic Arch

Sergeant Sims shouted, "come on, let's get back and pick up your gear. We're gonna be late." They ran through passageways leading to their compartment below.

"Let's go 2nd Platoon! Move out!" Frenchie bellowed. "Up to the hanger deck to draw ammo on the double!"

"Help me with my pack, will ya Frank?" Mike groaned. "I can't get these damn straps adjusted right."

Their packs weighed an average of fifty to sixty pounds, and Mike's straps were too tight, cutting off the circulation in his arms. Frank loosened the "M-buckle" that held them in place.

"Thanks, that's better." Frank noticed that Mike didn't look so young any more, as Mike plopped his camouflage helmet on his head.

Jim finished hooking his cartridge belt to his suspender straps, Frank picked up his new M-16, freshly cleaned and oiled, and the three followed the other men through the passageways leading to the hanger deck. On their way, they passed sailors who watched quietly and occasionally, one would give a thumbs-up and say "good luck."

Ken was waiting for them in the troop mustering area where hundreds of Marines were milling around, picking up bandoliers of ammo, looking for their units, shouting, cursing, pushing and shoving. Ken said, "You guys get over there and pick up your M-16 ammo and grenades. Start loading your magazines as soon as you get your ammo, but don't lock and load your weapons, yet.

And the bug juice is right over there." The small plastic container of insect repellant was typically carried in one of the oversize pockets of their jungle utilities along with grenades, and extra ammo.

They started for the stacks of ammo cases when Sims came rushing across the hanger deck screaming, "Second squad, fall in over here! Come on men! Move! Move!"

"Just hold your horses, Sims, they haven't drawn their ammo yet," Ken snapped.

"Damn it Forman. Don't you talk to me that way!"

"Sims! Where is your squad?" Frenchie bellowed. He was really mad. His face was scarlet red as he ran across the hanger deck.

"Staff Sergeant LeBeaux, my three new men just got up here, and they gotta draw their ammo."

"Well get your ass in gear. Them choppers ain't gonna wait on your ass!" Frenchie snarled. Frenchie walked away and left Sims standing by himself.

"Okay, get over there, get your shit and get back over here fast!" Sims yelled.

Frank, Mike and Jim ran over to the stacks of ammo spread out all over the deck and each grabbed several ammunition bandoleers from the boxes of ammo. They each snatched six grenades out of a box, took them out of their containers, and stuffed them into the oversize jungle utility pockets. They were excited, nervous and breathing hard by the time they saw Ken. He was methodically loading M-16 rounds into his magazines.

"Shut   up   and   listen   up   for   roll   call!

Baker...Yo...Brown...Yo...Cannon...Yo..." Frenchie snapped.

Frank tried to rearrange his grenades so he could be more comfortable. His hands shook as he took the bullets from the bandoleers and loaded the magazines. He started to slide a magazine into his rifle, but Sims shrieked, "Not now, O'Brian! Not now! Wait until we get on the chopper."

"Morgan...Yo...Newman...Yo...O'Brian...Yo..."
Frank's throat was dry and his mouth parched. He thought about taking a drink of water from one of his two canteens, but he thought someone might yell at him.

After roll call, they lined up single file in a stairwell that led to the flight deck. It was still dark outside; and inside the stairwell, red "night lights" glowed. The lights were supposed to help the men adjust their eyes to "night vision."

They stood and waited, leaning against the bulkhead, trying to relieve the weight of their packs as the helicopters on deck revved up their engines, vibrating the bulkhead they were leaning against. Frank looked at his watch in the eerie red glow and noticed it was 0622. They'd been waiting for about fifteen minutes when a whistle screeched over a loud speaker attached to the overhead of their compartment, followed by a loud voice that barked, "Now Hear This. Now Hear This. Land the Landing Force. Land the Landing Force."

The waiting was over. A sailor wearing goggles that made him look like an insect, pulled open the door and in came a rush of wind and the thunder of the chopper engines. "Okay Move! Move!" he screamed.

Frenchie jumped through the door opening and pointed in the direction of a chopper, blades whirling. Sims and Ken scrambled to the top of the stairs with Frank, Mike and Jim following closely. The deck was covered with CH-34 helicopters, rotors cutting the air, waiting for the troops to climb aboard. The "Whop...Whop...Whop...Whop" rhythm of all the helicopters lined up across the flight deck was deafening. Everyone bent over slightly as they ran across the deck. Nobody wanted to get smacked by a chopper blade.

Most of second squad piled into one chopper with Frenchie sitting at the door. Sims sat next to Ken facing Frank, Mike and Jim. As soon as Frank sat down, he reached for a magazine, loaded his weapon, chambered a round and made sure the safety was on. His hands were shaking, and Ken looked at him and smiled.

"You got plenty of time, yet!" he yelled, over the roar of the engines, shaking his head.

Frank held his rifle between his legs, grasped the barrel tightly, and hoped no one else saw his hands shaking. They waited while all the other birds were loaded with troops in the first wave. It was dark inside the chopper, and it vibrated violently. The noise was deafening as the pilot revved the engine.

"Here we go!" Ken yelled. He and the rest of the Salts locked and loaded their weapons.

LZ Robin

The chopper lifted off the tarmac, and then banked sharply as it cleared the ship. There was a sickening lift upward. As they gained altitude, Frank could see other choppers following. They climbed higher and higher in the hazy light of dawn until the carrier looked very small.

The wind rushed through the open doorway, and they could see the amtracs plowing out of the stern of the *Cleveland* heading for the beach. The landing craft looked like toy boats bobbing around in a deep blue bathtub. They were loaded with Marines, crammed tightly together in a breathless, roaring steel box that bounced and swayed in the ocean. Frank was glad he was in the chopper and not an amtrac. Back in the States, during practice landings, men in amtracs were constantly getting sick and throwing up. He remembered the putrid smell and the screaming need to escape the steel box.

The choppers flew in a wide circle and waited for the boats below to deploy on line. He tried not to think, he'd done everything he could for the time being. He occupied himself by silently singing the lyrics of his favorite song, *Hang On Sloopy, Sloopy Hang On.* Frank snapped back to the present when the chopper banked into a steep turn and headed for the beach.

"Keep your weapons on safety until you hit the ground, and be careful that you don't blow away one of your buddies!" Frenchie screamed.

Frank felt the safety latch on his rifle and knew that it was on, but he couldn't remember if he had chambered a round. "Oh, shit! Did I lock and load? Damn! I can't remember!" Slowly and cautiously, he eased the bolt back and he breathed a sigh of relief when he saw the brass end of a shell tucked snugly in the chamber. He laughed to himself thinking, *You dumb ass!*

Ken sat quietly across from Frank and Mike as the choppers began the run for the beach. He leaned his head back as if he was trying to take a quick nap, slowly closing and then slowly opening his eyes. If he was afraid, no one could have seen it.

Frank was scared, and he hoped that no one could tell. Mike sat pressed against his left side and Frank felt better, thinking, here we go. *We're on our way! After all the training. Now it's time.* Foamy waves pounded the white beach as the choppers raced by and Frank could see the broken tree lines that lay beyond the sandy stretches. Thicker clumps of trees broke the neat lines near the beach and an occasional clearing could be seen as the birds flew by. He couldn't see any movement on the ground.

Mike elbowed Frank and shouted, "We're going in! We're going in!" but Frank's stomach knew he was falling. It twisted and turned and rose violently in his chest and throat as the bird plunged down in tight, swinging circles. He gripped the barrel of his rifle with his left hand and his right hand found the trigger.

Great clouds of sand swirled into the air as the choppers hit the ground. Frenchie screamed, "Move! Move! Move!" as he threw men out the door. Frank's feet hit the ground, and he fell to his knees under the weight of his pack. He blinked his eyes and squinted, trying to keep the sand out.

Mike hit him on the shoulder and screamed, "come on" as he ran past him. Ken was running toward a tree line, with Mike and Jim close behind. Frank struggled to

165

his feet and heard the "Whop…Whop…Whop" sound of the choppers lifting and heading back to the *Iwo*.

He was running as fast as he could in the soft sand, his chest heaving and his lungs gasping for air through clenched teeth. It was like moving in slow motion, and he felt he could never catch up with the others to reach the woods. Sims slammed into him from behind screaming, "Get to the woods! Take cover! Take cover! We have to secure the LZ."

Frank saw other men jumping off the helicopters as they swooped in from the sky. The Marines ran for the trees -- thirty seconds had been an eternity. Frank finally reached the safety of the trees where he dove for cover. He glanced to his right and saw Ken, Mike and Jim lying flat on the ground, looking into the woods. Sims was farther to the left, on his knees, looking into the trees. No motion in the tree line. The last of the choppers had unloaded the troops and pulled out of the landing zone. All was quiet. They were in luck. *Thank God*, Frank thought, *it's not a "hot" LZ.*

Both Charlie and Delta Company Marines landed in the secure LZ without incident. Alpha and Bravo hit the beach farther east, and they also found that the NVA had chosen not to fight. Everyone breathed a sigh of relief as the companies began to organize into a combat wedge for moving across country.

2nd Platoon of Charlie Company was walking point with Sims' 2nd Squad. Ken, Frank, Jim and Mike took the lead. Frank's Platoon was spread out in an "echelon left and right formation" that looked like the delta wings on a jet aircraft. 1st and 3rd Platoons were in "column formations" guarding each flank, and the company commander and his team were in the center of the formation. When everyone was set, Frenchie ordered Sims's squad, with Frank walking point, to move out marching west toward Mai Xa Thi where they expected to make contact with the NVA.

Grunts

The NVA used the weather and terrain in Quang Tri Province as "weapons" that could inflict casualties on the Marines. Just because the NVA didn't fight at the LZ, didn't mean that the Marines wouldn't suffer.

Quang Tri Province is in the north central coast region of Vietnam. The province is almost at the same latitude as Mexico City back in the Western Hemisphere. It was "winter" in Vietnam, and November was the middle of the monsoon season, which can bring torrential rain that is so heavy you can't see the man standing three feet away. Besides being constantly soaked, the Marines had to deal with the heat and humidity. Temperatures during the day could easily reach 100° and, with the humidity, it felt like 110°. Then there was the wet sandy terrain, which caused the loaded down Marines to sink in the sand, and each step became a struggle to put one boot in front of the other.

The rice paddies stretched for miles in all directions. They were filled with human and buffalo shit that made the Marines gag and retch. Some began puking as the Platoon moved cautiously so as not to slip and fall down into the filth. The paddies were crisscrossed with dikes that the

Marines avoided because they knew the rice paddy dikes were a favorite place for mines and other booby traps to be planted by hostile peasants or NVA soldiers. This made crossing miles of rice paddies pure torture.

At night, the temperature dropped to near freezing, cold winds would blow out of the north, and the unrelenting rain caused the Marines to get uncontrollable shakes. Two man foxhole teams would huddle together under ponchos in an effort to keep dry and share body heat. They avoided digging in nearby paddies or other standing waters. They didn't want to wake up with leeches attached to their private parts. Morning was a brief blessing when the temperature would begin to climb and warm the frozen, soaked, miserable Marines.

At dawn on the second day of the operation, Frank and his buddies gobbled cold C-Rations and "saddled up" for another all day march. The Marines moved out across reasonably flat terrain, sand dunes rising and falling gently, broken by trees growing in neat lines, defining long, unused, but still watery rice paddies. Occasionally, they would pass thick clumps of trees with heavy underbrush. The terrain would change to open rice paddies where they became targets for snipers hiding in nearby tree lines. The best defense for not being the target of a sniper was to keep your eyes open and constantly scan potential hiding places.

The Marines moved cautiously in this quiet, but hostile terrain, knowing that the enemy was not far ahead. Sheets of rain would pound the Marines for hours, then suddenly break, bringing clear blue skies and scorching heat to bake the exhausted men.

The quick pace Frank set as point became agonizing, and the weight of his pack and equipment drove his boots into soft sand, slowing him down and making him struggle to maintain his pace. Scattered rice paddies sucked him into the manure, holding him fast. Pain raked his legs, back, shoulders, and arms as he pulled his boots up, out, and threw them forward. His head jolted and shook inside his helmet with each step. Bugs swarmed around the men, and they swatted the pests away from their faces. Men splashed on bug juice, but it was of little help and the torment continued.

By mid-morning, the orange morning sun rose from the horizon and climbed high in the sky, becoming a merciless white ball of fire. The sand absorbed the rays and turned it into hot coals that burned to the touch. Heat waves, rising from the watery paddies, distorted trees in the distance, causing Frank to see the tree line as if he were looking at them through distorted glasses.

"Veer slightly to your right, O'Brian," barked Sims. "You're headed in the wrong direction." Sims carried the compass, and any deviation from the exact line of march was noted by the command marching in the middle of the wedge, monitoring progress. The company commander would radio the point unit, order the adjustment, and they would move on.

Frank turned slightly to the right, took a few steps, and saw that Sims was satisfied. He picked out a single tree in the distance as an objective he would march toward. His mouth was too dry to curse or complain.

169

They marched on for a few uneventful hours, crossing dunes, sloshing through paddies and creeping through woods. Frank remembered the long marches and endless runs they had made during training and laughed. Nothing compared with this! The pain racking his body became dull and bearable, and he was able to push a little harder.

"Don't look down at your feet, O'Brian," Sims snapped. "You're walking point, and you better watch where you're going."

"Screw you!" Frank wanted to scream.

"I'm not kickin' a trip wire or steppin' on a punji stick."

"The asshole's right, Frank," Ken said quietly as he jerked his foot out of a paddy and threw it up on another dike. "Charlie likes to take pot shots at the point, especially if you aren't looking around all the time. If you're looking at the countryside and he decides to snipe at you, you may see the muzzle flash. And if he misses, you get a chance to ding him. But if you're lookin' down all the time, Charlie thinks he gets a free shot at you without you ever seein' him."

"That's just dandy," Frank croaked, "but I don't wanta end up getting my legs blown off by a damn mine."

"Knock off the talk up front," Sims began.

"Aw hold your water, Sims, I'm tryin' to teach O'Brian somethin'."

"What you gotta learn to do," Ken continued, "is train your eyes to search the ground immediately ahead for wires and spikes and then scan the terrain farther out in front of you for signs of Charlie or movement in the bush. Ya learn to develop a rhythm. Glance down ten feet out, slowly scan from left to right, moving back to your feet, and then, when you know it's okay, force your eye balls back up and scan from the left to the right farther out. Try it, counting to yourself like it was cadence or somethin' and see if it doesn't work."

Frank checked the ground in front of him, moved his eyes back to his feet, continued to take steps, forced his eyes up and out, picking out details of the countryside surrounding them and repeated the routine. He developed a rhythm and he caught himself calling cadence to himself like the DIs in boot camp.

The sun crested high above, and finally the word was passed to take a short chow break for lunch. Frank had just passed a line of rubber trees, and he stood stuck in the mud in another paddy. He retraced his steps, found a piece of dry ground under the shade of one of the trees, and dropped into an exhausted heap. Mike and the others joined him, and each groaned and grunted as their packs fell. He leaned his M-16 against a tree and opened his flak jacket to allow air inside. The stench from his body was nauseating. They all faced forward and watched to their front. Each gulped noisily from canteens while they dug into their packs for a can of C-Rations.

"Shit! Ham and mother fuckers!" Forman spewed the vulgar nickname the Marines gave the putrid meal of ham and lima beans, "this is raunchy enough to make a maggot gag." Ken also began to complain as he sorted through his pack, examining the green cans, and throwing the rejects back into his knapsack. "Think I'll settle for a can of peaches, crackers and jelly."

Jim stood in the paddy behind the dike and took a long overdue leak. He ignored the fact that he was standing, knee deep in the water where he was peeing. Lumps of buffalo crap floated around his legs.

"Remember not to fill your canteens from that side of the dike," Ken laughed, "unless you're anxious to drink Thompson's piss."

Ken didn't smoke but everyone else did. He said, "it's bad for your health and we got enough problems." They all laughed and proceeded to light up during the break. Cigarettes were an escape from their misery and Frank enjoyed the sensation of filling his lungs, and the taste of the tobacco rolled across his swollen tongue and escaping through his parched lips.

Before they saddled up and prepared to move out, each filled his half empty canteen with the water in the paddy on the other side of the dike. Ken passed out Halazone tables that were supposed to purify the rancid water, and then he showed them how to hold a thumb over the lip of the canteen to prevent pieces of buffalo dung from getting in.

In less than fifteen minutes, they were on the move again, and the excruciating pain returned. It came in waves, and it took over an hour to become dull and bearable again. Frank concentrated on training his eyes and it helped him to ignore the weight of the flak jacket, pack and rifle.

"There's a village just ahead, O'Brian, about a 'click' or 1,000 meters, away so keep your eyes open," Sims commanded from behind. Mai Xa Thi was reported to be supporting VC and NVA units in the area. Contact with enemy units was likely.

Bet your ass I'll keep my eyes open, he thought, *but a thousand meters is a long way off.*

"We gonna stop at the 'Vill' for the night?" Ken asked.

"Gotta sweep and search it first, then move a little beyond it, before we set in," Sims answered.

"A little beyond ain't soon enough," Mike chimed in. "My ass is draggin."

"Alright!" yelled Sims. "Knock off the bullshit and keep your eyes open!"

Mai Xa Thi

They climbed out of one paddy, over another dike, and then plunged into another paddy. As Frank moved to the top of the next dike, he made out the shape of several grass shacks just ahead. "There's the 'Vill' Sarge."

"Yeah, I see it."

They were in the open, approaching from the west, with the sun at their back. It was difficult making out images, but Frank could see movement near the outskirts of Mai Xa Thi. People were running back and forth, and as the Marines got closer, he could see a water buffalo standing inside a wooden pen staring out at them.

To Frank's right, the "pop" of a rifle being fired and the crack of the bullet cutting through the air made everyone drop to their knees. They were chest deep in a paddy when one of the Marines on the flanks screamed and rolled backwards off the dike he was crossing. He screamed, "goddamn you, you sons of bitches!"

"You hit?" Frenchie screamed.

"Yeah, I'm hit! Some gook bastard shot a hole in my canteen!" The Marine with the shot-up canteen was one of the FNGs. There was nervous laughter from Marines nearby who were relieved that no one was actually wounded. The Salts just shook their heads.

No one returned the fire because they couldn't see where the shot came from. The Marine with the "injured" canteen continued to curse while Frank scanned the village. No movement in the village. Frank's stomach turned over, and the hair on the back of his neck rose.

Sims was behind a paddy dike near Frank, peering carefully over the top, when Frenchie came running up to the point with a radioman in tow.

"Everybody stay low and keep your eyes open," Frenchie ordered calmly.

"Candy Tough, Candy Tough, this is Charlie Two, Charlie Two, Break," the Platoon Sergeant called into the radio headset.

Frank heard the squelch coming from the radio as Frenchie released the headset switch and listened. Lieutenant Mosley ran up and joined him, looking carefully into the nearest tree line, waiting while Frenchie raised the Company Commander, Captain Olson.

"Skipper's on," Frenchie told LT, handing him the mike. "Candy Tough, we got a sniper on our right front, and we've taken one incoming round, Break. No casualties, Break."

Another squelch and LT paused and listened, while Frank stayed low, searching the trees for movement, but he saw nothing. "Copy, Candy Tough, Break."

"Frenchie, get one squad on line and send them into the Vill. Recon by fire first, and move the rest of the Platoon into position to give them cover. Sims! Get over here!"

"Yes, Staff Sergeant LeBeaux," Sims answered as he cautiously moved away from the dike.

"Get your squad on line, recon by fire, move into the outskirts of the Vill. The rest of the Platoon will cover you."

Sims was shaking visibly as he put his fire team into position.

Frank and the others moved forward in low crouches until they were on line, while the rest of the Platoon crawled into position to give them covering fire. A machinegun team moved up and joined them, the gunner busily mounting an assault pouch and loading a fresh belt of ammunition.

"On my command!" croaked Sims, his voice high pitched and excited, "open up on the tree line closest to us! That's probably where the sniper is."

"Fat chance," Ken mumbled. "He took his best shot and by now, he's 'di-diid' outta the area." "Di-di" or "di di mau" was troop slang for the Vietnamese word "to run" or "haul ass".

Frank's hands were wet with sweat and his stomach muscles tightened when Sims ordered, "Open Fire!"

The burst of fire chopped the earth and cut limbs

from trees, but there was no return fire. Everyone changed magazines, and it was quiet except for the constant chatter of the machine gun.

"Okay! Move! Move!" Sims screamed.

Together, they stood and began to run as fast as they could toward the village, firing short bursts from the hip. The weight of their packs and the mud in the paddy made their movements fell like they were moving in slow motion.

Still nothing moved, and there was no return fire.

They ran into the tree line, shooting and screaming, but no one was there. About twenty feet past the trees, Frank looked to his right and saw Ken take aim at a frightened water buffalo standing wide eyed in a wooden pen. "RRRRRIIIIIPPPPP" belched Ken's M-16. The water buffalo bellowed and fell forward crushing down the pen. Ken had splattered it in the head.

"What'd ya do that for?" Frank shouted.

"Damn 'boos' are meaner than shit," Foreman was laughing and snickering. "They don't like round eyes. And if they get a chance, they'll stick one of them horns up your ass." His laughter was contagious, and the rest of the fire team began laughing too. "Besides, it really pisses off these gooks when you blow away their buffalos. A 'boo' to them is like a car is to us back in the world. It's real important."

They began to pull back to the tree line, but Frank and Ken didn't get away from the dead 'boo' before Sims ran up to them.

"Okay, who shot that water buffalo?"

"Hell if I know Sarge. The machine guns musta hit

him by accident when we was comin' through the woods," explained Ken with a smirk on his face.

Sims walked over and examined the fallen buffalo.

"Looks like a nice neat group of M-16 rounds, right between the horns. Forman, you're the only one close enough to...."

"Awl shit Sarge. Wasn't me. Honest. I didn't shoot him. Ask O'Brian."

"That's right, Sarge. The 'boo' was dead when we got here. Musta been stray rounds or somethin'."

Sims stormed back to the tree line, got on the radio and called the Lieutenant and Platoon Sergeant to report the incident. Frank and Ken laughed when he was gone, and then they took Mike and Jim over to see the dead buffalo.

"Roger Charlie Two. The area is secure. No casualties, but we did accidently kill an water buffalo in the village."

Weapons Cache

The Marines swept into the village without any further resistance and found peasants huddled in family bunkers, waiting for the shooting to stop. There were more than two hundred of them, hiding in shelters that were holes dug deep in the ground with several feet of dirt covering the tops. Most were reinforced with thick trees, and the occupants were safe except for direct hits with artillery shells or bombs.

Their huts, or "hooches", were thatched walls with poles tied together, supporting thin, but efficient roofs that kept the rain out. Woven grass mats lay around the dirt floors. Handmade clay pots were strewn everywhere and ancient tools used for digging, planting and harvesting were stored outside the huts. Filth, flies and crawling insects were everywhere.

The Marines herded the villagers together, and the South Vietnamese scouts and interpreters, called "Kit Carsons", began interrogating the young and middle-aged men about the sniper. The Kit Carsons were supposed to be VC who changed sides, and they acted as guides and interpreters for U.S. military. They methodically began checking ID cards, asking questions, yelling and hitting the peasants who didn't give satisfactory answers or show proper respect.

"No! No! We haven't seen any NVA or VC. They numba ten, no damn good! Marines numba one! Friend! Sniper? Oh, no! No one shoot from village! Marines numba one!"

While the questioning continued, Frank and the other men began a thorough search of the village. Ken showed the new guys how to check for dirt in the grass hooches that looked like it had been freshly turned. They checked in stacks of hay and in the gardens that were scattered throughout the village. Sims watched Forman closely to make sure he didn't destroy anything else.

The owner had discovered his dead water buffalo, and back in the village square the chief started raising hell about the dead "boo". Ken and a few other Marines were searching hooches nearby. They watched and laughed as the old farmer screamed and garbled something to the other villagers about the dead animal. All the villagers became very excited and agitated over the incident, and there was a lot of screaming and yelling.

"Hey Ken!" Mike shouted from inside a bunker. "What do ya think they were digging around in here for?"

Forman bent over, crawled through the narrow door into the bunker, where Mike squatting down and holding an oil lamp, looked at the floor of the bunker. The dirt was freshly churned, and Ken took a probe rod and stuck it into the loose dirt while Frank and Jim watched from outside.

"What the hell's goin' on in there?" Sims asked, standing behind Frank. "I think maybe Mike found somethin', Sarge."

Ken pulled the long metal probe rod out of the earth and sank it again. This time it hit something buried two feet below the surface and wouldn't go any further. Frank heard Ken chuckle and he said, "Yea, Yea." Ken pulled the rod back out and then tapped it in again. They could hear the unmistakable sound of metal touching metal. Ken pulled the rod back out and tried again, this time about a foot away from the last hole. Another tap. More metal against metal.

"Hey, Sims, go tell LT that I think we found somethin'. Find out which one of those slant eyed bastards owns this bunker."

The interpreter asked the villagers who owned the bunker, and found it was the old man who had been raising hell about the dead boo. Sims and two other men dragged the old man, his wife and three kids back to the bunker where Ken was waiting outside with a hoe in his hand.

"Get your ass inside 'poppa-san' and dig up that floor!" Ken shoved the hoe in the old man's hand and pointed to the door of the bunker. The old man took the hoe, threw it on the ground, screamed at Forman, shaking his finger in Ken's face. Frank, Mike, Jim and other men stood watching the old man scream at them. "You Numba Ten. Garble...Garble...Garble. Fuck You Maleen. Garble...Garble...Garble. You Numba Ten."

Before Sims could stop him, Ken reached down, picked up the hoe and smacked the old man across the forehead, sending him sprawling to the ground.

"Teach ya to tell me to get screwed, you little zipper headed bastard!" He swung the hoe back and started to hit the old man again, but Sims caught the hoe and held it back. The old man's head was bleeding and other villagers gathered nearby, moaned their objections.

"That's enough, Forman!" Frenchie snarled, joining the group.

Ken dropped the hoe under the steady gaze of the Staff Sergeant. Frenchie reached down and jerked the old man back to his feet, pointed to the bunker, handing him the hoe. Frenchie spoke a few quick words that sounded like the gook's gobbling, and the old man complained. But Frenchie looked at him, snapped a few more words that sent poppa-san scrambling into the bunker.

Mike stayed inside the bunker watching the old man dig, and fifteen minutes later, Mike began throwing an assortment of weapons through the door. Most were Russian AK-47's, or SKS assault rifles, but a few were

Czech automatic rifles. More digging produced cases of Russian rocket propelled grenades and Chinese Chicom hand grenades.

Frenchie sent Sims to the village square to tell LT about the find and lead him back to the hooch. LT and Captain Olson returned with Sims to find the Marines had surrounded the hooch where the weapons had been found. The poppa-san's wailing inside the bunker could be heard throughout the village, and his family and the other farmers took up his crying.

Frenchie, LT and Captain Olson discussed the find, and Olson ordered the Marines to begin a thorough search of each hooch. The Kit Carson Scouts roamed the village screaming and kicking the peasants. In a few hours, the village square was strewn with stacks of weapons and ammunition.

The Skipper called Battalion Headquarters and, after an hour delay, ordered Charlie Company to bring in the ARVN unit from the nearby Marine firebase at Gio Linh. The Marines didn't want to have to deal with a hostile peasant population that might get violent. Better to let the Vietnamese methodically question the villagers and decide what to do with the enemy sympathizers.

As the sun dipped in the sky, the ARNVs walked into Mai Xa Thi to take over the search and interrogate the villagers. They started kicking and beating the peasants almost immediately. There followed a lot of crying, begging and unintelligible screams.

The Marines had accomplished their mission, and now they moved on to find the regular NVA units that were operating in the area. As Charlie Company moved out of the village, they could hear the screams and cries as the ARVNs taking revenge on the villagers.

Wasted

It was dusk by the time they moved another thousand meters. The officers and staff NCOs positioned the men in a defensive perimeter, assigning them to two-men fighting holes. Frank and Mike were together.

They dug a hole wide and deep enough for both of them to stand in. Dirt was piled in front of the hole, and Mike found camouflage nearby while Frank put the finishing touches on their nighttime home. The sun disappeared suddenly, and in the pitch black, mosquitos began to swarm and attack the men. Sitting on the edge of their foxhole, they squirted bug repellent into their hands and rubbed it on their faces and exposed skin. It didn't help much.

Ken and Jim were in the next hole to their right having the same problem. On their left, other men in second squad were dug in. And behind them all, in the command post unit, Sims, Frenchie, LT, and the corpsman settled in for the night.

Frank and Mike felt around in their packs until they found C-Rations for supper. They couldn't read the labels in the dark, so they had no idea what they were eating until they twisted open the cans and dug in with their plastic spoons. Frank got beefsteak, potatoes and gravy, and Mike ended up with "weenies and beanies". They sat together, eating, watching, listening and waiting.

The night air was cool, and although it was a moonless night, the stars were bright and provided enough light for the men to see remarkably well. They were positioned in a sandy area overlooking the watery fields and in front of them stretched more open paddies. They had a clear field of fire if the NVA doubled back and attacked, but Ken said the NVA were probably going to try to run to the north. If they saw anything of them, it would just be the rear guard, again.

Frank heard movement to his right, and he instantly swung his rifle in that direction.

"Hold it! Don't shoot! God damn it, it's me! Ken."

"Oh, okay. Come on over."

"Scared the shit outta me," Mike complained in a whisper.

They sat together and talked quietly. "Remember, you got a listening post about two hundred yards out to your right, near that dike over there," Ken pointed. "If you see anything or hear anything moving in that direction, don't throw a grenade until you're sure it's a gook. Always throw grenades before firing your weapon at night. Muzzle flashes give away your position, so it's smarter to use grenades, unless you're forced to shoot."

Frank and Mike shuddered. It was getting colder, with the wind blowing in from the sea, picking up moisture from the rice paddy water and cutting through their damp uniforms, chilling their bones.

"In about an hour, we'll stand down to fifty percent alert. One of you can sleep for an hour while the other watches. Decide who's going to take first watch and you'll switch one hour on, one off throughout the night until just before dawn. Then we'll go back to a hundred percent," Ken told them. Just after sunset and just before dawn they were told, were the most likely times for the enemy to attack. Standing watch, off and on throughout the night was standard procedure.

Frank decided to take first watch. Ken checked to make sure they had their grenades spread out in front of them, ready to throw, before he returned to his hole. "Frank, make damn sure you don't fall asleep during your watch!" Ken began to crawl away, and Frank said, pointing at Ken, "and you -- no snoring! A gook can hear you snoring a mile away."

While the troops stood to hundred percent alert, Marine 155 mm pack howitzer artillery batteries fired "harassment and interdiction" (H&I) missions that plastered the countryside around the Marine position. The H&I's fell indiscriminately throughout the night and kept enemy units from concentrating near the Marine positions. They could hear the distant thunder of the guns firing, followed by the ear splitting scream of the huge projectiles flying overhead, and then the deafening crash of the rounds pounding the ground.

Mike crawled a few feet behind the hole, zipped up his flak jacket, curled up in his poncho, and fell instantly into a deep sleep. Frank sat staring into the darkness, scanning the rice paddies and jungle foliage in front of him. He thought he saw something move near a dike to his left. He knew he heard someone walking through the water. He reached for a grenade and held it in his hand, his left index finger hooked through the ring on the pin, but the walking stopped suddenly and the figure near the dike disappeared. He held his breath, strained his eyes and ears and found nothing. He exhaled through his nose, watching and waiting. Nothing!

From behind him came a deep chesty snore. Frank jumped, swung around and found Mike with his mouth half open, gulping in the night air. There was another snore that sounded like a clap of thunder before he reached over, grabbed Mike by the ankle and shook him. Mike sat straight up, teeth clenched in the starlight, a hand grenade held in his fist. "What the fuck is it? Is it time for me to watch? I just laid down!"

"No, you were snoring, asshole. Loud enough to wake the fuckin' dead. Hold it down, will ya?"

Mike fell back to sleep quickly and quietly, his breathing deep and rhythmic, but he didn't snore anymore. Frank continued to watch.

The "Boom...Boom...Boom" of the 155's fired intermittently, and the high explosive rounds hammered the terrain around the Marine perimeter. Then Frank heard the rounds slamming into the other side of the company perimeter, followed by a terrible high-pitched howl. The explosions stopped, but the howling continued. He could hear yelling and the sound of Marines running through the brush.

"What the fuck was that?" Mike said. His voice was groggy, but he was wide awake.

"Don't know," Frank whispered. The screaming

continued and shortly thereafter, Frenchie made his way from foxhole to foxhole, telling the men that a FNG from 1st Platoon was hit by a "short round", an artillery round that falls inside the Marine perimeter. Frenchie was mad and visibly upset. He said that the unlucky Marine had been hit with shrapnel in the side of his head, and that part of his skull was blown off.

Charlie Company's nighttime perimeter could not be a symmetrical circle because of the terrain and the thick foliage. That meant that the firing coordinates for the H&I needed to be carefully calibrated to allow the rounds to hit close enough to the perimeter to break up any enemy concentrations, but fall far enough away to avoid hitting the Marine's positions. This time, unfortunately, the firing coordinates were off. As Frenchie said, "shit happens."

It was a moonless night, pitch black, misting rain, and there was no way to get a medevac helicopter in to take out the critically wounded Marine until morning. Corpsmen tried to make him comfortable, filling him with morphine but it did little good. The wounded man screamed continuously all night, passing out for a few moments, and then waking up screaming again. When dawn finally arrived, a chopper landed in a nearby clearing. As the Marines carried the stretcher across the clearing, the screaming stopped. The wounded Marine died just as they were loading his stretcher onto the medevac chopper.

"Wasted," Ken said that morning. No one ate. Everyone was quiet. Later in the morning, Charlie Company saddled up and moved out.

Hackers

Nights ran into days and the constant strain of imminent enemy contact, the exhaustive walks, the sapping sun, lack of sleep, and a steady diet of C-Rations generated a whole new set of values and priorities for the men.

Frank tried to ignore the gut wrenching stress of constant danger that came with every step. The enemy was there, watching and running just ahead of the Marines, and every tree line offered a potential sniper or ambush squad the chance to kill and maim. The weight of his equipment and the pain of cutting pack straps helped him forget the danger, but training his eyes and ears to walk point, offered the best escape.

He had never known this type of unrelenting heat before, even at home in the hot, humid climate of the Deep South. As each morning passed, the air temperature rose gradually and relentlessly until the blast at high noon was agonizing. The reflection of the water added momentary, painful blindness to bodies already suffering with red, sunburned, exposed skin. Water, clean and pure, was nowhere to be found.

They drank with the water buffalos in the fields, and sometimes they were able to fill their canteens from putrid wells in the villages they passed. The constant C-Ration diet, bland and tasteless, worked with all the other elements to punish the men as they struggled through each day.

The Marines continued to march west toward Con Thien, a Marine combat base on the DMZ located just a few meters from North Vietnam. The mission was to patrol around the firebase where the Marines were being pounded by NVA artillery, and to disrupt and stop any planned NVA ground attack.

The pounding rain, followed by scorching heat, made the misery of the marches seem endless. Some of the Marines passed out with heat exhaustion, and the corpsmen ordered medivacs to take them to the rear for treatment. Many felt like climbing aboard the medevac choppers to escape the suffering, but no one wanted to be caught faking heat exhaustion. Frenchie made it clear that any "non-hackers, slackers or chicken-shit malingerers" would find their "miserable asses transferred to Graves Registration in Da Nang."

Americans KIAs in Vietnam toward the end of 1967 through the Têt Offensive in 1968 averaged 400 to 500 each month. Many were Marines fighting on the DMZ, and Graves Registration was the Navy mortuary. This was the place where dead Marines were taken, and mortuary personnel identified, embalmed, and placed the remains in metal caskets for transport back to the States for burial. The smell of decaying bodies was vicious, and it permeated the building and every person who worked there.

Stories about Marines assigned to this gruesome duty were well known in Charlie Company. "Non-hackers" sent there lived and worked in a "slaughter house" that defied description or imagination. They would meet incoming choppers or trucks, and off-load the dead bodies and severed limbs. After they were removed, the mortuary personnel were required to wash down the chopper's litter platforms that were drenched in blood and body fluids, and then perform the same wash-down tasks on the flatbeds of any trucks used to transports bodies. They also were tasked with the duty of identifying the body parts that went with each dead Marine, sorting arms, legs and heads into their waiting body bags.

Gruesome didn't come close to describing their horrific jobs, and everyone would do anything to avoid this fate. And no one wanted a "non-hacker" to return to a line company after he had "learned his lesson". They were outcasts, shunned by the other troops, thought to bring bad luck, and most still carried the stench of death in their clothes, hair, and on their skin. Just thinking about Graves Registration made Frank determined to march on with the weight of his pack, rifle and equipment. He was determined to find the strength to avoid being labeled a "non-hacker".

Resupply and mail

By the end of the fourth day, everyone was out of food. But before dusk, they settled into a night perimeter tucked between two hills that rose to the east and west, where resupply choppers dropped in more C-Rations, fresh water, and the all-important mailbags. The Marines were grateful for the basics, but really excited about the delivery of mail -- and more cigarettes. The Platoon Sergeant responsible for their supplies, distributed the new "bounty" to the Platoon.

"Hey, Morgan, I'll trade ya two packs of Winstons for those two Camels," Ken offered. They were sitting around cleaning their weapons, eating, drinking, smoking and gloating over their good fortune. Their foxholes were dug, so it was time to relax before the sun went down.

"Nope. Can't stand those 'cunt smokes'. I'll keep my 'humps'."

"Aw, come on, man, I can't stand tearin' the filter off these things to make them fit to smoke." Frank and Jim chuckled at the trading session while they reread letters from home.

"I'll even throw in a can of peaches."

"Nope."

"And a pound cake."

"You're gettin' close. Throw in that half a pack of Luckies you got, and it's a deal."

"Screw you man, that's too much."

"No deal," Mike shrugged, and walked off.

After distributing the C-Rations, the supply sergeant conducted mail call, calling out the names of those who had mail from home. Frank got a letter from his mother. This break from the misery and monotony of "the walk in the sun" was a welcome relief.

His mother wrote that everything at home was fine, she worked as a real estate agent and was happy to say she closed a deal on a house for an Air Force captain who was being transferred into the area and would get a couple of thousand for the realtors' fee. Rusty, one of Frank's best high school buds, dropped by to see if she had heard from Frank. Frank's collie, Tammy, was fine, but she missed him like everyone else. His mother promised to fix his favorite meal for him when he got home and she assured him, his room was just the way he had left it. She sent her love, asked that he write soon and wrote that she was praying for him.

Frank folded the letter, tried not to get it muddy, stuck it in his pack, and watched the sun setting across the rice paddy. Home seemed like it was on another planet. He thought of the house, his room with a bed, clean sheets, warm blankets, a bathroom around the corner with clean, running water, all you could drink, the kitchen at the end of the hall with food, so much food stored in the cupboards. And best of all, it was safe there. No one was shooting at you, trying to kill you, and no dead bodies. And he began to laugh to himself at the stark contrast he was imagining as he sat in his two-man foxhole.

Mail from home meant a lot. It was contact with the "outside", a thin thread connected to a sane world. It was a reminder that there was something besides the present, that there was an end to it all. He had to hang in there, and everything would be all right.

"Hey, Mike, let me use your writing gear before it gets dark," Frank asked.

> *Dear Mother, We made a landing the other day and now we're marching through the countryside on a long patrol. The enemy is nowhere around. I guess they heard we were coming, got scared and ran back North. It really is safe in this area so I don't want you to worry about me. I told you about meeting Mike again in my last letter and he's sitting right next to me. I'm using his writing*

gear. He really is a good guy and so are the other men in the unit. We all hope that soon we'll be going back to the ship. I sure could use a shower. Congratulations on selling that house. When you see Rusty again, tell him to drink a cold Bud or two for me. Give Tammy a hug and tell her not to bite anybody unless she has to. I've got to go now. Take care, don't forget to lock your doors at night and I'll write again, soon. Love, Frank

"Alright! Stand to! Come on! Get on your flak jackets and helmets, and get into your holes!" Sims marched up and ordered them back to reality.

As darkness approached, Frank and Mike sat next to each other, legs dangling into the foxhole, talking quietly. Grenades and extra ammunition sat within their reach, and the mosquitoes came out and began their never-ending attack.

"I wonder how far we'll go tomorrow," Mike said.

"Christ, I don't know. Gooks have probably found a way to get across the river and head north by now."

A crescent moon brightened the starlit night making it easy to see. In the distance, the rumble of an artillery battery firing alerted them that those rounds would soon start falling around their position. They sat and waited until they heard the now familiar, but still frightening, rush of the incoming shells. Like freight trains, they roared overhead and burst in yellow flames not far from their position. The cracking explosions were deafening.

"Those 155's are somethin'," Frank observed.

"Get some arty!" Mike cheered in a whisper. The short but violent barrage ended as abruptly as it had begun.

"What'd your Mom have to say, Mike?"

"Nothin' special. Dad's okay. Everything's just the same. What about you?"

"More of the same."

Frank checked his watch and saw it was almost time to stand down to fifty percent. Mike would get to sleep first while Frank stood watch for an hour.

"You want first watch?"

"Yeah, Frank, I guess it's my turn."

He crawled a few feet behind the foxhole, spread out his poncho, laid back and made himself comfortable. Frank had grown used to sleeping on the ground, his flak jacket and poncho providing a warm shell that helped keep out the damp night air. His eyes fell shut and he slept.

Arc Lights

To support the Marines fighting along the DMZ, the Air Force launched B-52 bombers flying out of Guam and Thailand, code name *Arc Light*, to attack NVA positions. The racks of 750 and 1,000 pound bombs inflicted heavy casualties on enemy regiments moving toward the Marine "strong points." It was now mid-November, and Charlie Company established a defensive perimeter east of Con Thien.

Frank dangled his feet into his foxhole, the sky to the north lit up with white flashes of light that were as daylight. After the white, almost clear flashes, came the ear splitting, sustained booms that rolled across the landscape. The ground began to rise and fall in waves that felt and looked like a blanket being shaken up and down again and again. Frank's foxhole collapsed and he rolled away, lying flat on the ground next to Mike. The *Arc Light* attack went on for a while, and the Marines rode the reeling earth until at last, the flashes stopped and the "earthquake" passed.

Night vision was key to Marines being able to make out images, often shades of black with black backgrounds that moved in the night. The iris of the eyes were wide, allowing any faint light or black contrast to be visible to the Marines on watch. *Arc Light* strikes were similar to illumination artillery fire with white phosphorus burning brightly, hanging from a parachute high above the Marines. The pairs of Marines in their foxholes took turns, one watching for anything or anyone who may be "lit up" in the bright lights. The other Marine kept his eyes tightly closed, and buried his head in his poncho to block out the light. After the *Arc Light* strikes were over, the Marine who preserved his night vision took over watch.

Frank was on his second watch when the 155mm howitzer battery at Dong Ha began to fire H&I that landed very close to the Charlie Company's perimeter. H&I was intended to fall on potential NVA troop concentrations that might be assembling near the Marine position to kill, wound, and disrupt any assaults that might be attempted. Great firing precision was required to make sure the nighttime firing coordinates were correct so that the high explosive rounds would fall on the NVA, and not the Marines. Friendly fire was the most horrific way for a

Marine to be "dinged, fucked up or wasted."

Charlie Company was lucky that night. No contact and no short rounds from the 155s. Dawn brought more rain and the promise of another long march through harsh terrain.

CHAPTER X – FIGHTING ON THE DMZ

Between the 3ʳᵈ and 19ᵗʰ of December 1967, the NVA fired 578 rounds of 85mm, 130mm artillery, 122mm and 130mm rockets, 82mm mortars, and 57mm recoilless rifle fire into Alpha-3.

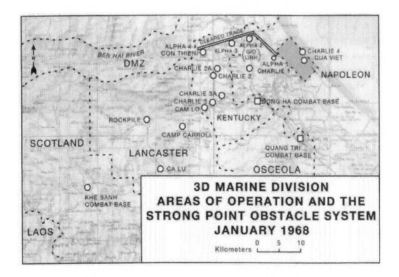

Operation Kentucky V

The US Military Assistant Command in Vietnam (MACV) had assigned the 3rd Marine Division the mission of stopping the NVA infiltration across the DMZ. The Marines also were assigned the mission of providing security and the labor for the construction of a string of bunker systems across the DMZ. The *Operation Dye Marker* was an interdiction strategy developed in the Pentagon to stop the infiltration of NVA units crossing the DMZ to fight in the south. It called for the construction of an intricate bunker system equipped with electronic sensors, ground radar, and new night vision technology. All intended to detect troop movements, and allow the Marines to call in artillery, mortars, naval gunfire and air strikes to destroy approaching enemy units.

By November 1967, the Marines had built and defended bunker systems from Charlie-4 and Firebase Cau Viet in the east, to Alpha-3 and Firebase Con Thien, to the Khe Sanh Combat Base located below the DMZ and near the Laotian border. The bunker system also provided the NVA with choice targets where they could pound the Marines with artillery, rocket and mortar fire. The Marines hated sitting in bunkers, becoming stationary targets inside the "strong points". By tradition and training, Marines are assault troops intended to maneuver in the field, pursue the enemy, and attack.

The Marine generals fought to have the Marine battalions conduct search and destroy operations, but they lost the argument with the Pentagon civilians and White House strategists. McNamara had his bunker system.

Ho Chi Minh and General Giap planned to repeat the same successful strategy that led to the French disaster at Dien Bien Phu, by laying siege to one of the American "strong points" and destroy the American Marines. The North Vietnamese leadership knew that, like the French politicians and citizens, a bloody devastating defeat would cause Americans to withdraw their support of the war and seek peace that, in turn, would lead to the reunification of North and South Vietnam.

In November 1967, Mike's Battalion launched *Operation Kentucky V*. They patrolled the area around Mai Xa Thi, but the enemy decided not to engage. Most Marines carried over 50 pounds of equipment and extra ammunition in terrain that changed from steep hills covered with thick jungle canopies, to sucking rice paddies, to loose sand dunes. The temperature was over 100° and the humidity was so high that even the air felt like it was sweating.

The Marines struggled and fought their way through the airless, semi-darkness of the jungle to the crest of each hill before running down the steep reverse side into the darkness below.

It was late November when Mike's Platoon stopped for a break. He asked to no one in particular, "how about some 'slack'?" (the grunt's term for rest, hot food and time out of the field). "Wonder when we're going back to the ship?"

With their packs strewn about the ground, they sat on fallen trees, resting, smoking and trying to catch their breath. The air under the tree canopy was hot, humid, and the stench of rotting foliage filled their nostrils.

"Hell, if I know," Ken answered as he pulled off a soggy pair of black socks and wrung them out. "A guy in 3rd Platoon said he heard that we weren't goin' back."

Ken's mud caked boots sat next to him on the fallen tree as he stretched his pink, stinking feet and wiggled his toes trying to air them out a little. No one complained about the nauseating stench of his feet because there was no distinguishing it with the raunchy smells of the jungle.

"Scuttlebutt. Probably just more scuttlebutt," Frank said. His recently issued machete laid across his knees, and he poured cool, dirty water on his blistered, torn hands. Walking point meant he had to chop and cut a path through the jungle, and his aching arms and shoulders felt as if they were being ripped from his body.

"I hope the scuttlebutt was wrong."

They had averaged just three hours of sleep each night. And if it weren't for the corpsman making each man swallow the huge, orange-colored yellow fever pill issued each Sunday, they would have lost track of time. No one bothered keeping up with the days of the week. It just didn't matter.

Ken helped the new men improve their diet in the bush by teaching them to steal some rice from villagers, and mix it with their C-Rations. He then would share sauce from a bottle of Tabasco Sauce he had received in the mail. It helped spice up the bland, tasteless C-Rats. For dessert, they picked breadfruit from trees that grew wild in the jungle and sucked the delicious orange and tangerine-like juice until they drained the last drop.

"What I wouldn't give for a hot shower, some decent food, and a full night's sleep," Jim said, stretching, groaning and yawning.

"No slack. No slack, man. There just ain't no slack," Ken said, laughing and shaking his head, finding humor in their predicament. Knowing everyone suffered together was the only ointment they had for their wounds.

"All right! Saddle up! Let's go, we're movin' out!" Sims commanded, from the other side of the bushes.

Ken cursed and frantically began putting his socks and boots back on while his buddies laughed.

The troops staggered another three hundred yards up a steep incline, to the crest of another hill, where Frank stopped and looked around carefully, before starting down the other side. His eyes and ears had become keen, able to pick out telltale signs of the enemy's presence. He scanned the countryside, mountains on all sides, a small stream cutting through the valley below, and found nothing unusual. There was no movement below, and it was absolutely quiet. They moved on, and at dusk climbed another hill and prepared for the night. Frenchie made his rounds, checking each position, talking with the men.

"When are we goin' back to the ship, Sarge?" Mike asked.

"We're not, Morgan."

"Aw shit! That fuckin' guy in 3rd Platoon was right." Frank's heart sank. "Forman said he'd heard we weren't goin' back."

"He's right, but tomorrow, we're marchin' to a clearing about two clicks north, where we're gonna be picked up by choppers."

"Shit, that's fuckin outstanding," Mike shouted. And then he thought about it a little more. "If we're not goin' back to the ship, where are we goin'?"

"Dong Ha, a firebase west of here, near Highway One."

"You mean we're goin' to the rear? Where they got showers, food and bunks and shit?"

"Yeah, for a few days, anyway. Since its winter, we're going to be issued new poncho liners. That'll help us keep warm and fight off the uncontrollable shakes. Then we're goin' to a new fire support base they're building on the DMZ, called Alpha-3."

"We gonna get some slack before we go?" Mike asked anxiously.

"Yeah, Morgan, you gonna get to clean your scuzzy ass, and feed your face and catch up on your Z's before we go out again."

Frenchie moved on to the next hole, to Ken and Jim, and passed the good word, while Frank and Mike sat and talked quietly about Dong Ha and Alpha-3. The sunset and darkness covered the jungle.

"Wonder what the fuck it's like at Alpha-3?"

The Rear

The next morning, the men moved more lively, half-running to the clearing where the helicopters would pick them up. They climbed aboard, smiling and laughing as the "birds" lifted them out of the jungle, into the clear morning sky. The memories of twenty-five days in the field slipped away as the choppers touched down at Dong Ha.

They marched in platoon formations down a dusty road, through the deadly outer defenses of the base, where two rows of triple razor-sharp concertina, backed by countless sandbag bunkers, waited to greet attacking NVA soldiers.

Frank had never seen barbed wire rolled in razor sharp "doughnut" coils, stretched and stacked ten and twelve feet high, anchored to the ground with steel stakes. Mines and booby traps saturated the open ground in between the rows of wire. Then on top of the bunkers sat M60 machine gun firing positions that scanned the open terrain beyond the concertina coils.

"Charlie'd have to be outta his fuckin' mind to hit this place," Mike observed. "Yeah," Ken agreed. "This is the rear for 1st Battalion, 9th Marines. Life's tough all over."

Frenchie was close enough to hear the comments and snarled, "You dumb shits. The 1st Battalion, 9th Marines, or 1/9, is rotating in and out of Con Thien right now. This is their rear area CP. You know, their command post or headquarters."

Frenchie said, "Do you know what they call 1/9 and why?" Laughter stopped and everyone listened. Frenchie continued, "General Giap hates 1/9 because they kill lots of gooks. Giap calls the battalion 'Di Bo Chet,' in English, 'The Walking Dead.' By late 1967, 1st Battalion, 9th Marines had a higher casualty rate than any other Marine battalion in Nam. The NVA really have a hard on for 1/9." Frenchie walked away shaking his head.

There was no laughter as the ragged 1st Battalion, 3rd Marines marched to the middle of Dong Ha. They passed secure and extensive defenses, hard-backed hooches with sandbags piled against outside walls. The 9th Marine's headquarters, supply and logistic troops lined the road, gawking at the 1/3 grunts as they marched by. Frank became conscious of his own filth and the beard he was growing, when he looked at the other men, standing and watching, with their clean uniforms and freshly shaven faces.

Automatically, the grunts straightened up, lifted their heads, fell into step, and marched to an unheard cadence. Their aching, worn out bodies and rancid smell reminded the 1/3 grunts that they were real Marines, not REMFs – "rear echelon mother fuckers" as Ken liked to call the Headquarters Marines who lined the road.

The 9th Marines Headquarters troops welcomed the 1/3, and no one complained when the filthy grunts used up all the hot water that was available at the showers. And when they went to the mess hall, the line of Headquarters Marines waiting up front stepped aside and let the worn out infantrymen go first.

Each man piled his tray high with sliced beef, powdered whipped potatoes, canned vegetables, bread and globs of butter. The troops gorged themselves, and the mess sergeant smiled when they returned for seconds. Frank stuffed his mouth with chocolate cake and washed it down with several cups of cold milk. Some guys over-ate and they got sick and threw up. But most finished their meal, then went back to the area where they were billeted.

Alpha and Bravo Companies rejoined Charlie and Delta Companies at Dong Ha. That night, for the first time in over a month, the battalion slept inside hard-backed hooches. The combination barracks and tents protected the weary men from a torrential downpour that began just after sundown. They slept on wooden floors because bunks and mattresses were not available. No one complained. They were dry, didn't have to dig muddy foxholes, and didn't have to stand alternating watches every hour. Most importantly, the enemy wasn't trying to crawl into their position. Frank and his buddies crashed in the warm, dry barracks. Resting their heads on filthy packs, they didn't wake up until well after sunrise.

Two days passed, where the only things "stressful" were the trips back and forth to the showers, the head, and mess hall. Otherwise, they would sleep morning, noon and night, totally unmolested.

On the third day, Sims and Frenchie broke the tranquility by telling everyone to clean up their equipment and weapons, and get ready for an inspection that afternoon. Amidst groans and curses, they turned to washing packs, flak jackets, cartridge belts and other pieces of equipment that could be dragged into the showers. They dried their gear in the noontime sun, while everyone stripped rifles, and machineguns, cleaning the weapons meticulously piece by piece.

That afternoon, when Frenchie and the Lieutenant had completed the inspection, Ken grumbled, "must be about time to move out again. Always happens this way. Just about the time you begin to feel like a human being, back to the bush we go with the other animals."

"Yeah, I hope we don't have to hump across country day after day this time," Frank said.

"Did ya hear those guys in the mess hall talkin' about Con Thien?" Mike joined in.

"They said two companies from the 9th Marines have been under siege up there for over a month. Gooks are poundin' the shit outta them with arty and rockets every day. They call it the 'meat grinder'."

"Another guy said he heard that the 4th Marines got their asses kicked at a place south of Con Thien called Dai Do," Mike continued. "Said a whole battalion got ambushed by a regiment of NVA. Had 'beaucoup' wasted, and a shit-pot more of them got fucked-up."

"Doesn't surprise me," Ken said. "2nd Battalion 4th Marines call themselves 'the magnificent bastards.' But they also have very bad luck. They could get themselves ambushed goin' to the PX in Da Nang."

They all laughed at the rumors. But deep inside, each felt uncomfortable about the stories circulating among the troops. There seemed to be a sharp increase in enemy activity along the DMZ. And with Christmas and New Year's right around the corner, none of them wanted to celebrate the holidays caught in "a world of shit".

Siege

On the fourth day, they saddled up, climbed aboard open-back trucks, called "rough riders", and formed a convoy heading north on Highway 1 toward the DMZ. Packed with troops, the trucks kept a safe distance between each truck in case one hit a land mine, the trucks in front and behind wouldn't get hit.

The men leaned back and tried to enjoy the ride, and not think about the danger of hitting a mine. There were plenty of trucks ahead of them and if anybody got blown away, it would probably be one of the trucks up front.

They raced through villages where kids ran along beside the trucks yelling and begging for food and cigarettes.

"Cigarette! Cigarette! Chop! Chop! Marines Numba One! Marines Numba One!"

"Go fuck yourselves ya little slant eyed bastards!" shouted a few guys at the back of the truck.

"Why're ya breakin' their chops?" Ken shouted over the roar of the truck motors.

"Most of those little bastards are the sons of NVA and VC fighting along the Z, and they'd blow you away if ya gave them half a chance." Answered a Salt from 1st Squad.

Frank, Ken, Mike and Jim sat silently while the jeering and taunting continued. The kids were begging for food, so one of the Marines dug a can of ham and limas out of his pack and threw it into the crowd. The can bounced off a little boy's head, and he dropped to the ground like a sack of rocks. The other kids jumped over his sprawled body and scrambled for the can.

Some of the guys howled with laughter, but abusing the kids was really stupid. As the trucks pulled away from the kids, they shot the Marines the finger and screamed,

"Fuck you! Fuck you GI!" You numba ten! Numba ten!"

"No wonder they try to kill us every chance they get," Ken said.

They crossed a bridge straddling the Cua Viet River and, in the distance farther north, they could hear giant artillery pieces firing. The thunder became louder and louder until they crested a hill where below, they could see a Marine 155mm howitzer battery blasting away. Crewmen scrambled behind each gun, passing huge shells that were thrown into smoking, open breaches. They wore protection over their ears and, as the NCO commanding the weapon lowered his arm, a lanyard was pulled, causing an explosion that sounded like lightening striking nearby. The barrels rocked back and balls of fire belched from the muzzle while the grunts covered their ears. The concussion rocked the trucks as they headed farther north.

"Get some Arty!" Ken shouted, when they were far enough away to hear again. He stood and cheered the artillerymen, yelling, "Get some! Get some, Arty!" As they drove down range from the guns, the rush of shells passing overhead made Frank nervous, but it didn't bother Ken and the other Salts.

Before noon, the trucks stopped in the middle of a muddy field, and the Marines climbed down. They sloshed around in deep, red mud until they were in a tactical formation with Frank and others taking the point.

The wedge was aimed north, northeast where battered hills and once green woods waited. It was desolate. The Air Force has sprayed Agent Orange all across the DMZ killing all living things including plants, animals and trees. Bugs seemed to have survived. Besides Agent Orange, the land was pock- marked with crater after crater of shell and bomb holes. It made the DMZ look more like what "no-man's land" in World War I must have appeared.

Charlie Company moved out, Sims giving Frank directions, as the trucks roared off back down Highway One. They marched through the unearthly landscape, up one hill and down another, without stopping for a break. It was not until early afternoon when they finally stood at the foot of a hill. Around the top, men scurried back and forth hauling timber, sheets of steel and sandbags. Running east and west, intersecting the hill on both sides, was a wide, open area where nothing stood. It looked as if a giant plow had cleared a two hundred yard wide stretch of dead trees away.

"Welcome to Alpha-3!" Ken spat.

It was late afternoon by the time Charlie Company broke from the jungle to an open area, and Frank could see the rough outline of a perimeter that surrounded a muddy hill with a sandbag bunker at the top. Ken walked up to join Frank on point and said, "Word is we're going to provide perimeter security for the 11th Engineers while they build the Alpha-3 bunker system."

Captain Olsen, LT, and Frenchie arrived and began to discuss the best way to place Charlie Company into a defensive perimeter. They pointed at likely approaches for NVA attacks and discussed the best way to create interlocking fields of fire, a "killing-ground" that would allow the Marines to fire on NVA soldiers trying to breach the perimeter.

Frank was impressed that, as tired and worn out everyone was -- and all he wanted to do was drop his pack and sit down to rest -- Captain Olsen and the company leadership continued to walk around the perimeter, placing each pair of Marines into their most advantageous position.

Frank and Mike were placed on a slight rise where the ground to the left was slightly lower and they had a clear view of any approaching enemy. To their left and right, the other 2nd Platoon Marines were strung out every 20-30 feet into adjoining foxhole positions. Everyone gratefully dropped their packs and broke out entrenching tools to begin digging foxholes.

It was still daylight as the Marines dug in and rested. In the next foxhole, Frank and Mike heard the portable radio one of their buddies carried into the field. The small transistor radio picked up signals from Da Nang where Radio Vietnam played popular music and broadcast news from "the world." They also liked listening to Radio Hanoi where "Hanoi Hanna", a woman DJ and supposedly an American traitor, broadcast music and taunted the Americans with her sexy voice.

Frank and Mike listened to Hanoi Hanna welcome the 1st Battalion, 3rd Marines and specifically Colonel Stark to Alpha-3. "Our brave soldiers of the 320th NVA division are surrounding your position, and our brave patriots will kill all of you," she cooed.

At dusk, when the word came down to "stand to" at one hundred percent alert, Sims and Frenchie made the rounds of the perimeter checking on each position.

Frenchie heard about Hanna welcoming the battalion to Alpha-3, and he just said, "screw Hanna, and just enjoy the good music she plays."

They quickly settled down to a brutal but dangerous routine. Frank and Mike worked on improving their fighting holes, and stringing rows of coiled concertina wire in front of their position. Because the NVA used specially trained troops, called "Sappers", who could silently crawl through concertina wire, penetrate the perimeter, and kill unsuspecting Marines, Frank and Mike attached to the wire in front of them, empty C-Ration cans with rocks inside. If the cans were brushed or moved by a Sapper, the rattle from the rocks would alert them that an attempt was being made to penetrate their position.

They did their best to avoid the working parties assigned to fill sandbags and build the command bunkers at the top of the hill. The command bunker was a favorite target for the NVA artillery spotters sitting in the hills surrounding Alpha-3. Ken referred to the command bunkers as "artillery magnets".

Thick sheets of rain fell constantly, filling the foxholes with mud and waste-deep standing water. The nights were bitter cold with a stiff wind blowing out of the north. The Marines pulled the hood of their ponchos over their heads and tried to stay warm with their new but soaked poncho liners. No one had much luck in keeping warm. They all just shivered with what they called "uncontrollable shakes" throughout the pitch-black night.

Alpha-3 was located almost in the middle of "McNamara's Line." The strategy was to build "strong points" and lay mine fields along a 11 kilometer long, 600 meter wide cleared land, bulldozed by the 11th Marine Engineers. Called the "Trace", it ran east to west, and parallel to the DMZ. The Trace provided a cleared field of fire and line-of-sight visibility so the Marines could monitor and detect enemy troops moving from North to South.

The Air Force continued to spray both the DMZ and the Trace with Agent Orange. Ken said, "the Department of Defense bought tons of this shit from Dow and Monsanto. The idea was to remove the foliage the NVA were hiding in, thereby making it easier to see and kill them." But the constant spraying did not stop the NVA. They used the protection of the surrounding terrain by jumping from shell hole to shell hole, "leap-frogging" across the Trace. And if the NVA found an area that would not permit leap-frogging, they avoided that portion of the Trace by moving their troops through Laos and Cambodia.

Agent Orange was nasty. It may have been orange when it was sprayed, but on the ground, it was a dead gray, smelly and sticky. It got into your eyes, mouth, and all your orifices. It got into your water, C-Rations – everything. Wherever Agent Orange was sprayed, the foliage died and the birds abandoned the area. Rumor had it that the Air Force kept spraying so the Defense Department civilians could place more orders with Dow and Monsanto. But that was just what Forman said. Frank was yet to experience Agent Orange.

The NVA did their best to make good on Hanoi Hanna's promise to try and kill everyone. Snipers picked off unsuspecting Marines. Artillery was fired from across the DMZ, while mortars and rockets were fired from closer positions just outside the wire. In the morning, the NVA would hit the Marines with mortars, then rockets at noon and at dusk, and then massive artillery rounds at the Marines' evening chow -- and intermittently throughout the night. Casualties mounted.

The 11th Marine Engineers used bulldozers and endless work details to build huge bunkers on the crest of the hill. The bulldozers dug deep holes, while engineers covered them with thick beams, sheets of steel mats and layer after layer of sandbags. They were designed to take direct hits from enemy artillery pieces, providing complete safety for the occupants.

While the Marines defended the hills and worked on the bunkers, the 320th North Vietnamese Division infiltrated the charred, pockmarked hills facing the Trace, and they began to dig in. Although the area was constantly pounded by B-52s, Marine Phantom jets, naval gunfire, artillery and gunships, the NVA still managed to haul large artillery pieces far enough south to strike the Marine positions.

The enemy troops crawled across the Trace in force and surrounded the hills, laying siege to Alpha-3. At Con Thien, west of Alpha-3, the 9th Marines had already tasted the sting of the enemy's strategy to control the DMZ by laying siege to the *Dye Marker* strong points. It was as if the NVA strategists were planning for another "Bien Dien Phu" victory, but this time, against the Americans.

Monsoon and Incoming

They had been at Alpha-3 a week. The rain, mud, cold nights took a toll on the Marines.

"Come on, O'Brian!" Sims barked one gray morning.

Frank and the other Marines in 2nd Squad headed up the hill, like a row of ants, circling the crest. They had the bad luck to be assigned to another work detail building bunkers. They worked in pairs, Frank used his entrenching tool to shovel dirt and mud while Mike held open sand bags to swallow the dirt. They tied the bags and then stacked the growing mountain of bags on the roof of the bunker. Before dusk and the stand down order, they staggered back to their foxhole on the perimeter.

"Christ! I hope the gooks don't decide to hit us tonight," Frank said. He shuddered in the wet, cold night air. "There ain't a lot between us and them but 20 yards and the barbed wire."

"If they got any sense at all, they're back home in their barracks, tucked in where it's nice and dry and warm," Mike answered.

"Yeah, but I doubt it. Bastards are probably watchin' us right now, as we set in for the evening."

Four man patrols, listening posts, were sent out on all sides of the perimeter. If the enemy decided to attack, one of the listening posts would hear their movement and call in artillery before the enemy got close to the perimeter.

That night passed without incident. The men were wet, cold and miserable. In the gray dawn, the rain continued to fall in sheets while they ate cold C-Rations for breakfast. After chow, they continued to make improvements on their foxhole.

The next few days and nights were quiet, but the rain did not let up. The men strengthened the perimeter by adding additional concertina barbed wire, but not without a great deal of difficulty. They wore thick gloves for protection from the razor-sharp barbs, but bouncing the hoops of wire and stretching them out cut their arms and legs. Once in place, they drove strong stakes deep into the side of the hill and tied the barbed wire securely into place.

When the rain finally stopped and the sky cleared, a huge UH-46A "Sea Knight" helicopter flew in, carrying a load of lumber, steel mats and sandbags, all in a huge canvas pouch suspended from the chopper's underbelly. The bird was in the process of dropping the load on the crest of the hill when everyone heard the rapid "Thump! Thump! Thump!" of incoming mortar fire.

Frank looked around, and saw everyone diving for cover. He jumped into his hole, landing on top of Mike. Each put on their helmet, and then waited nervously for the rounds to hit.

"Crunch! Crunch! Crunch!" The shells hit and exploded near where the helicopter was planning to set down to unload the supplies. Still ten feet in the air, the pilot immediately released the cable holding the construction material, and it came crashing down. He revved his engine, and the chopper abruptly pulled away from the hill.

"Thump! Thump! Thump!" Three more rounds were fired, followed by a volley of three more.

"Holy shit! I wonder if they're gettin' ready to attack in broad daylight." Mike blurted through clenched teeth.

"I doubt it," Frank yelled back. Then another "Crash! Crash! Crash! Boom! Boom! Boom!" "They're probably tryin' to get the bird while its still on the landing pad."

When the mortar rounds stopped falling, Frank and Mike raised their heads up, saw the barbed wire in front of them, but no enemy soldiers in sight. They breathed a sigh of relief -- the gooks weren't trying a frontal assault, at least not then.

Luckily, no one was hurt in the mortar barrage, and the chopper lifted off with its wounded Marines. But before dark, six rockets slammed into the muddy hill, killing two Marines and wounding five others. Medevac choppers were called back in to take out the dead and wounded. They managed to land, load up the dead and wounded, and take off before the darkness set in.

Rockets were more frightening than mortars because rockets flew in a flat trajectory rather than an arch, and rockets are much faster than mortars. When the troops heard a rocket report, everyone knew that you had to get down fast because the missiles hit their target at about the same time they heard the sound of their report. The "Bang! Whoosh! Crash!" sounds of a rocket meant someone was probably going to die.

That night, the NVA began to systematically walk artillery rounds across, through and behind the hill. Frank and Mike had never experienced being bombarded by mortars, rockets or artillery, and they trembled in their holes. As the shells slammed in, booming, one after another, they could hear men yelling that they had been hit. And the cry for corpsman was heard throughout the night. Still, the enemy did not make a frontal attack on the wire.

"Get some!"

The next morning, the men laid more concertina wire in the rain, while others, working on the crest of the hill, frantically built the main bunkers, covering them with thick timbers and several layers of sandbags. When the rain let up, Marine F-4's screamed out of the haze, dropping napalm and 500 pound bombs on suspected enemy gun emplacements. Giant rolling balls of yellow flames and black smoke billowed across the hills all around the Marines at Alpha-3. Ear splitting shock waves followed the explosions, and the Alpha-3 men cheered and yelled their support for the attacking F-4s.

"Get some Phantoms! Get some! Knock yourselves out!"

The grunts urged the pilots on to "get some NVA," waving their entrenching tools in the sky, shouting encouragement to the Marine pilots.

After the F-4s had departed shortly before noon, Alpha-3 was mortared again. This time, three more Marines died. The NVA had their own version of "get some".

The Marines worked as fast as they could, reinforcing the perimeter by placing, just outside of the perimeter, command-detonated Claymore mines that could be triggered from the firing system located inside the perimeter. When detonated, the Claymore mine explodes in a forward direction, filling the "kill zone" with thousands of white hot, buckshot pellets.

Around Alpha-3's perimeter, the Marines also planted S-Mines, better known as "Bouncing Bettys". Smaller than a Claymore, these mines were pressure-detonated explosives, meaning Charlie would have to step on the mine to detonate it. The Bouncing Bettys were designed to explode waste-high, sending out hundreds of metal balls right at groin level. The object was to cripple and maim versus kill. Because it often would take as many as four NVA soldiers to carry one of their wounded from the battlefield, the Marines wanted to keep the NVA busy carrying away their wounded buddies.

More rolls of concertina wire were thrown up, and foxholes were dug deeper and deeper. Friendly artillery, shooting from miles away, pounded the surrounding hills after the F-4s left. Again, the men cheered, "get some arty! Pound those sons-of-bitches! Get Some!"

In the evening, the sun didn't seem to set, it just grew darker and darker until the gray haze vanished and night set in. It was pitch black, except for the occasional illumination shells that slowly drifted down in the wet sky. The Marines sat watching the darkness, listening for sounds of NVA movement beyond the wire.

Lightning flashes to the north told them that B-52s were dropping 1,000-pound bombs on the NVA. The ground shook as if there was an earthquake, and the deafening roar and concussion of the bombs exploding, rolled over their perimeter.

It was a special treat for the Marines to watch "Puff the Magic Dragon" hit the surrounding hills at night. "Puff" was a DC-3 aircraft equipped with a pair of electric machine guns mounted at the cargo doors. It could be heard, droning overhead. The AC-47 would bank sharply to point the guns at the ground, and then the gunner would hit the trigger. The electric Gatling machine guns could put one bullet in every square inch of an area the size of a football field in just a few minutes. Every fifth round fired from the Gatling guns was a tracer, and at night the column of hot lead falling from the sky looked like a solid pillar of fire. It was almost like a hose of bright white water, washing the countryside, weaving back and forth. The guns fired so fast, it sounded like an extended, never ending groan. The Marines in the perimeter chuckled quietly to themselves as Puff worked out, spraying the area outside of the perimeter with deadly fire.

Foot Rot

Trapped in absolutely miserable conditions -- burning up during the day, and then freezing at night with the uncontrollable shakes -- Frank began to wonder if the suffering would never end. The soaking rain drenched his clothes, and his boots, socks and feet had absolutely no chance of getting dry. He was bone weary because of daily physical demands and the constant threat of being blown up in an enemy barrage.

The lack of sleep began to take its toll on all the men, and the Marines began to move as if they were in a daze. Everyone eventually lost track of time, and they only knew it was Sunday because that was the day the corpsmen force-fed the malaria pills to the troops.

Frank's Company corpsman was named Bowman, but everyone called him "Doc Bow". Each Sunday, Doc Bow would require everyone to stand in front of him, open his mouths, and Doc would pop in the malaria pill that was almost too large to swallow. Doc would then force the Marine to gulp water until he could confirm the pill had been swallowed. Some Marines tried to spit out the malaria pills in the hope of contracting the disease and getting to spend time out of the field in the hospital. But Doc Bow knew that game, and he made damn sure that game didn't work.

Adding to the nightmarish conditions, the endless monsoon rain caused soaked feet to rot. Immersion foot, or jungle rot, made the skin change colors from white to a sick pink, and the flesh wrinkled. The lack of dry air and sunshine caused their feet, already torn and sore with giant blisters, to drain, bleed and become infected. Frank could barely walk by the time he decided to go to the platoon corpsman for help.

"Okay, let's take a look, O'Brian." Doc Bow held Frank's bare right foot on his lap and looked at the blisters. He was all business, and he seemed concerned at the sight of Frank's foot. Doc Bow twisted Frank's foot from side to side, thoroughly inspecting Frank's extensive jungle rot. Doc spread and peered between each toe, causing Frank to yank back in pain.

"Shit Doc! Take it easy. My fuckin' foot hurts like

a sonofabitch!"

"Don't whine O'Brian, I'm not impressed. If you fuckin' people would do like I told you, you wouldn't have screwed up feet like this."

Frank gritted his teeth and winced as Doc Bow cut around the blisters and squeezed the pus out. He felt like smacking Doc in the mouth. "All you've got to do is take off your boots, ring out your socks, and air your feet for an hour each day and this shit wouldn't happen."

"Fat chance! Everybody's always workin' on the perimeter, goin' on workin' parties, running patrols, sittin' in the fuckin' rain on either a listening post or on watch and you want me to take an hour to air my feet! You tell me when Doc! Just tell me when!"

Doc Bow wiped the bleeding foot with gauze, digging deep and pushing hard, before he applied antiseptic that burned like hell.

"God damn it, Doc! I told you to take it easy!"

"Listen, asshole, I'm a corpsman, not the chaplain. If you got personal problems, I suggest you go see the Padre."

When the treatment was finished, Frank limped back to his foxhole, cursing the Doc with every hobbled step. With every step, water soaked through his boots, soaking his dry socks, and making his fresh wounds sting. Mike, Ken and Jim sat near the foxhole taking a smoke-break as Frank approached. "Doc Bow is one rotten son-of-a bitch!"

"What's the matter, Frank, he piss in your canteen?" Ken asked. The others laughed.

"No, smart ass. That shit bird corpsman just cut away chunks of skin from both of my goddamn feet. That's what happened."

"Yeah, I know what ya mean," Jim agreed. "The prick did the same thing to me the other day."

"I don't think Doc Bow wants the reputation of a gentle healer," chuckled Ken. "He doesn't want to increase his work load. Interferes with his naps."

Frank sat down, lifted his feet and rested them on top of a mound of dirt. He tried twice to light a cigarette in the rain before he was successful. The smoke helped.

Claymores

That night, there was activity along the wire as NVA Sappers crawled around in the rain, surveying the defenses in an effort to penetrate the Marine perimeter. Occasionally a Sapper would get tangled in the wire, and he would be detected when he brushed tin cans tied to the wire that had been filled with rocks. As the Sapper attempted to free himself, his movement would cause the cans to rattle and expose his location. Well-thrown grenades blew away the Sappers, and silence would return to the perimeter.

Frank and Mike stayed awake throughout the night, listening to enemy soldiers move around just outside the concertina wire. They had been told that a favorite Sapper tactic was to find a Claymore mine planted in front of a Marine position, and quietly turn it around facing the Marine position so the forward blast would be directed at the Marines manning the position. After the Sapper turned around the mine, he would move back, shake the bushes and the unsuspecting Marine would trigger the mine, blowing himself away.

At night, the only way to detect whether a Sapper was attempting to turn a Claymore was to tie the wire connected to the Claymore to a stick stuck in the side of the foxhole. If the wire attached to the stick moved, the enemy was attempting to turn the mine.

Crouching down in his foxhole, Mike pulled the Claymore wire tight, and wrapped it around the stick he had jammed into the side of the foxhole. He couldn't see the barbed wire in front of their foxhole, and could just barely make out the wire leading to the Claymore. After hours of listening and watching, Frank felt, then saw, the Claymore wire move ever so slightly.

"Claymore," he screamed, warning the men in adjacent holes to get down. The wire moved again and became taut by the time Frank grabbed the firing mechanism and triggered the mine. A deafening explosion rocked the earth, whistling BB-like steel fragments flew through the night, and then there was silence.

"Anybody hit?" shouted Mike.

"Jesus H. Christ!" Ken yelled back. "What the fuck are you two doin?"

"Are ya okay?" Frank asked.

"Yeah. Yeah. Yeah," came the answers from holes on both sides.

"I think I caught a gook trying' to turn my claymore around."

Sounds of laughter filled the dark. "You think you

got what?" Ken cracked up.

Sims came stumbling down the hill. Everybody heard him coming. "What the fuck's goin' on? What the hell are you doin'?" he gasped as he hit the ground and crawled up to their hole.

"Got a gook, Sarge," Mike explained. "O'Brian caught him tryin to turn our claymore."

"Did ya see him, O'Brian? How could ya see him?" He answered his own question. "It's dark'ern a well digger's asshole out there. Why'd ya blow it? Why'd ya blow it?" he stuttered.

"Saw and felt the wire move," Frank pointed to the now used firing mechanism, still hanging from the stick.

"Big damn deal! Ya see the wire move so ya blow a Claymore?" Sims chided. "Ya couldn't have known that anybody was out there, if ya didn't hear anything."

"I didn't want to wait until I heard somethin'. I knew somebody was screwin with my mine when I saw the wire move. How'd the wire move if it wasn't a gook?"

Sims stormed back to the command post cursing O'Brian and Morgan for blowing a mine without knowing for certain that the enemy was out there.

The next morning, Frenchie and Sims joined Frank, Mike, Ken and Jim as they inspected the wire in front of their foxhole. The blast had gouged another crater in the landscape, and all around the hole lay bits and pieces of bone, flesh, and shredded uniform. None of the pieces were very large, but Ken searched thoroughly until he found one of the bigger ones.

"See Sims. Told ya there was a gook out here,"

Frank said triumphantly. "Not much evidence," Frenchie chuckled, shaking his head. "Good goin O'Brian."

"May not have even been a gook," Sims complained.

"Here Sims!" Ken threw a seared handful of flesh at the squad leader. Sims jumped back and dodged the bloody clump. "Put that in your C-Rats if ya don't believe it was a gook! Maybe it was a stray water boo!"

"Goddamn you Forman. You better knock it off!" Sims screamed. Everybody, including Frenchie laughed. Frenchie gave Frank credit for a confirmed kill, and that improved everyone's morale.

Phil

The next morning, December 5th, 1967, new replacements arrived to bring the platoons to full strength. Throughout the morning, the FNGs filtered down to join platoons and squads guarding the perimeter. A few of the FNGs were assigned to Sims' squad, but he didn't assign them to Frank's point fire team. Ken and the others stood around and laughed while Sims gave his patented "welcome aboard" lecture.

Two replacements joined a working party, laying more wire that afternoon.

"Where ya from Ted? Ya did say Ted was your name, right?" Ken asked. The two new guys stood back and watched as the veterans bounced a hoop of wire, pulling the individual strands apart. Their eyes darted around, taking in the strange countryside and the grisly Marines stretching the wire.

"Jersey. Newark, New Jersey," Ted jumped back as a strand of the wire snapped loose, tearing at Mike's arms.

"Come on. Grab a hold of this shit," Frank said. "It won't hurt ya. Much!" Everyone laughed.

"What about you bub?" Frank asked the new guy.

"Name's Phil," the replacement answered. "I'm from Little Rock."

"Where the hell is Little Rock?" Mike asked, laughing good-naturedly.

"Arkansas. Little Rock, Arkansas," Phil answered defensively. He didn't know that the men were just kidding.

Everyone was laughing when they all heard the telltale, "Bang....Whoosh....Crash....Bang....Whoosh.... Crash." Two rockets slammed into the hill, and they dove for cover. However, the FNGs were taken totally by surprise, and their reflexes were slow. Not moving, they just stood and watched the explosions hit near the crest of the hill.

"Thump....Thump....Thump." Mortar fire joined the rockets.

"Get down! Get down!" Mike screamed as he and the others scrambled frantically toward a nearby foxhole. The two new guys finally followed, as mortar shells continued pounding the hill.

The big NVA artillery batteries, far to the North, joined the mortars and rockets. And again, the NVA began to systematically blanket the hill. The shells roared overhead slamming into the ground, deafening explosions throwing chunks of earth in all directions. As the tempo of the barrage picked up, the men crouched down in their foxholes with their backs firmly pressed against the dirt walls. Ken, Jim, Frank and Mike exchanged worried glances as the pounding continued. As the attack continued, all they could do was hide in their holes, protected by their helmets and flak jackets.

For a while, Frank chain-smoked and ignored the new guys. Frank thought, *if I get it, I get it. May as well have one last smoke.*

Mike was the first to notice Phil, huddled in a corner, his head pressed against the wall, his body shaking uncontrollably, tears running down his face, and his chest heaving.

Mike nudged Frank and nodded in Phil's direction. Ken and Jim spotted him, but the other new guy, Ted, didn't notice anything. He sat motionless, staring off into space.

"Ooohhhhh Maaammmaaa! Maaammaaaa! Heeeelp me." Phil cried quietly. "Take meeee Hooome. Pleeese Maaammmaaa. Pleeeeesssseeee, Pleeese" His pleading cries kept growing louder and louder.

Everyone in the hole was watching. In the small confines of the foxhole, Phil's wails cut into everyone, becoming louder than the thunder above. The others felt anger, disgust, rage and pity. But nothing, and no one, could help Phil return to his mother. Not now.

Frank crawled over and tried to pull Phil away from the wall, but Phil pushed his head back and refused to be moved. Frank grabbed his shoulders and shook him as the ground trembled underneath them. "Come on man. Hang in there. It will be over soon!" he screamed over the din.

Phil didn't hear. He kept crying for his mother, louder and louder. Frank tried to put his arm around him and hold him, but Phil pushed Frank back. He shook and trembled, saliva running from the corners of his mouth. His eyes were wide and wild as he pushed past Frank and tried to climb out of the hole.

Ken caught Phil's leg and dragged him back down as shells exploded nearby. "Get down! Get down you, stupid shit!" Ken shrieked with revulsion. He threw Phil down on his back and began to slap him viciously. But Phil continued to scream for his mother until Ken finally beat him into silence.

Phil lay motionless in the mud, staring up at the disgusted look on Ken's face. He blinked his eyes and looked around as if he didn't know what had happened. Frank thought that perhaps he really didn't know.

Slowly, Ken got off him and let him pick up his helmet and return to his corner. The barrage continued. Nobody knew how long it lasted. They didn't speak another word until it was over, and everyone avoided looking at Phil.

When the barrage was over, everyone returned to stretching and pulling the barbed wire. Everyone -- but Phil! Moving in a crouched position, he slowly moved toward Doc Bow's position, crying as he struggled up the hill. Phil never came back.

CHAPTER XI -- A WALK IN THE SUN

And When He Gets To Heaven,
Saint Peter He Will Tell,
Another Marine Reporting Sir,
I've Served My Time In Hell.

Line from a Marine epitaph.

Surrounded

The days and nights of December 1967 crawled by while the NVA pounded Alpha-3. The Marines responded by calling in their own air and artillery strikes that punished back the enemy soldiers. Each time the NVA tried to mount a coordinated frontal assault, the American bombs and artillery shells found the troop concentrations and wiped out their positions. Casualties increased and the struggle became more and more costly for both sides.

Although the monsoon rains fell continuously, construction on the heavily fortified bunkers near the crest of the pockmarked hill finally neared completion. A steady stream of choppers flew in and out, delivering more supplies, and carrying out the dead and wounded.

Grunts on the line worked from dawn to dusk reinforcing the perimeter, stretching more rolls of barbed wire, and planting hundreds of mines and booby traps. Their bloodshot eyes sank deeper into their bearded, shrunken faces, but their spirits were lifted each time mail was delivered.

Letters from Frank's mother talked about having his brothers' home for Thanksgiving and how much they missed him. Frank borrowed Mike's writing gear, got into their foxhole, pulled a poncho over his head and wrote:

Dear Mother. Thanksgiving sounds great. How I look forward to next year's dinner with you and my brothers. I hope you are doing well and selling a lot of houses. Is Tammy looking after you and guarding the house? I'm doing OK. It rains a lot but we are pretty safe here. We are reinforcing our position so it's very unlikely that the NVA will try anything. How are my brothers doing? Studying, making good grades and working? Tell them hello. Mike wants his writing gear back so he can write home so I'll say goodbye for now. Keep us in your prayers. Don't worry. I am fine. Love, Frank

Night Ambush

"These damn C-Rats are giving me the trots," Mike complained. He'd suffered with diarrhea for weeks. It was noon, and the sun was well hidden above the thick, relentless rain clouds, as they sat on mounds of mud, eating lunch.

"Try swallowing a glob of peanut butter in one gulp," Ken suggested. "That'll plug up your ass fast enough."

Frank finished warming a can of ham and eggs over the blue flame of a chemical heat tablet used for preparing food. Water ran into his makeshift stove, an empty twisted can, and drowned the fire.

"Shit!" Jim spat. "I wanted to use that heat tab when you was done. I'm outta the heat tabs."

So was everyone else. They laughed as Jim tried to eat his cold pork steak, gagging on each bite.

Sims crossed the hill, headed in their direction. He found an unoccupied mound of mud nearby and sat down. No one offered him anything to eat or even a smoke.

"How's everything goin', men?"

They ignored him, hoping he would go away.

"We're goin' out on a reinforced squad size patrol tonight," he finally blurted out. "It's our turn to go on an ambush."

"Awe, Jesus! Cut us some slack!" Ken spat. "Couple of nights ago, guys over in Delta Company ambushed another Marine patrol wandering around in the dark, and a few guys got dinged before they finally figured out they were fighting Marines instead of gooks."

"Brilliant," Mike said. "We're surrounded by two thousand pissed off gooks, and we're going to go out at night and ambush them. All fifteen of us!"

"Maybe he's just screwin' with us again," Frank speculated, as if Sims wasn't there. "You just bull shittin' us, right Sims? Huh? Aren't ya?"

"You guys are un-believable," Sims stormed. "Don't you understand that everybody's gotta go out on night ambushes? That's how we catch Charlie tryin' to get himself together for an all-out attack."

"Come on Sims. Don't have a hissy fit," Ken said. "It ain't that we don't understand, it's just that we don't think this miserable hill's worth fightin' over."

"Yeah," Mike joined in. "If the little bastards want the goddamn hill so bad, give it to them. It sucks! They'd find out soon enough!"

"We could go back to Dong Ha where they got hot chow, hooches and a beautiful perimeter to defend," Jim said. "It's crazy goin' outside the wire at night."

"And at Dong Ha, you'd have to run night ambushes to keep the gooks from attackin' that perimeter, too," Sims argued.

Running night patrols was part of the plan, and there was no changing the plan. The men complained and bitched all afternoon. But just before dusk, they picked up their gear and got ready to move out. Other troops moved into their vacated foxholes for the night.

While Frenchie watched and listened, Sims briefed the men on the patrol route and the location where they would set up the ambush.

"O'Brian, you'll take point when we get outside the wire. We'll move out in a staggered column. Go about half a click west, skirting the south side of the Trace, then we'll turn south and go about two hundred meters 'till we get to Hill 395. There'll be a stream runnin' past the east side of the hill, and we'll set up on this side of the stream, just a little ways back. Any questions?"

"Yeah. I gotta stomach ache! Can I be excused? I'd like to go home," Ken said. The joke was needed, and the laughter broke the tension.

"Forman, you're a real smart ass," Sims scowled. "You better be takin' this shit serious.

"What do we do if we run into gooks?" Jim asked.

"Throw grenades and run like hell!" Ken answered.

Sims glared at Ken and shook his head. "If we run into the enemy out in the open, we hit them fast and run back to the perimeter."

"Like I said, throw grenades and run like hell!" Ken concluded.

"Shut up Forman!" Frenchie snapped. He'd had enough of the jokes. "Sims, check your compass and make sure it's illuminated." Sims opened the cover and saw that the dial on the compass was bright enough to be easily read.

"Radio?" Frenchie pointed. Sims took the headset, depressed the switch and whispered, "Charlie Two. Charlie Two. This is Charlie Two Alpha. How do you read me? Over."

No one could hear the answer being transmitted from the platoon command post toward the top of the hill. "Be advised Charlie Two, I read you five by five."

Frenchie reminded Sims that he should give a situation report, or "sit-rep", every half hour. "To maintain operational silence, depress the headset switch twice if everything is quiet, and three times if anything moves."

Rain continued to fall on the pitch-black night as the column of grunts, three four-man fire teams and a machinegun team, made their way down the hill. Troops on watch in the lines were alerted that an ambush patrol was leaving the perimeter. "Hold your fire! Ambush out!" was the command passed from hole to hole.

When the patrol reached the wire, they had to find the zigzag opening that would lead to the other side. Frank walked right into the first barrier, scratching his face and rattling the C-Ration cans tied to the wire.

"Holy shit! Watch where you're goin' up there!" Sims hissed.

"Moron! Thinks I ran into the goddamn wire on purpose?"

"Frank," Ken whispered from behind, "I'll go to the right, checkin' the wire, and you go to the left. One of us will find the opening. Be back in a few minutes." He turned and told Sims, "wait here, until we find the opening."

Frank moved parallel to the wire, but he was unable to see where he was going. He could only feel his way along the strands with an outstretched arm, trying not to rattle the cans as he felt his way forward. He hoped the Marines in the foxholes near the wire had gotten the word that his patrol was out there trying to find their way out of the perimeter.

The minutes ticked by as Frank moved slowly away from the rest of the squad. His hand reached out and found nothing. The rain pelted down, and he reached out again -- still nothing. He took a few more steps in the same direction, felt empty space that covered just a few meters until he reached the next strand of wire. Frank had found the hole in the wire.

Following the wire, Frank retraced his steps until he met back up with the squad. "Found the opening! Let's go," Frank whispered.

"Hold up a few minutes," Sims said. "Forman's not back."

They waited in the dark, but Forman didn't return. Frank was getting worried, and Sims was getting mad. Finally, Sims agreed that they should follow the wire to the right, where Ken had gone, to see if they could find Forman. Frank took the lead.

He followed the wire, feeling his way along, with the others close behind. Time was slipping by and they were supposed to be outside the wire by now, well on their way to the ambush site. But they couldn't go anywhere until they found Forman.

"Ooooohhhh! Shit! Goddamn it!" Frank heard muffled moans and swearing just ahead. He knew it was Ken, but he couldn't see what had happened to him. There hadn't been any shots or explosions.

Frank tripped and almost fell over what felt like a pair of boots sticking straight out of the ground. "Oh shit! Who the hell is that up there?" Ken called in a muffled groan.

"It's me, asshole," Frank whispered, kneeling on the ground. He felt around in the mud and all he could find was a pair of boots sticking straight up. Ken was upside down!

"What are you doing?" Frank whispered.

"What is it, O'Brian? What's goin' on?" Sims asked

from behind.

"It's Forman. He's upside down in a foxhole. He's stuck in the mud."

"Goddamn it! Quit shootin' the shit and get me outta here!" Forman whispered to Frank.

Apparently Ken had followed the wire, feeling his way along, unable to see anything in front of him. He had tripped and fallen head first into an abandoned one-man fighting hole that had filled with mud and water. He was lucky that he hadn't knocked himself out and drowned in the mud. Frank, Sims, Mike and Jim, heaved and pulled until they yanked Forman out.

"Holy shit! I thought I was gonna die down there," Ken whispered. He was a little groggy and dizzy from the sudden headfirst fall that caused the blood to suddenly rush to his head. "Just give me a minute and I'll be okay. Where's my rifle?"

They felt around in the mud, found Ken's weapon, cleaned it off as best they could, then moved out again. Frank retraced his steps for a second time and found the opening in the wire. He crept through the zigzag passage, feeling his way along again until the squad cleared the perimeter. Sims checked the compass, gave Frank the direction to take, and they cautiously moved out. Each step was slow and methodical.

Having watched and scanned the hill terrain hour after hour from inside the wire, Frank could visualize the terrain as he moved forward. The Trace was cleared of any fallen trees but filled with shell and bomb craters. Sims kept adjusting the line of march, pushing Frank farther and farther to the right.

They had gone less than three hundred meters, when Frank insisted they stop. "Sims. I'm tellin' ya," he whispered. "We're going north, across the Trace, not west. We're not skirting the south side, we're headed for North Vietnam!" Frank's sense of direction, even at night, was uncanny.

"Bull shit, O'Brian. I can read a fuckin' compass, we're goin' in the right direction, and I have been counting our steps. Now move out!"

"What goin' on," Ken whispered.

"Nothin' Forman. Just shut up and move out!"

"Watch your mouth, Sims!" Ken growled.

They marched on, and Jim continued counting the steps. As Jim's count approached five hundred steps, Frank found that he was entering a badly damaged forest with tree trunks blasted and splintered by bombs and artillery strikes. The remnants of the forest were on his right, which sounded alarm bells in his head. *Oh shit! If the goddamn woods are on my right, that means we're on the north side of the Trace. Sims got us on the wrong side of the Trace. Jesus, we're damn near in North Vietnam!*

"Sims! Sims!" he hissed. Goddamnit. We're in the area of the blasted trees on my right. On the north side, goddamn it! Just like I told ya!"

Sims opened the compass and looked down at it again. He shook his head.

"What's goin' on?" Ken whispered. Everyone was getting very tense.

"What are these goddamn stumps doin' here?

They're supposed to be off to the left." All of a sudden, it registered.

Ken leaned in close to Sims' ear and said, "You've really fucked up this time, Sims? Didn't ya? Huh? Huh?"

"Okay, hold it a minute. Let me think," Sims responded.

"That may take all fuckin' night!" Mike whispered.

It wasn't funny, not funny at all. But it was now obvious to everyone on the patrol that Sims hadn't read the compass correctly, and he had led them to the northern side of the Trace, right in the middle of a favorite NVA staging area! Their prospects of getting out of there in one piece were slim and none: if they didn't run into a large enemy force and get wiped out by the enemy, they could be hit with friendly artillery fire or an air strike.

"Alright. Here's what we'll do. I'll call Charlie Two and tell him that we've reached our objective. We'll stay here for the night, and nobody will know we fucked up!"

"You're out of your goddamn mind Sims," Ken spat.

"I'll tell ya what we're gonna do. You get your ass on that radio. Tell LT that you screwed up, and that we're on the wrong side of the Trace. Then we'll beat feet back across the open space we've been waltzing around in, and head for the real objective." Ken's voice was quiet, but firm.

Sims made the radio call, reported their position, and headed the patrol south. Frank prayed that someone alerted the tank crews and the sniper teams with Starlight scopes that Marines were going to be crossing the Trace – not NVA. They waded through mud and puddles soaked with Agent Orange. It stank and they all felt like puking.

An hour later, they found the stream next to Hill 395. There, the patrol got down in prone positions in a long row that ran parallel to a path crossing the stream. They set up an L-shaped ambush formation that provided a cross fire for anyone coming down the trail. The machinegun team took up a position in the middle of the L, so they could have a wider killing zone. Frank, Mike, Ken and Jim were straddling the side of the trail. And before they settled in, Frank and Ken crawled down to the path to set up a Claymore mine.

They alternated taking short naps as they lay in the mud. Thankfully, the rain let up slightly. The troops snuggled up inside ponchos trying, without success, to keep dry, with hand grenades nearby, weapons loaded and ready to fire. It was quiet throughout the night, and finally the gray haze of morning began to appear. No contact. Everyone was relieved as they moved back to Alpha-3 and made their way back through the coiled concertina wire.

When they crossed over on to their side of the wire, Ken turned to Sims and said, "Please, please, next time we go out on patrol, give that compass to someone who knows how to read the goddamn thing!"

Begging for a Rain Suit

Dawn on December 10 saw the monsoon rain continuing, often falling in wind-driven blinding sheets of rain. The Marines hunkered down in their foxholes, sinking into the ankle-deep river of water and mud. It was cold, and the constant pounding of the Marine location continued with the NVA's mortar fire in the morning, rockets around noon, and artillery barrages at night. The sound of Hanoi Hanna's music played over radios, and she repeatedly promised that the Marines at Alpha-3 would all be dead before Christmas.

The Marines' M48 Patton main battle tanks, with their powerful armament, were dug into the northwest sector of the perimeter, providing the tank crews with an unobstructed view of the Trace. The tank's 90mm gun could traverse up, down, right and left to have a clear shot at anything that moved near the Trace perimeter. At night, Marine sniper teams would sit on the tank turrets, watching through their night scopes for any troop movement in the Trace. The NVA thought they could infiltrate from the north to the south in the cover of darkness. They must have been surprised when, in the pitch black, a rifle report was heard and one of their comrades fell to the ground with a bullet in his head or chest.

The four-man tanker crews had it pretty good, shielded from sniper fire by the steel tank hull during the day, and dry, warm and toasty inside the tank at night. Unlike the Marine grunts that only had standard-issue ponchos, the tankers had "rain suits" that kept them very warm and dry. Frank decided to try to beg one of the tankers into parting with an extra rain suit that Frank was sure they had stashed away someplace in the tank.

"Nope. Sorry but we don't have any extra rain suits," the tanker responded, standing on the turret, looking down at Frank.

"Aw come on, you guys have to have one hidden

away in there someplace," Frank said.

Suddenly, all hell broke loose. "Boom – Whoosh – Bang!" A B-40 NVA rocket exploded behind where Frank was standing. The time between the reports of the rockets firing, the time it took for the projectile to fly through the air, and the ear splitting explosion on impact, was just a few seconds. The tanker dropped out of sight, slamming closed the tank hatch. It appeared that the NVA gunners were zeroing in on the tank positions.

When the shelling started, Frank was caught in the open – his foxhole was too far away, and there was no place near the tanks to take cover. So he dove under the front of the tank and crawled back into the mud between the tank's treads, with just his head sticking out. The rockets continued to fall all around them, and Frank prayed that the tank would not be hit. He thought, *My God, no one would ever find my remains if the tank is hit and blows up.*

Mercifully, the barrage ended and the tank survived. And so did Frank! He quickly made his way back to Mike and the safety of their foxhole -- but without a tanker rain suit.

Several days later, mail and new socks -- two pair for each man -- were flown in on resupply choppers. Rumor had it that hot Christmas dinners would also be flown in to them if they were still at Alpha-3. But for now, Frank was just content to read his mail.

> *Dear Frank, I watch the evening news each night and the reports are so frightening. We are all so worried about you. I pray that you'll be all right.*

I'm still working hard and hope to have another closing by Christmas. Hank got married. A girl he met at college and he plans to continue his education. He drops by every chance he gets to ask about you. Tammy bit the neighbor that bum! She's a good judge of character. Your brothers will be home for Christmas and we will all miss you and be thinking of you every minute. Please write and let us know how you are doing.
Love, Mother.

For the next several days, they sat around the foxholes, cleaning weapons, reading mail, writing letters, eating, sunning their sore feet and taking naps. The bunkers on the hill were almost finished and the engineers were busy, putting the finishing touches on their work. Frank stretched, yawned, thought about taking a nap, but decided to write a letter home, first.

"Mike! Mike!" Frank threw a clod of dirt at his sleeping buddy. "Where's your writin' gear? Can I use it?"

"Leave me the alone you inconsiderate shit! I'm trying to get some sleep. Look in my pack. It's behind the hole." He closed his eyes and was gone again.

Ken finished scraping the bottom of a can of hot beefsteak and potatoes, and belched. The fumes from his heat tab burned Frank's eyes. "Hey, pig! Why don't ya move your stinkin stove downwind? The fumes are makin' me gag," Frank complained.

Dear Mother, Don't know why the news reports are so bad. Everything's fine here. We're still in a safe area and the NVA are nowhere around. Hank's married! I can't believe it. Hope he's happy. Why'd Tammy bite the bum next door? Glad you will all be together for Christmas. That's nice. They say we're going to have a hot turkey dinner for Christmas too. We're all looking forward to it. Don't worry about me. Love, Frank
P.S. Please send a few pair of socks and some canned ham.

Watch your step

It was sunset, December 15, when Frank looked up the hill and saw his squad leader and Platoon Sergeant approaching their foxhole.

"'Aw shit!" Ken spat, looking up the hill. "Here comes Frenchie and Sims. Must be some really bad news." Mike woke up, stretched and yawned.

"What's up, Sarge," Jim asked Frenchie, ignoring Sims.

"How are you men doin'," Sims asked. "Looks like you're rested up."

"Not hardly," Frank answered. They sat down among the men, as Frenchie lit a cigarette. The Platoon waited for the bad news.

"The gooks have artillery spotters in the hills to the west and south, right out there," Frenchie pointed. "And we're goin' to go find em."

"Aw shit! I knew it!" Ken kicked at a stack of

equipment. "Another reinforced squad playin' cowboys and gooks."

"No. No. No." Frenchie explained patiently. He didn't blame the troops for complaining. They'd done well since arriving at Alpha-3. It had been tough, and he was proud of them. Sims shifted nervously, trying not to look at the men.

"It'll be the whole company, Charlie Company, reinforced. We'll move out in the morning and sweep around our side of the perimeter. Won't be gone for more than eight hours."

Ken responded sarcastically, "I guess we'll surprise the gook forward observers. They probably won't see all two hundred of us comin' at em. Right?"

"We probably won't actually catch em," Sims said. "But we'll push them back, farther away so it'll be harder to call in arty strikes accurately."

Mike joined in the sarcasm, "That is a brilliant plan. After we sweep by Charlie, he'll come trippin' on back behind us to take up his original position. He'll probably call arty in on top of us, when we get outside the wire."

"Sarge, why don't we send a squad out to snoop and poop around the countryside until we find the bastards," Ken suggested. "We could blow em' away, and that'd put a stop to the arty for a while."

"That ain't the plan," Frenchie said. "We're gonna do it this way." Frenchie and Sims went to the next hole to pass the word.

"Screw the plan!" Ken stormed. "Probably some birdbrain colonel in the rear dreamed up this shit. Thinks we'll bag a couple of gooks by sendin' out a whole damn company."

Just after dawn the next day, 2nd Platoon saddled up, grabbing their helmets, flak jackets, light packs with one meal stashed away, weapons, and two full canteens of water. They lined up in a single file near the opening in the wire, with Frank, Mike, Ken and Jim on the point. It took almost half an hour to form a tactical wedge for the full company. When everyone was in place, the Skipper gave the command to move out. The skies had cleared, and the day promised to be a scorcher.

Sims gave directions, but Frank knew that the patrol route was almost identical to the one they had taken the night of the ambush. He followed the southern edge of the Trace for about half a click, then turned left, heading for Hill 395. The sun was bright, and it began to get really hot. Sweat began to pour anyway as he scanned the barren hills on either side of them. It was quiet, except for the sounds made by two hundred marching men!

We're gonna go right through the ambush site, Frank thought. Wonder if our guys remembered to pick up those Claymores we put out the other night?

"Remember to stay away from the trail, Frank," Ken said from behind.

"Hold down the noise!" Sims snapped. They moved forward in silence.

The flanks swept the surrounding hills as Frank neared the stream. He stopped just to the left of the path, and looked at the far bank. Nothing moved.

"Sims! Sims!" Frank called, bringing the squad

leader up. "I think we oughta' check out the other side before everyone starts to cross."

"Good idea, O'Brian." Sims turned to Forman and said, "You and your fire team check out the other side of the bank. Signal for us to cross if it's all clear."

"Brilliant idea, Frank," Ken bitched as they waded out across the stream. "Shittin Sims woulda' never thought of it on his own."

Frank didn't answer. They would have been the first to cross the stream anyway and, at least now, they had machine guns covering them from their rear. It was less than ten meters to the other side of the stream. But with the muddy water rushing around their knees, Frank slipped and almost fell in the mud as he struggled to reach the other side. The safety on his M-16 was off. The others followed him a few yards past the stream, staying away from the trail, each crouching, looking and listening. Nothing moved. It was quiet.

After crossing the stream, they fanned out to the right and left, moving a little farther into the dead forest. But still they found nothing. Ken returned to the bank and motioned for the others to across.

"Wonder why the NVA spotters haven't called arty in on top of us by now. I know the bastards are there, watchin," Ken said.

Frank walked on. "We're probably spread out too much to give 'em a good target."

All two hundred men crossed the stream and began marching south, swinging around the Alpha-3 perimeter in the direction of Gio Linh, the nearby ARVN base. The sun was high, and they'd gone about three hundred meters past the stream when suddenly an explosion ripped through the right flank of the Platoon.

"Hit the deck! Incoming arty! Incoming!" Sims screamed. But when the men dove for cover, many of the Marines landed on buried land mines and were blown up.

"Corpsman! Corpsman! Oh, God help me!" screamed one of the wounded. Several were in shock, lying out in the open, with feet, legs, hands and arms blown away.

"Mines! We're in a fuckin' minefield!" Frenchie bellowed. "Don't anybody move except corpsmen! Get to the wounded!"

Frank and the others lay face down on the ground not moving. Frank felt the familiar rapid pumping of his heart and the rush of adrenaline up his spine to his head. He looked to his right, barely moving his head and saw a tripwire under the barrel of his rifle.

Oh, God. If I move, I'll be blown to bits! I don't wanna die! I don't wanna die!

Frank fought to control his panic as the screams of the wounded cut through the air. All around him, other Marines lay motionless, afraid to move. He could hear Mike praying and Ken cursing, but Jim was quiet. Frank's eyes focused on the black wire just under his blue steel rifle barrel. Slowly he lifted the barrel off the trip wire.

"Holy shit! Somehow I didn't trigger that son of a bitch," he sighed, thinking out loud, "how the hell do ya walk out of a minefield?"

"Carefully, very carefully!" he thought he heard Ken answer.

"Okay! Okay! I want everybody to try and stand up! Slowly!" Lieutenant Mosley barked. He stood next to Frenchie about twenty yards behind the point. "Carefully! Push up and stand right in your own footprints!"

The screams of the wounded were ungodly as the uninjured men followed LT's orders, while corpsmen began running through the minefield to get to the wounded.

"Doc Bow! Doc! Get your ass over here!" Frenchie bellowed from the right flank where the Platoon Sergeant was working on one of the wounded.

Doc Bow ran, high stepping across the field, trying to avoid triggering more mines. He looked like a drum major at the head of a high school band. Guts. Doc could be an asshole at times, but he had guts. When a Marine was down, Doc came running.

One of the wounded men in 2nd Platoon was a guy Frank knew. Another "O'Brian" from Boston lay motionless and bloody only a yard or two from where Frank stood. The guy's right leg was severed just above the knee, and shrapnel had clawed away part of both thighs and his stomach. He was in shock, and he moaned quietly. Doc Bow tied a tourniquet around the stump, and then gave him a shot of morphine. Doc wiped the blood from his face and tightened the tourniquet.

"Give me some help getting him on a poncho," Bow said to Frank and three other Marines nearby. "The medivacs will be here in a few minutes and we'll need to get him on the chopper."

Frank carefully crept over to where his wounded buddy lay. The wounded Marine's eyes opened and he recognized Frank. "You are going to be OK today," he said, with a pained smile on his face. "One O'Brian getting fucked up in a day is enough."

Frank knelt down, took his wounded buddy's hand in his and squeezed. "I can hear the birds coming in. We'll get you out of here and you'll be fine. You'll be home way before the rest of us."

Frank, Mike, Ken and Jim helped with the dead and wounded. They rolled a dead Marine onto a poncho, and began carrying him to the waiting medevac chopper. They struggled to keep from dragging the dead Marine across the ground, hoping they would not trigger another mine. Frank was amazed at how heavy a dead body was. He had carried wounded in the past, but the dead seemed unbelievably heavy.

Medevac choppers hovered just above the ground to avoid setting off more land mines, but low enough to allow the dead and wounded to be carefully loaded aboard.

After the last helicopter lifted off, Frenchie yelled, "Everybody turn around so we can reverse march back to the stream. Step in the fresh footprints we made marching in. Everybody's got to retrace our steps back to the stream. We gotta get the fuck out of here."

Slowly and carefully, Frank, Mike, and the other Marines in Charlie Company began to retrace their footsteps back toward the stream. Frank silently prayed to himself with each step – *Yea, though I walk through the valley of the shadow of death....*

Frank watched every step, looking at the ground cover, searching for any telltale sign of mines or booby traps. He planted his boots in the footprints the Marines had left when they walked in – toe-to-heal since the boot prints were reversed.

I shall fear no evil, for thou art with me. Oh, God, please help me! Please! Hang on, Frank, hang on! I'm not lettin' anybody down! Frank prayed. He could see the stream just ahead.

It was quiet; no one talked as the company slowly retraced their footsteps back to the stream. "Just a little further. We're almost there. It's safe on the other side. At least I think it's safe."

"Slow down Frank," Mike said from behind. "You're goin' too fast. Watch where you're walkin'."

Frank stopped for a moment and looked ahead. The stream was less than twenty meters away, and the ground was well churned by boots that had passed there earlier. He looked behind and saw that Mike and the others were strung out, keeping plenty of distance between each man. They moved slowly cross the stream. Now safely on the other side of the stream, the Company stopped to rest and regroup.

By late afternoon, they made their way back inside their perimeter. Shaken and exhausted, they took off their gear, dropping their weapons and equipment where they stood. The men were quiet, and most smoked one cigarette after another as they thought about what had happened. One Marine was KIA, and nine others were severely wounded in the minefield.

As the sun began to set, Frank asked himself, *how did I get out alive? I was walkin' point, but I never saw a trip wire until people started dyin'. Seems like I would have kicked one. And why didn't my rifle barrel trip that land mine when my rifle had the wire attached to it?* Frank was alive and so were Mike, Ken and Jim. Maybe they would all make it. Just maybe!

ARVN screw-up

A few days after Charlie Company's patrol around Alpha-3, Frenchie passed the word that the minefield they had walked into had not been planted by the NVA. It turned out that the ARVNs located nearby at Gio Linh had planted hundreds of "Bouncing Bettys" mines to protect their perimeter. But the ARVNs failed to pass on this critical information to the nearby Marines! Frank heard the news and thought, *Holy shit. I could have been killed by friendlies! No shit! What a war!*

CHAPTER XII -- CHARLIE-4

The object of war is not to die for your country,
But to make the other bastard die for his.

General George S. Patton

Starlight

On December 14, the rain finally stopped and the sun broke through the clouds. The Marines were grateful to dry out. They kept busy by either working on the Alpha-3 perimeter, or filling sandbags and stacking them on the newly completed bunkers. The clear skies also allowed Marine F-4 Phantom to fly bombing missions hitting the NVA hidden in the hills nearby.

The F-4s dropped napalm and high explosive bombs that drew cheers from the Marines at Alpha-3. Frank, Mike and all the other Marines would wave their entrenching tools in the air, saluting the Marine pilots and screaming "get some" – "fuck em up" - at the top of their lungs, as if the pilots could see or hear them.

The Marines were hoping the Phantom airstrikes killed a lot of the NVA so that it would make it impossible for them to mount a frontal assault on Alpha-3.

At the end of the day, the Marines at Alpha-3 were so exhausted that it made it hard for them to stay awake during their night watches. "Christ! Whose turn is it to take first watch?" Mike asked. He and Frank sat next to their hole, finishing their C-Rats in the quiet evening.

Frank thought for a moment. "Hell, I don't know. I lost track." He stuffed empty cans back into a C-Rat box and tossed it behind the hole. "Which do ya want? It really doesn't make a difference to me."

"I'll take second, if you don't care."

They sat with their weapons, helmets and flak jackets on, waiting until the word was passed to "stand down" to fifty percent alert. When it was time, Mike crawled behind the hole, and quickly fell into a deep sleep. Frank stared into the night, listening to the soundless quiet and was glad the NVA had pulled back. The NVAs arty didn't fall that night. A cold wind sent a chill through him, but he didn't care. Shivering helped him stay awake.

Knowing the NVA would use the cover of darkness to infiltrate across the Trace to the South Vietnam side of the DMZ, the Marines sent out listening posts and night ambushes every night to interdict the enemy soldiers. They also used a new, classified night vision sniper scope called Starlight that allowed the sniper to see the enemy even in total darkness. Ken was the Platoon sniper, and his M-16 was equipped with the Starlight scope. Every night, Ken would find an elevated "perch" where he would sit, wait, and watch for enemy movement outside the perimeter of Alpha-3.

During his second night watch, Frank heard two shots ring out just 50 meters from their foxhole. They seemed to come from one of the tanks that were dug into the perimeter, facing the Trace. Tracer bullets have a small pyrotechnic charge at the base of the lead bullet that causes it to burn brightly at night. Marine snipers like Ken used the tracers to "mark" or pinpoint an enemy target at night.

When fired, tracer rounds looked like two, very long, yellow pencils that flash and quickly burn out. The only problem with firing a tracer round at night is that the tracer immediately gives away your position to the enemy. The NVA can easily spot the source of the brightly light bullets and return fire on that spot.

After Frank heard the two tracer shots ring out, he heard the unmistakable "pop-pop-pop" of several AK-47 rifles firing into the perimeter. All of the AK-47 firing came from the same area near the tank. Then all went quiet.

Frank and Mike stayed crouched in their foxhole, listening for movement outside of their position. Nothing. They finally decided that an attack was not imminent so they continued to alternate sleeping and watching throughout the night. After Mike finished the fourth watch, he woke Frank. It was almost dawn and time to "Stand-To" at one hundred percent alert. They sat together through the final hour of darkness, watching the sun come up over the Trace and the DMZ.

They spotted Ken, walking toward their position with his rifle and the attached Starlight scope slung over his shoulder. He looked angry and exhausted. "What's up

Ken?" Mike asked. "Somebody piss in your canteen?"

"Nah, that stupid shit tanker almost got me killed," he said. "Last night I had a great shooting position on top of the tank. The plan was for me to spot the NVA and then mark their position with a few tracer rounds." Ken dropped into their foxhole and propped his rifle on top of the parapet. "Then the tank was going to blast away at the gooks with their main gun."

"So about midnight, I spot a half dozen or more gooks clustered about 100 meters outside of the wire. They were huddled together talking, which made them an easy target. Who knows what they were planning, so I squeeze off two quick shots and two gooks drop like a bag of rocks."

"Good for you. Nice shooting," Frank said. Ken didn't brag about his kills, but everyone knew he was a deadly shot.

"Yea, but then that stupid tanker pops out of the turret and he says, 'Hey, I missed the shots you just took. Sorry – I was asleep. Can you do that again?'"

"By then, the NVA were returning fire and the top of the tank was getting dinged all over the place." So I said to the tanker, 'Screw you, ass hole. Get up here and take a few shots yourself.' And with that, I got off the perch and hid down behind the tank until dawn. Got a few hours of badly needed sleep."

Frank and Mike were both bent over laughing. "That tanker was probably the same prick that wouldn't give me his extra rain suit," Frank said. "Too bad he didn't take you up on taking shots. Probably would have gotten dinged."

They were all still laughing when they saw Sims and Frenchie making the rounds, talking to the 2nd Platoon Marines in each foxhole. Frenchie lit a cigarette and took a long drag. "Was that you taking shots last night Forman?" They sat and listened while Ken retold his story to Frenchie and Sims.

Frenchie laughed, but Sims seemed to side with the tanker.

"Now I've got some good news! We're pullin' outta this shit-pit!"

They wanted to cheer, but they were all too tired and drained.

"Bout damn time," Mike said. "We goin' back to Dong Ha, Sarge?"

"No, but we're goin' to a place almost as good. Placed called Charlie-4, over near the ocean, just north of Cua Viet. But still on the DMZ in Quang Tri Province."

"Is it anything like Alpha-3?" Frank asked. "Ya know, like thousands of gooks all around? Gettin' hit every day? Night ambushes? Shit like that?"

"Nah, I hear it's pretty quiet on the eastern end of the DMZ. Bunkers are already built. Of course it could stand a little Better Homes & Garden improvement. But the wire's in place. And there are wide-open dunes surroundin' the perimeter, perfect fields of fire. And best of all, it hasn't been hit but once in the last month and a half."

"They'll be due to hit again, just about the time we get there," Ken observed.

Mike Boats

On December 16th, a battalion from the 9th Marines moved into Alpha-3 to relieve Frank's battalion. They saddled up, and began to file out past the concertina wire for the last time, they hoped. To no one's surprise, the NVA began to fire a few artillery shells into the hill as a parting shot at the old defenders, and a greeting for the new Marines.

The battalion followed a different route leaving Alpha-3 from the one they had taken coming in, nineteen days earlier. The line of march was supposed to be clear of mines, but Frank, walking point, watched carefully and prayed with each step. Lush trees and foliage appeared as they headed south, away from the lifeless, decimated DMZ.

Gentle hills rose and fell as the morning passed. Two hours after the march had begun, they turned west, passing south of the ARVN combat bases at Gio Linh and the Marine hellhole at Con Thien.

They found breadfruit trees that they plucked clean as the unit swept the countryside. The men sucked the juice out of the breadfruit as they marched past the remains of an old, burned out Catholic chapel that stood abandoned in the jungle.

Years before, the French colonial missionaries had built missions in the remote Quang Tri province as part of a campaign to convert the predominantly Buddhist population to Catholicism. The walls of the chapel had been blown down, and tangled vines grew out of control everywhere. But the door and steeple remained standing. And on top of the steeple, a cross cast a shadow over the men as they marched past.

At Highway One, six-wheeled military trucks, called "Rough Riders," met the battalion to the cheers of the men! Riding in trucks, rather than marching, was a luxury, and it meant they were in or near the rear, far away from Alpha-3.

When the convoy reached the bridge that crossed the Cua Viet River, the troops got off the trucks and climbed aboard "Mike Boats", shallow draft landing crafts that would take them down to the mouth of the river. They dropped their packs and equipment, stretched out on the deck, and "crashed" in the midday sun. The Navy boatswain's mate who piloted the boats gunned the engines, and the trip began.

"Shit! This is like bein' back home, cruisin' on the lake or somethin," Jim sighed. The men relaxed, smoking one last cigarette before going to sleep.

"Jesus, this really is great," Ken yawned. "Must be some kinda mistake or somethin'. If we're not walkin' that means somebody screwed up."

"Nope. It's no mistake," Mike said. "I got it all figured out. We're bait! They needed some troops to float down the river for Charlie to ambush. Give away his position and all of that shit!"

"That's real funny, Mike," Frank said. He leaned back, resting his head inside his helmet and fell asleep. Two hours passed and they slept soundly before Frenchie woke them.

"Get up! Come on, get off your ass!" Frenchie shouted. "We're almost there. Saddle up! Come on, get up, goddamnit!"

The landing craft slid on to the white, sandy beach, the ramp dropped and the sleepy men stumbled off. Frank looked around, got his bearings and saw they were on the north bank of the river. A barbed wire enclosed combat base, Cua Viet, sat on the south side of the river. A brisk, salty breeze blew in off the ocean, and the pounding surf was just a few hundred yards away. It was early in the afternoon, giving the men three or four hours to enjoy the sun before dusk.

Warrior Corpsman

A group of fifteen Marines sat in the shade of a nearby tree, waiting for Charlie Company. They were replacements fresh from the States, loaded down with new equipment, clean-shaven and smooth cheeked. They stood watching uncomfortably as the grunts got organized, not sure of what to do. Frank remembered the first day when he, Mike and Jim had watched a Marine unit return to the carrier after months of combat. They now had some new FNGs to take their place in the hierarchy of the company.

"Hey, Ken!" Frank called, as he threw his pack on and fastened his cartridge belt, "check out the guy carryin' the Unit One pouch over his shoulder."

"Must be our new corpsman," Ken answered.

"Yeah, but he's carryin' an M-16, not a .45," Mike observed. Standard equipment for corpsmen included the Unit One Medical Pouch, and only a side arm, usually a .45 caliber pistol. But this new corpsman carried an M-16, plus two bandoliers of ammo, crisscrossing his chest, and grenades bulged from inside the pockets of his jungle utility jacket. He was assigned to our Platoon, and Frenchie introduced him to the men.

"Sergeant Sims, this is Doc McKay, our new corpsman."

"Welcome to 2nd Platoon, Doc. Glad to have you," Sims began. "My men are the best in the Corps, with just a few exceptions," and off he went, giving his usual "welcome aboard" speech. The men stood and listened, trying not to laugh, while Sims droned on.

After a few minutes, Sims and Frenchie went off to check with the Company Commander on where the Platoon would be spending the night. The troops introduced themselves to the Doc.

"Ken Forman," he stuck out his hand, as he did with all new men. "I'm the exception Sims was talkin' about." The others laughed, and so did Doc McKay.

"I'm Frank O'Brian, and this is Mike Morgan and Jim Thompson." They all shook hands and made idle talk as the old guys sized up the new corpsman. He was just under six feet tall, slight build, with brown hair and eyes, set in a boyish face. He was uncomfortable with the grunts, but he hid his nervousness well. He held his rifle comfortably and seemed to be at ease with the weapon.

"From Cleveland, huh Doc?" Ken was saying. "I don't think there are any other guys in the outfit from Cleveland, but one guy in third squad is from Toledo, I think."

"Hey, Doc," Frank said. His curiosity had gotten the best of him. "How come you carry an M-16?"

"Thought it might come in handy," he answered. Doc McKay seemed a little shy, and he didn't offer any further explanation about his rifle.

The Enemy's Kids

On December 18, the unit moved out, marching north, with the China Sea on their right flank. The countryside was similar to the area they had landed in months before, rolling sand dunes, broken tree lines and worn out, unused rice paddies.

The weather was good, the sun shining, but not too hot, in the late afternoon. Everything seemed peaceful and quiet. Frank set a moderate pace. The village where they would spend the night was only an hour away.

Ha La Trong, population about three hundred, was a typical small Vietnamese village, located on the eastern end of the DMZ. As they approached the village, Frank saw civilians heading for home, coming in from the few remaining fertile rice fields. Farmers, skinny, stoop-shouldered old men, walked their water boos.

Some had little children riding on the lumbering animals. Women, old and young, scurried around, gathering firewood needed to cook the evening meal and to keep shacks warm during the night. Children ran around, laughing and playing as the sun began to set. They started begging for food and cigarettes as the Marines entered the village.

A quick, but thorough search of the village did not turn up any hidden cache of weapons or ammunition. The village chief watched as the Marines and the Kit Carson

Scouts checked everyone's ID card and found everything in order. It was a routine that the Marines, Scouts and villagers had gone through many times before.

The Marine perimeter circled the village. As 2nd Platoon dug their foxholes, Doc McKay joined the men on the lines, sharing a hole with Jim. He preferred being with the men, rather than setting in for the night with the platoon command post group behind the lines, as was the custom for corpsmen. Sims tried to change his mind, but Doc was stubborn. He did his fair share of digging with his entrenching tool, and he paired off with Jim.

The sun dropped below the horizon, changing the sky from a bright blue to a constantly deepening, darker blue. Jim and Doc McKay sat beside their freshly dug foxhole, eating their evening meal and talking. Several children hung around begging for food, so Jim tossed them a can of unwanted ham and lima beans, and told them to "di di mau", Vietnamese for "beat it" or "get lost."

The kids stayed and continued to beg until Doc mixed some Kool Aid for them and threw in three C-Ration cans of weenies and beanies, pork steak, and ham and eggs. The kids jabbered with joy, laughing and thanking Doc. They stumbled and tripped over the Doc's equipment as they rushed to thank him for his generosity, then disappeared.

The word was passed to "Stand-To" at one hundred percent alert. As Jim and Doc started laying out their ammunition and grenades, Doc discovered that three of his hand grenades were missing.

"Goddamn slant eyed little bastards," Jim stormed.

"I should have known better than to let the little shits hang around the gear."

"I'm sorry, Jim," Doc stammered. "I didn't have any idea they'd steal from us. I never saw any of them reach down and pick anything up. Honest! I didn't know!"

"Don't sweat it, Doc," Jim said. "It's not your fault. You didn't know any better, and I did. I'm madder at myself than I am at the kids. It was stupid! Stupid on my part."

They passed the word to be on the alert for grenades being thrown from inside the village. Most villages along the DMZ were filled with civilians who supported the VC, and the village of Ha La Trong was no exception. The children had taken the grenades home to mothers, fathers, brothers or sisters who were either sympathetic to the VC, or who were VC hiding among the villagers.

It was no surprise when the grenades were "returned" to the Marines that night -- without pins! Three explosions rocked the perimeter as the deadly stolen grenades fell near or in foxholes. Quick reflexes and good luck prevented any casualties.

Two grenades had been thrown near Marine positions, but the men heard them hit, and they were fast enough to get down inside their holes before each explosion. The third one was lobbed into a foxhole, but the man on watch heard it hit and got out of the hole, hitting the dirt before the explosion.

A particularly vicious search of the village took place the following morning. Most houses and gardens were severely damaged or totally destroyed by the furious Marines as they again looked for signs of weapons or ammunition.

In retaliation for the attack the night before, Ken and the others began breaking furniture and water jugs, kicking down thatched walls, and stomping through carefully planted gardens. Everyone, especially the village chief, was questioned again, but nobody knew who had thrown the stolen grenades. After his house was burned down, the village chief and his family were sent to the rear to be questioned by Intelligence. Three water boos lay dead in their pens, as the Marines marched out of the village. The men laughed about the destruction of the village and the dead boos -- but Doc McKay and the other FNGs didn't understand.

Sandcastle

Frenchie had been right about Charlie-4. It was a lot better than Alpha-3. The men were impressed with the three rows of concertina barbed wire staked into place around the perimeter. Cleared, wide-open fields of fire surrounded the wire. Mines and booby traps were in place. But best of all, the bunkers looked like sandcastles ready for new "tenants". Instead of living in open foxholes, the men would have pillbox-like bunkers to stand watch in. They were surrounded and covered with several layers of sandbags, and each bunker had a wooden floor.

Frank and Mike were assigned to a bunker on the northeast side of the perimeter, with Jim and Ken next door. They settled into their new homes, making ingenious improvements on the already "lavish" accommodations.

Doc McKay was a frequent visitor and usually he could be found at one bunker or the other, working with the troops.

Using sandbags, they built fighting positions on top of each bunker, so that at night the Marine on watch could sit on top and have a better field of fire. The man off watch would sleep inside the bunker -- dry, warm and safe. Empty ammo cans were built into the sandbag walls where grenades and extra magazines would be kept out of the weather.

Approaches to each bunker were examined carefully and, where necessary, additional mines and booby traps were planted. Barbed wire in front of each position was staked down more securely, and additional C-Ration cans with rocks inside were tied to the wire. Any NVA crazy enough to try to infiltrate the lines would be heard, seen and quickly blown away.

Charlie-4 had many civilized conveniences, including a huge canvas field mess tent where the troops enjoyed two daily hot meals, breakfast and dinner. Powdered eggs, greasy bacon, powdered milk and hot coffee were a hell of a lot better than C-Ration ham and eggs. The dinner menu rotated between chili, beef stew and ham with powdered mashed potatoes and back again to the chili, which caused many problems at night in the small, close-quarter bunkers. At lunch, the men were usually out on patrol or on working parties, so they had to settle for C-Rations.

Every day, one of the platoons went out in a

northerly direction on a patrol, then would swing inland to the west and set up ambushes for the night. They followed various routes back south, and swept around the south side of the perimeter before coming back in. For weeks, the patrols made no contact with enemy units. As they all knew, it was too good to last.

As far as Frank, Mike, Ken and Jim were concerned, working parties were to be avoided if at all possible. To that end, they became masters at avoiding any strenuous work detail. With Doc McKay's help, they were responsible for cleaning latrines and burning the barrels of waste produced each day by the constant stream of Marines using the luxurious outhouse facilities. While not the "ideal" job, they believed it was better than filling sandbags and loading them on amtracs all day in the scorching sun.

Doc would select a "shitter" that needed cleaning, and his four buddies would slowly begin to clean it. The bad part was removing the barrels from underneath the boards that the men sat on. They would tug, pull and gag, until the barrels were clear of the "shit house". Gasoline was poured into each barrel and lit. Once the barrels were burning, the four of them would go off to find a shady place, upwind of the fire, and sleep. Sims always tried – unsuccessfully -- to catch them sleeping while the "shitters" burned. But each day, one of the four would stand watch, while the others slept.

New leadership

Mid-December brought some troubling changes to 2nd Platoon. Lieutenant Mosley, the experienced and trusted Platoon Commander moved up to be Charlie Company's Executive Officer. This was good for the LT because his new duties took him farther away from the danger of leading search and destroy operations.

2nd Platoon got a brand new Second Lieutenant, fresh out of the Marine Basic School at Quantico. The new Lieutenant was a Midwesterner from Chicago named Newman, which seemed appropriate to the men. The new LT would have to be "snapped in" and trained, and it depressed the troops to think of a "boot" Lieutenant calling the shots in the bush. But then, there was more bad news.

Frenchie had finished his second extension to stay in Vietnam, and he was headed back "to the world" to spend Christmas with his family. Frenchie was the real leader in the Platoon, and the troops would follow him anywhere. He had saved them many times because of his commitment to keeping the men safe while still accomplishing the mission. But everyone knew that Frenchie had pushed his luck too far by now. It was time to get out of the field. The Platoon's respect and trust for him was deep and well earned. They loved Frenchie, and he loved his men.

Frenchie's replacement turned out to be downright frightening. He was a newly promoted Staff Sergeant who had just finished a tour on the "Grinder" as a DI at Parris Island. Very quickly everyone agreed that Staff Sergeant Wright was really full of himself, and that he would likely be very dangerous out on patrol because he didn't know what he didn't know -- and didn't seem to care.

Ken said Wright was like Sims on steroids, and Wright had a very bad habit of talking to the 2nd Platoon Marines like they were his "shit bird" recruits. Big mistake, because no one knew how his "style" was going to play out when the shit hit the fan. Everyone tried to avoid both new leaders.

After months with Lt. Mosley and Frenchie, it was a real concern to have two new, inexperienced leaders - and in the case of the Platoon Sergeant, a really bad attitude to boot. While everyone tried to make jokes, it really wasn't funny. They agreed to call the new officer "LT", but the new Staff Sergeant would be "Sergeant DI". For sure, it was a "very bad bag."

Field Testing AR-16A1

The word came down from Battalion that the Colt Manufacturer's representatives for the M-16 would be visiting Charlie-4 to check on the progress of the "in the field testing" of the rifle. At that time, it was believed that the M-16, with its 30-round magazine, was prone to jamming, and that the jamming was thought to be caused by lousy weather, or dirt in the chamber, or infrequent cleaning and lubrication, or sand on the ammo itself – all common conditions in the field.

Sergeant DI made it a daily ritual to order 2nd Platoon to stop whatever they were doing and clean their weapons and ammo. When the Platoon went out on patrol, the weapons and ammo would always get dirty. Keeping weapons and ammo clean and working properly was next to impossible, but so critically important to the Marine behind the gun sight.

Frank had a tough choice to make. He only had one toothbrush. Either he could use the brush to clean his rifle with bore cleaner and hope it actually did some good, or brush his teeth. He chose to clean his rifle -- and to hell with his teeth.

When the Colt reps arrived, Charlie Company was taken out to empty sand dunes where they lined up and fired their M-16s at imaginary enemy soldiers. 1st Platoon went first, and the reps were obviously angry when most of the rifles jammed. 2nd Platoon went next, and Frank, Mike, Jim, Ken and Doc test-fired their rifles. Even though each of them had cleaned their weapon that morning, all of their M-16s jammed because the cartridges "froze" or jammed in the chamber. When this happened, it required the shooter to use a cleaning rod to poke the cartridge back out of the chamber, then clean the chamber with bore cleaner, before trying to fire again. Everyone was grateful that they were only shooting at imaginary enemy soldiers.

The Colt reps reported to Captain Olson that his Marines didn't clean their weapons, and this was the cause for the M-16s to jam. It was said that the Colt reps were lucky to get back on their helicopters in one piece! The Skipper was furious with the Colt reps because Skipper knew that a jammed M-16 was no match for the NVA AK-47s and the SKS assault rifles. He and his Marines knew they were at a serious tactical disadvantage.

But Marines had to fight with the weapons they were issued. And many tried to take AK-47s off of dead NVA, so they would at least have a fighting chance. But the vast majority of Marines were stuck with the faulty M-16. The joke was that Mattel made a toy M-16 and Colt made the real thing, but the difference was: the toy worked!

Napalm

On December 18, 2nd Platoon left the perimeter to take over the patrol of the Tactical Area of Responsibility (or "TAOR") from 1st Platoon. LT was visibly nervous, and he raced around with Sergeant DI checking and rechecking everyone's weapons, gear and reviewing maps. LT seemed happy to see Sergeant DI had a compass and, presumably, knew how to use it. The Platoon's radio operator was experienced and had worked closely with Lieutenant Mosley. He rolled his eyes as he followed LT around, hanging his head and trying not to laugh.

Thank God for the Skipper. Captain Olsen talked quietly with LT and Sergeant DI to make sure they knew where to go and what to do. He tried to hide his obvious concern from the men of the 2nd Platoon. He also stopped and inspected weapons as he walked through the Platoon. All were clean, or as clean as they could get under combat conditions.

Frank again took the point, and he set a steady pace heading north through very familiar terrain. Sergeant DI kept telling Sims to have Frank change directions, first moving left and then to the right. This not only slowed down the patrol, but it made a lot of unnecessary and dangerous noise. None of the men were happy or impressed with his "tactics".

2nd Platoon passed 1st Platoon heading south to

Charlie Four, while they continued north to the farthest point in their patrol route. They marched another 1,000 meters north and remained near enough to the China Sea to hear the pounding surf. Frank turned west and passed the abandoned Blue Pagoda, one of the patrol objectives. Then he turned north again, and headed toward the outer limits of the TAOR.

Just beyond the Pagoda, he entered the shallow waters of a depleted rice paddy field. Frank avoided the paddy dikes because the NVA and VC liked to bury mines or shallow pits containing deadly punji sticks.

Just past the paddy field, Frank climbed a gentle rise in a sand dune. He looked carefully over the top of the dune and saw several NVA soldiers digging foxholes near a tree line less than a 100 meters away. The terrain between Frank and the NVA was almost completely clear, with only a few places to take cover.

Frank ducked back down below the sand dune and waved Sims forward to have a look. Sims was excited. The NVA soldiers were clearly visible in their tan uniforms and pith helmets. Their shirts were off, and they wore blue T-shirts. Like the Marines, they were sweating from the heat of the noonday sun.

"Holy shit. I have to report to Lieutenant Newman and Sergeant Wright," Sims said as he scampered down the dune.

Ken, Mike and Jim joined Frank and peeked over the top of the dune. "Shit. This is a bad fuckin bag. A very bad bag," Ken said.

LT and Sergeant DI followed Sims to the top of the

dune, and all three slowly raised their heads up to see the NVA. They seemed to freeze for a moment, and just long enough for one of the NVA to see three boobs with their heads stuck up over the sand dune.

The NVA soldiers grabbed their weapons and immediately opened fire with automatic weapons. LT, Sergeant DI and Sims dove for cover, and LT sputtered, "Shit! Did anyone see how many there were?"

"No Sir," said Sergeant DI. Sims hadn't counted either, but they seemed to agree that the NVA unit was more than a squad. LT called the Skipper on the radio and reported the contact with the enemy. The Skipper asked for details, listened to LT's report, and then ordered 2nd Platoon to attack.

Now that the Marines had successfully completed the "search" part of their mission, it was time to begin the "destroy" phase. Unfortunately, the NVA knew the Marines were just about 100 meters away, and they would be ready for an assault.

LT and Sergeant DI brought up the rest of the Platoon, and put the three rifle squads on line. There were two machine gun teams and a rocket team assigned to 2nd Platoon. LT placed the machine gun teams in the center of the line where they could lay down a heavy, sustained fire on the enemy. The machine guns and rockets would provide suppressing fire, while the three rifle squads attacked the enemy position.

The Skipper had ordered an airstrike on the NVA position, with LT coordinating the strike with an Air Force Bird Dog, a Cessna Piper Cub single-engine spotter plane with a pilot and an Air Observer (AO). The Bird Dog began to fly back and forth across both the Marine and NVA positions. The AO could be seen sticking his head out of the window on the co-pilot side as the plane flew back and forth, very close to the ground.

Frank and his fire team were on the left flank. To mark where they were positioned, Ken spread out the bright yellow air panel flag and weighted it down with rocks. The squad on the right flank did the same thing with the other air panel. The bright yellow markers were intended to show the AO in the Bird Dog to determine the exact map coordinates of the Marines' location, which the AO would convey to two F-4 Phantoms circling overhead. This would reduce the risk of the Marines on the ground being hit by friendly fire from the F-4 Phantoms.

The automatic rifle fire from the NVA was sporadic, and the Marines did their best to stay low and maintain cover. Ken was next to Frank as the Bird Dog flew over the Marine position. They saw the AO hang out of the co-pilot's window and throw a red smoke grenade down on the enemy position. The NVA opened fire on the Piper Cub with automatic weapons, but the AO could only fire back with his Colt 45 caliber pistol. It was quite a sight, and Ken said to Frank, "that AO has got a lot of balls taking on automatic fire with only his 'pea-shooter'!"

The Bird Dog gained altitude and then headed south out of the NVA position that it had marked with the red smoke grenade. With the NVA's position clearly marked for the F-4 Phantoms, Ken stuck his head up to get a clear view of the NVA and yelled, "get some" to the Bird

Dog as it flew out of harm's way.

Suddenly, a single shot rang out, and a Corporal named Jones fell backwards with a bullet hole in his left cheek. Jonesy, as his men in 3rd Squad called him, was "short" -- he had only thirty-five days and a "wake-up" before catching his bird back to the states. Jonesy was married, had a one-year-old son and lived in North Carolina. Blood gushed from the wound, and Jonesy mumbled, "Aw shit. Aw shit!" through his broken teeth and shattered jaw. The bullet had exited through the back of his neck.

"Corpsman! Corpsman!" Frank, Mike and Jim screamed. Doc McKay ran from the middle of the formation. He dropped down next to Jonesy and began to examine his wound. Sims, Sergeant DI and LT soon followed.

"What the fuck happened here?" Sergeant DI screamed.

"Looks like Jonesy didn't keep his head down and a sniper got him," Sims shouted.

LT was ashen faced. He got back on the radio and reported to the Skipper that a Marine had been shot. He wasn't sure what to do next, and he seemed both afraid and confused.

Doc McKay tried to cut a hole in Jonesy's throat to insert a tube down his windpipe to allow him to breath. A tracheotomy was a difficult surgical procedure in a clean operating room and nearly impossible under battlefield conditions. Doc did his best, working as fast as he could while Jonesy made gurgling sounds, blood running out of his mouth and down his cheeks. His eyes were wide open and he was struggling to breath, to gulp in air. As he lay there, he was drowning in the blood that was flowing from the gaping wound in his face, down his throat, filling his lungs. Finally, Jones stopped struggling. And his eyes suddenly rolled back into his head. Jonesy died in Doc's arms.

Doc McKay threw down his scalpel and bandage and screamed, "Bastards. Goddamn sons a' bitches!"

Jones was one of the Platoon's Salts that everyone looked up to. They respected his knowledge and courage. He was less than two months away from "catching his bird back to the world," and he had just started his "short-timer" calendar. He counted the days and talked incessantly about returning home to his family. Now he would return home in a casket with an American flag draped over it.

Sergeant DI called in a medevac chopper to take Jones' body to Graves Registration in Da Nang. Frank, Mike, Jim and Doc rolled Jonesy's body onto his poncho. Keeping low, they half carried, half dragged, his body about 30 meters behind the Marine position to the waiting chopper. Frank, Mike, Jim and Doc carefully lifted his bloody body through the chopper's open bay door. Frank watched with tears in his eyes as Jones flew away.

The Bird Dog was still flying nearby, and the two silver F-4 Phantoms circled over the Marines and the medevac chopper. There was no time to mourn Jones. It was time for "payback" and Jonesy's Brothers in 2nd Platoon were anxious to deliver.

The wind was blowing out of the north, and the

red smoke the AO had thrown on the NVA position now began to blow back across the Marine's line. LT radioed the AO to call in an airstrike on the NVA position. Sergeant DI ran up and down the line screaming, "Fix bayonets – fix bayonets." Frank thought that if it weren't so sad, it would have been funny. What Sergeant DI didn't realize was that none of the Marines had ever been issued bayonets for their M-16 rifles. So much for fix bayonets!

The Bird Dog made a final pass, and Sergeant DI excitedly ran up and down the line yelling, "Okay, get down and stay down! The Phantoms are going to make their run! Keep your heads down! Keep your heads down!"

The Marines rolled into their shallow foxholes and waited. The yellow air panel was on Frank's left, and the Marines on his right, including Mike, Jim and Doc, were scrambling down the side of the sand dunes and hugging the ground facedown.

Frank lifted his head, looked to his left, and saw the first jet drop from the sky at a lightning speed. The pilot hit his afterburners and screamed across their front, skimming the treetops, dropping two napalm bomb canisters. They tumbled to the ground, a direct hit on the NVA position.

The noise was deafening as balls of flame erupted on top of the NVA, sucking oxygen out of the air and scorching the earth. Billows of black smoke darkened the sky, and the men could hear animal-like shrieks coming from the enemy positions.

"Get some, Phantoms! Get some!" the Marines shouted.

275

The black and red smoke mingled together and slowly blew back over the Marine position. The men cheered as the enemy screams rose louder and then fell silent.

"Crispy Critters! Crispy critters! Burn those bastards!" they yelled.

The smell was nauseating, and Frank tried not to gag. Black and red smoke burned his eyes, but he knew that the sting was nothing compared to what the napalm had done to the NVA soldiers. He looked to his left again and saw the second Phantom drop out of the sky and hit his afterburners.

Frank looked to his left and screamed, "Oh my God! No! No! He's coming in on top of us! He's headed straight toward us!"

"Get down!" he screamed, "Everyone, get down! Get down!" But no one heard him over the roar of the jet. Frank held his hands over his ears and watched in horror as two silver cigar shaped napalm bombs filled with jellied gasoline dropped from the sky. They tumbled end over end and landed, right on top of the Marines' position.

I could hold my rifle up and hit that one, Frank thought. The canisters seemed to tumble in slow motion.

The two napalm bombs hit the ground together, about 30 meters to Frank's right, splashing fire into bright orange puddles. Napalm sucks oxygen from the air and sears the lungs. The fire missed Frank, but he gasped for breath as the jellied gas splashed on the two machine gun teams and rocket team in the middle of their position. Nine Marines took a direct hit and jumped up in what seemed like a wild slow motion dance. The burning Marines flailed their arms, beating themselves, whirling, running, screaming, trying to escape the flames.

Frank and the other Marines jumped up and joined the deadly dance trying to catch the burning men to throw them to the ground and extinguish the fire. Doc dragged two into the rice paddy just behind their position, throwing them into the shallow water. They howled with agony and trashed around in the putrid water.

Other Marines threw burning men to the ground as the shrieks rose to a crescendo. Men threw sand on the living torches, but the flames kept burning. The sand would not smother the fire. But instead, the sand stuck to blistered flesh and burned into the open skin.

Frank pulled one flaming Marine into the paddy and threw him into the water. The fire went out but the charred man kept thrashing, howling and crying. Knowing he couldn't do anything more for the Marine, Frank ran back and chased down another burning man.

Hell. I'm dead and this is hell. It's gotta be. Hell's a bad fuckin' place. When do I burn? When do I catch fire? raced through Frank's mind.

The frenzy seemed to last an eternity. When it finally came to an end, it left nine badly burned Marines laid out on ponchos in the sand. None had any hair, eyelashes or eyebrows left -- their hair had just burned away. Gone! Some were blind because their eyes had burned out. Empty eye sockets were all that remained where once bright, blue and brown eyes had been. The sight and smell made the 2nd Platoon Marines vomit.

Doc McKay struggled to control himself as he worked on one of the really badly wounded who was unmercifully left alive. The man's flesh on his face was burned away and he snapped his exposed teeth at the corpsman, like an injured dog, until Doc pumped the burned Marine full of morphine.

Medevac choppers flew in, and their rotors threw up a sand storm that tore at the wounded making their screams and howls raise to a new crescendo. The Marines loaded their Brothers on the choppers as gently as possible. The birds lifted off and flew away, back to the field hospital at Dong Ha.

LT called in artillery on what remained of the NVA position, but the frontal assault on the NVA position was called off. As the sun began to set, the surviving Marines saddled up and began the march back to Charlie-4. Frank staggered in a daze, unable to comprehend what he had just lived through, and the horrible wounds his fellow Marines had suffered.

Mail

Two weeks passed, and the 2nd Platoon Marines began to recover from the horrific tragedy north of the Blue Pagoda. The Skipper talked to the troops, and he did his best to answer the question of how "friendly fire" could cost the Marines so dearly. There really wasn't an answer. The 2nd Platoon Marines spent time talking and mourning among themselves. LT and Sergeant DI had the good sense to leave the survivors alone for a while -- until it was 2nd Platoon's turn to patrol the TAOR again.

Dear Mother, How are you doing? Well I hope you are well. How is Tammy? Have you seen Fred, Will and Rusty? I hope they stop by to visit.

Are Sean and Kevin going to make it home for Christmas? Please enjoy the holiday and don't worry about me. We are still in a very safe place, and the NVA are way off to the north. In case you see news reports, we had a very tough battle the other day and somehow the Air Force missed their target and hit some of the Marines in my Platoon. I am fine, but we suffered some casualties. Friendly fire accidents are very rare, so I don't expect it to happen again. I just wanted to let you know I am fine in case you saw it reported in the news. There will be a Christmas cease-fire so everyone is looking forward to getting some sleep. And maybe the mail will bring some good stuff from home. Take care and don't worry. I'm fine. All my love to you, Sean and Kevin. Merry Christmas. Frank.

Christmas Eve 1967

With Christmas only a few days away, Frank and Mike took their turns standing night watch. But in the quiet of the night, Frank couldn't get the horror of the napalming out of his mind. He kept thinking, *we marched north. We attacked the enemy. Jonesy gets wasted. We called in air strikes. What went wrong? What the hell went wrong?* He had to stop thinking about it because none of it made sense. But Frank was sure of one thing: he and his buddies were grateful that they had survived.

On Christmas Eve, resupply choppers brought boxes of presents and letters from home. Ken got a special Christmas gift. Doc happened to see Ken when he was taking a crap on a nearby sand dune. Doc couldn't help but notice that Ken's rectum was eaten raw by, what Doc surmised, were worms. Everyone had been drinking water from shell craters since that was the only water available. Obviously, Ken drank some worm-infested water, and the worms took up residence in his intestines.

Ken was put on a medevac chopper that very day and went to the hospital in Da Nang for treatment. He never returned to Charlie Company, and ended up getting to go back to the States early -- very early, the lucky bastard!

"Damn! Great stuff!" Mike yelled as he ripped open a box. "A plastic jug filled with Jack Daniels!"

"No shit man!" Frank, Jim and Doc laughed as they dug into their care packages from home. They sat behind the lines in a candle lit bunker near the command post, sharing their packages. That night, they didn't have to stand watch in the lines.

"Don't open the booze now, Mike," Frank said. "We'll have a Christmas party tonight. Whata ya say? I got a canned ham, two cans of peaches, and Jim got some good shit too. Hey, Jim, what all did ya get?"

"Three Jiffy Pop packages and some canned nuts."

"Glad ya finally got some nuts." Mike said. They all laughed and dug deeper in the boxes.

"Scotch! I got a fifth of scotch!" Doc whooped.

Cans of Vienna sausage, Sloppy Joes, spaghetti and meatballs, spam, Jiffy Pops, nuts, booze and fruit began stacking up. Frank thought, *these were morsels from "the world" -- cans and bags that had once been at home in dry, warm, safe places.* They chain smoked cigarettes, drank, told dirty jokes and laughed.

They all fought to control the pain in their chest -- homesickness. They tried not to think about how far, how unbelievably far away, home really was. Each of them had a family celebrating Christmas together back home. But that was okay. The Marines had each other. And for them, that was family enough.

At midnight, the men wished the company commander "Merry Christmas" by putting on a first class fireworks display. Flares, rockets, illumination grenades, and countless rounds of ammunition were shot up into the pitch-black sky. It was Christmas Eve 1967.

In the morning, Frank, Mike and Jim suffered with what they believed to be "terminal" hangovers. They had roaring headaches, stomachs were turned upside down, and each had a rancid taste in his mouth. It was almost noon before they were able to move. Each made countless trips to the latrines and most threw up multiple times. But they were able to sing their Christmas carol:

> *Jingle bells. Arty shells. VC in the grass.*
> *Take your merry Christmas,*
> *And shove it up your ass!*

CHAPTER XIII – AT THE TIP OF THE SPEAR

The opposite of fear in battle is love.

Dienekes, a Spartan Warrior before the Battle at Thermopylae

Tet 1968, "The Year of the Monkey"

By early January 1968, General Giap had completed his preparation for his Tet Offensive by moving over 70,000 NVA and VC soldiers into position to attack 100 cities and bases across South Vietnam. The North Vietnamese leadership believed that a decisive blow in South Vietnam would lead to a collapse of the government and an uprising of the South Vietnamese people.

The 320th NVA Division, including the K-400 Main Force Battalion, was assigned to attack across the DMZ on Eastern and Central Quang Tri Province. By mid-January, a company from the K-400 Battalion had moved into carefully camouflaged positions just north of Charlie-4.

The estimated three hundred to four hundred NVA regular soldiers were now within striking distance of both Charlie-4 and Cau Viet, the critical Marine Corps supply, communications and transportation base located at the mouth of the Cau Viet River. The green clad NVA soldiers dug defensive positions, hid from the aerial reconnaissance, avoided Marine patrols, and waited.

Marine Intelligence, which the grunts considered an oxymoron, had reported that they believed an NVA unit was moving south along the coast. For once, Intelligence was right, and *Operation Napoleon* was launched to provide security along the Cua Viet River.

FNGs

At Charlie-4, the 1968 New Year came and passed almost unnoticed, and without fanfare. The battle at the Blue Pagoda and the "friendly fire" napalm attack had taken something out of the men of Charlie Company. They didn't talk much, especially about that day. Intelligence reports said the NVA had been badly mauled, but no casualty figures were available. The NVA were known to pick up their dead and wounded before pulling back, and by now they were across the DMZ regrouping.

The daily drudgery of life at Charlie-4 continued with little change in the monotonous routine. Reinforced platoon size patrols constantly scoured the countryside, but the NVA seemed to have vanished. 2nd Platoon ran patrols every fourth day. And each time, their caution and anticipation increased. As each day passed, the men knew that contact with the enemy became more likely.

Sims finally caught Frank and the others sleeping during the day while burning "shitters," and he ruined their game by ordering them out on the working parties filling sand bags and reinforcing bunkers. Charlie-4's fortification was never finished, and the bunkers were never strong enough to suit the officers and NCOs.

The first week in January saw fresh replacements arrive, bringing the platoon's troop strength to forty-seven men. Frank's fire team had two new privates who had joined the Marine Corps six months ago, straight out of high school, on the buddy program. They were from Oregon, and somehow stayed together through boot camp, infantry training, staging, and then ended up in the same platoon in Nam. Both were named Bill.

One was Bill Hamby and the other was Bill Lester. Hamby was taller than Lester, so they earned the nicknames "Big Bill" and "Little Bill." You could still smell the fabric of their new jungle utilities. Now the fire team had two Mikes, two Bills, a Jim and one Frank. The two Mikes, Morgan and Thompson, were Salts since they had survived in-country for over 3 months. And Frank's in-country time was about to provide him with his own "Salt" status. Hamby and Lester were now the Platoon's two new FNGs.

Mail

It was near the middle of January 1968 when choppers flew in with fresh supplies and mail, which brightened everyone's day. Frank received two letters, one from his mother and another from his friend, Rusty.

Dear Son, we received your letter yesterday. It was covered with mud and your brother Sean said that you were obviously out in the jungle somewhere.

Warm socks and food is on the way and other packages will follow. Everything is fine at home, but we all worry about you constantly. Please take care of yourself. You are always in our prayers. Love, Mother

Frank folded the letter and put it in an ammo box built into the wall of his bunker. He never carried letters outside the perimeter because if he got killed, he didn't want the NVA to find a letter from home and start writing to his mother. It had been known to happen.

Dear Frank, married life sucks, and don't ever let anybody tell you it doesn't! I never realized how good I had it when I was single. Cindy's three months pregnant, and I've got to work two jobs and try to go to school at the same time. I barely have time to sleep, and money's always tight. I got thrown out of my fraternity because I couldn't pay my dues. Really pissed me off. How are things with you? Okay, I hope. You only got about eight more months to go before you come home, don't you? It will be good to see you again. We'll go out and get blitzed, whether Cindy likes it or not. Gotta go. Take care, Rusty

Extend the TAOR North

On January 18, it was 2nd Platoon's turn to patrol north of Charlie-4. They were ordered to expand the TAOR beyond the Blue Pagoda and "recon" the broken tree lines, worn out rice paddies, and sandy open areas north of their usual patrol route. "Recon" for Marine Intelligence meant grunts would patrol in a certain direction until they made contact with the enemy. Then the Intelligence guys would know if they were right!

"It's our turn to go out again today, isn't it?" Frank asked, trying to forget about home.

"Yeah, we're movin' out just before noon. 1st Platoon will be comin' back."

"I hope this one is just another quiet walk in the sun."

"I doubt it," Mike answered. "I heard Sims and Sergeant DI talkin' a little while ago about us pushin' the patrol route north." Mike was convinced that LT and Sergeant DI would get Marines killed or wounded.

When 2nd Platoon left the Sandcastle, Frank was point and he headed east, toward the ocean, crossing the now familiar sand dunes. The sun was high, and it beat down on them as they waded through small pools of water left by high tide. He swung north and walked cautiously through the tree lines until he reached an inlet, called Sea View, where he turned west.

The farther north he went, the more cautious he became. Frank knew that being familiar with an area caused carelessness and that was dangerous. Early in the afternoon, the Platoon stopped for a break. It was anticipated that 2nd Platoon would make contact with 1st Platoon's point element very soon.

As they moved forward, Frank tensed and raised his rifle, flipping the safety off as he squinted and looked at a tree line fifty meters to their front. Mike followed Frank's stare, and they both froze in place. A figure wearing a camouflage helmet was slipping from tree to tree. He appeared to be looking south, toward the tree line where Frank and Mike were positioned. They could see other troops following the leader. Frank breathed a sigh of relief when he recognized that it was 1st Platoon's point.

2nd Platoon moved out again, passing the 1st Platoon troops on their way back to Charlie-4. Their patrol had been uneventful, and the men stepped lively as they headed back to the safety of the bunker complex. Frank prayed that he and his buddies would follow their example tomorrow afternoon.

They passed the demolished Blue Pagoda, where the ground was chewed up from the artillery and bombs that had fallen three weeks earlier. The area still smelled of napalm, and the Platoon moved cautiously as they circled around the battlefield. West of the Pagoda, they marched through intersecting tree lines, where they would set up for the night in an "ambush" formation. But for now, they kept marching farther west, to the outer limit of the patrol route.

It was quiet, nothing moved, and the utter silence was eerie. At dusk, the Platoon backtracked to the intersecting tree line and quietly set up in the "L-shaped" ambush formation with the machine guns carefully positioned at the intersection of the "L", giving them the best field of fire. Tactics for triggering an ambush called for everyone to throw grenades first, then open fire with automatic weapons. The goal was to create confusion among the enemy soldiers while inflicting maximum casualties as quickly as possible.

As night fell across the forty-seven men, no one moved or made a sound. Throughout the night, they followed the usual routine of one man sleeping while the other watched. The moon was full, and it shone brightly on the white sand to their front. Frank stood his watches and thought of home. He sang favorite songs to himself, listened to the wind, watched the stars, and waited. It was quiet.

Frank had the last watch of the night while Mike lay asleep nearby. The night was cold and damp, with dawn still a few hours away. Standing watch at night, with a full moon, in enemy territory, increased the senses of sight, hearing, smell, and that "sixth sense" that somehow alerted Marines to danger.

Vietnam and everything about it stank. A Marine's sense of smell was vitally important -- it was easy to make out the odor of Americans with their diet and the smell of their sweat versus the telltale fishy smell of the NVAs and VCs. All grunts knew that you could smell the enemy before actually making contact.

Frank's hearing was "turned up" to its highest volume. It is next to impossible to move around in the pitch black without making some type of noise or sound. It also was important for Frank and everyone else on the patrol to remember where your fellow Marines were located at dusk so you didn't mistake a "friendly" sound of movement for that of an enemy soldier.

Even with the NVA he knew was nearby, Frank still

struggled to stay awake, and he fought the urge to close his eyes, layback, and fall into a much-needed deep sleep. Frank had a routine he used to keep awake. He tried to remember and recite to himself the lines of *The Desiderata*, a philosophy of life poem that his oldest brother Sean had given him before he left for Vietnam. The first lines were easy to remember and made Frank smile: *Go placidly amid the noise and haste, and remember what peace there may be in silence.* What Frank wouldn't give for a little peace and silence? He spent the hour before dawn saying his prayers.

There is no way to understand how men, just before a battle, instinctively know that something really bad is going to happen. Many of Frank's buddies that had been wounded told him that somehow they knew in advance when they were going to get hit. In a firefight, the life expectancy of a Marine walking point was measured in seconds.

Today, Frank had that feeling. Somehow, he knew that he would be either wounded or killed that day. He said a silent prayer: *Dear God. Give me strength and courage to fight and do my duty. I can't let my buddies down, so please help me. If I die, make it quick. If I'm wounded, please don't let it be too bad.* For Frank, knowing that the next day he would be tested brought a certain calm, a sense of inevitability. He was at peace with himself, considering where he was, and what the dawn would bring.

19 January 1968

The time was 0530, and only the stars were left to light the night. Frank gently shook Mike's foot, and he sat up instantly and reached for his weapon. Mike's tension passed when he realized it was Frank touching his leg. Sims crawled along the line of Marine position and whispered that they were going to saddle-up and move out in ten minutes. "We're getting ready to go," Frank whispered.

"Shit," Mike spat. "I just laid down." The two quietly gathered their equipment, locked and loaded their M-16s, and cautiously moved over to where the Platoon was forming up. It was early dawn, and Frank could barely make out the images of the other Marines in his Platoon. They were gathered together in small groups of fire teams and squads, preparing to move out. Frank and Mike joined the other members of their fire team, and Frank whispered to McKay, the new corpsman, "Hey Doc, when I get hit today and you hear me calling, coming running as fast as you can."

McKay smiled and nodded his head, "Sure."

Frank and Mike took their usual position at the head of the column. And as they moved out, Frank prayed softly to himself, *Our Father, who art in heaven, hallowed be thy name, thy kingdom come, thy will be done….*

"Thompson! You and your fire team go across first. Take a radio with you, and give us an 'all clear' after you've checked out the tree line!" Sergeant DI whispered in a raspy, shaking voice.

A fifty-meter wide-open sandy stretch of terrain lay north of the tree line. The plan called for the Platoon to cross the open area just before dawn. The soft grey light would allow the Marines to move inside the opposite tree line, and set up another ambush site. They would then hide and wait for the enemy to spring the ambush.

They crawled out of the cover of the trees and into the sand, moving on line. Mike was on Frank's right, followed by Jim, Doc and the radioman. The trees were blacker than the gray dawn, and grew more ominous looking the closer the men crept through the sand toward them. Frank's head began to feel light and his mouth dry. Adrenaline shot up his spine to the base of his skull. As he reached the trees and crawled into the darkness they created, he tightened his grip on his rifle. Ten minutes later, when the entire fire team reached the safety of the tree line, everyone breathed a collective sigh of relief.

The fire team followed Frank a few meters into the trees and, for a moment, no one moved. They crouched behind the trees, looking and listening for any sound or movement by NVA troops before the fire team began moving farther into the tree line. They then slowly fanned out, checking carefully for any sign of the enemy. They found nothing. Thompson radioed LT and advised him that it was "all clear".

2nd Platoon crossed the open area one fire team at a time, with each fire team melting noiselessly into the dark woods. They spread out to the left and right of Frank's fire team. Sergeant DI took third squad further into the woods on a recon patrol trying to locate a suitable ambush site, while Frank waited with the rest of the Platoon.

Sergeant DI and 3rd Squad had been gone only a few minutes and had moved only about fifty meters north, when the sky erupted into bursts of automatic weapons fire, and grenades exploding all around them. Men screamed and cursed as they dove for cover and began to return fire. Frank and the rest of the Platoon could hear the sounds of the firefight rise and fall in the familiar cadence of men shooting and then pausing to change magazines. It was the unmistakable "POP-POP-POP-POP-POP" sound of AK47s and the "RRRIIIIPPPPP" sound of M16s that create the cadence of a firefight. There were many more AK47s firing than M16s.

"Oh, shit! 3rd Squad ran right into Charlie!" Frank whispered through clenched teeth.

"I knew it, goddamn it! I fuckin' knew they were there!" Mike answered.

"Wonder how many there are?" Jim asked no one in particular.

Frank was close enough to the LT to hear the radio traffic. He heard Sergeant Wright yelling, "We're hit! We're hit! They're all around us! I've got two men hit, and they're layin' out in the open where we can't get to 'em! We're pinned down! We're pinned down! We need help!"

Shaken, LT radioed Captain Olsen back at Charlie-4 for instructions.

"Candy Tough Charlie! Candy Tough Charlie!" (This was the company commander's radio call sign.)

"This is Charlie Two! Charlie Two! Over."

"Go Charlie Two! This is Candy Tough Actual! Over." The term "actual" meant the Charlie Company Commander was speaking directly with LT.

LT reported, "We're hit! One squad went out on a recon patrol, and they got hit! They have wounded to our front that we can't get to. We're pinned down! What do we do? What do we do? Over."

"You get the rest of your people up there and get those wounded Marines back, goddamnit! Regroup and assault the enemy! Do it now!" ordered the Company Commander.

A damp, light fog hugged the ground, and the firing from the ambushed squad became sporadic. The wounded men, lying in the open, could be heard cursing and calling for help.

Frank felt light headed. He knew he and 2nd squad would be in the firefight next. The premonition of being killed or wounded almost overwhelmed him, but his heart pumped strength back into his body. He tensed and felt his entire being coil like a tightly wound spring. He could smell the damp woods mixed with the acid odor of gunpowder and explosives, and see a lot of bright muzzle flashes. *The enemy was close -- very close! There were a lot of NVA, and they were only a few meters away.*

Sims dropped down next to Jim and gave them details of the plan. "Okay, we're going to move out in a 'staggered column' formation," he said, excitedly. Sims was gasping for air. "We'll head straight toward 3rd Squad."

"Hold it, Sims," Jim interrupted. "We can't go up there in a staggered column. It'd be too easy for Charlie to ambush us. We oughtta to spread out in an "on Line" formation and assault into the fuckin' area! Whose dumb shit idea was it to move out in a staggered column?"

"Shut up, Thompson! You are as bad as Foreman. We're not going to argue! LT said we'll move out in a staggered column, and that's what you are going to do!"

"He doesn't know 'Shit from Shinola'! He hasn't been in country but a few weeks, and we're gonna get our asses blown off because of that dumb shit!"

The firing, only a few meters away, rose into another crescendo, and more screams were heard.

"It's stupid Jim," Mike said, "but we gotta get up there. We gotta move, now!"

"Frank, you take the point," Sims continued. "I'll be right behind you with the radio and a weapons team. The rest of the Platoon will be spread out behind us. Any questions?"

Frank and the others looked at each other, and shrugged their shoulders. Everyone shook their heads in the affirmative.

It had become easier to see in the morning haze in the twenty minutes that had elapsed since 3rd Squad made contact. Trees and bushes were more prominent, and the muzzle flashes ahead were clearly visible.

Frank crouched and crept forward, and the other men followed. Jim was a few feet behind him, with Mike, Doc and the two FNGs, Big Bill and Little Bill. Sims was eighth in the column, and they all moved cautiously from tree to tree.

Frank had only gone a few yards when the trees gave way to another open area, an old Vietnamese cemetery covered with mounds of earth. It looked like a field of oversize molehills. From where Frank stood, it was about twenty meters to the other side, and the cemetery was about thirty-five meters wide. Trees bordered each side of the graveyard. Frank stopped to reconnoiter the open area, and he called Sims forward. The shooting on the other side stopped and then started again.

"I'm gonna go around to the left, and keep out of the open," Frank said.

"No, you're not! We gotta get across now! Take your fire team across first, and we'll follow!" Sims spat.

"Listen, you dumb son of a bitch," Frank yelled in a low, harsh voice, "the goddamn NVA are waiting on the other side, and they're probably in the tree line on both flanks waiting for us to do something just that stupid!"

"O'Brian, you better shut your goddamn mouth and do what you're told. There's plenty of cover out there behind the burial mounds. Now move!" Sims shouted.

Frank looked across to Jim, Mike and Doc. They were squatting behind a fallen tree trunk next to Sims. Frank said, "We're wasting time arguing while 3rd Squad is pinned down on the other side, and wounded Marines are laying in the open needing help. Come on! We have to move!"

Frank and the fire team slipped out of the trees and started across the cemetery. It was light enough for them to see the trees on other side, but it was still hazy with a damp fog hugging the ground. Frank walked in a half crouch, taking a few steps, then stopping to look around and listen. The firing had stopped, and the only sound was an occasional groan or moan from the wounded. Frank's mind raced with the thought, *is that coming from wounded Marines or the NVA?*

With each step, Frank could hear his heart pounding in his chest. He was sweating in the chilled morning air. Beads of sweat poured down his face and back making him shiver. Nothing moved, and the stillness was deafening. Halfway across, he stopped and motioned for everyone to get down. He and Jim took cover behind one of the burial mounds, and Mike, Doc and the FNGs dropped behind another.

"I can feel the sons of bitches all around us, but I can't see them," Frank whispered.

"Yeah they're here. I can smell them!" Mike answered. The pungent smell of oriental sweat gave a remarkably strong, easy to detect, odor.

Frank and Mike got back up into a crouched position and the others followed, spread out behind them. Frank's eyes constantly searched the ground around him, consciously noting places where he could dive for cover. The graveyard was pockmarked with craters from artillery shells that had fallen in the past. To his left, he saw a row of burial mounds. Another blown down tree lay on the ground, and a shell hole was just to his left. His trained eyes moved from left to right, searching the woods that were now less than ten meters in front of him.

He moved forward, taking short steps almost in slow motion. His rifle was aimed straight ahead, safety off, and the selector switch on "full automatic." Out of the corner of his eye, he saw the unmistakable profile of a NVA soldier standing motionless, pressed against a tree.

Frank could see his distinct combat helmet. And for just a second, he thought the NVA soldier was standing next to the tree taking a piss. But then Frank realized that the NVA soldier, now only within five meters of Frank, was holding an AK-47 rifle that was pointed right at Frank. He was just waiting there, not moving a muscle. Frank pretended not to see him, and thought, *God help me!*

Frank didn't bother to raise his rifle to his shoulder to aim. He just swung it in the direction of the NVA soldier and squeezed the trigger. The full automatic burst of bullets pounded into the NVA soldier's chest, punching holes across the front of his uniform and throwing him backwards into the bushes. Frank was grateful that his M-16 hadn't jammed on him.

Instantly, gunfire erupted all around the cemetery as the other NVA soldiers opened fire. The distinct staccato "pop-pop-pop" rhythm of a lot of AK-47s firing together sent bullets ripping through the air. Frank thought it was like firecrackers going off on each side of his head.

Frank dove to the left trying to take cover in a shell hole, but instead of landing inside the shell crater, he crashed to the ground on top of its outer rim. He was exposed to enemy fire, and bullets were chewing up the dirt all around him. Frank rolled backward into the hole as if he had been hit.

Finding cover behind a row of graves, Mike, Jim, and the others fell to the ground. A blown down tree separated Frank from the other members of his fire team. Curled up in the shell hole, Frank checked to make sure he wasn't hit. He thought, *Holy shit! They're trying to kill me. These assholes really are trying to kill me.* Somehow, this was a shock to Frank.

The noise was deafening as the NVA continued to fire and the Marines answered with bursts from their automatic weapons. The NVA must have thought Frank was dead or severely wounded because they had stopped firing in his direction and focused their fire on the rest of the Platoon.

Frank took off his helmet and slowly raised his head just above the edge of the crater to look around. He was close enough to see several NVAs less than fifteen meters in front of him, lying on the ground and firing at 2nd Platoon. Farther to the right, near the corner of the cemetery, a NVA machinegun team poured a constant stream of fire into the Marines who had taken cover behind the burial mounds.

The NVA gunner swept his weapon back and forth, squeezing off short, disciplined bursts while his assistant gunner fed a belt of ammunition into the machinegun. They were clearly visible to Frank, and he could see they were only partially shielded by the trees and bushes.

Shit! Bastards! Sons of bitches! The fact that Frank would have to expose himself to enemy fire in order to shoot at them also came as a shock. But his training kicked in. He ejected the spent magazine from his M-16, slapped in a fresh one, and checked to make sure his weapon was on "full automatic."

Frank hesitated and prayed, *help me God!* Then he got up on his knees, snapped his rifle into his shoulder, and squeezed off a full automatic bust directly into the machinegun position. The assistant gunner dropped the belt of ammunition and jerked convulsively as the rounds ripped into his side. The gunner began to swing toward Frank, but it was too late. His mouth opened to scream, but a round from Frank's M-16 hit him in his face. Frank's rounds also hit the machinegun. It flew up into the air and fell harmlessly to the ground, resting on its' side.

The earth and sky around Frank suddenly burst into a blaze of return fire from the other NVA who had seen him fire on the machinegun team. Frank fell back into the hole and ducked down as chunks of dirt flew into the air and rained down on him. Now the NVA were again concentrating their fire on Frank, and he thought, *they're going to kill me. They're going to kill me.* Hugging the bottom of the shell hole, he prayed. He could hear screams of the wounded, both Marines and NVA, and the ear-splitting sounds of battle spread across the graveyard.

"Frank! Frank!" Jim screamed over the din. "Can you move? Can you move?"

"Hell, no! I can't move! They got me pinned down!"

"We're gonna open up to cover you," Jim screamed. "Get your ass back here when we open fire!"

Frank slapped in a fresh magazine, and put his helmet back on. *Jesus! They're gonna get me this time! Christ!*

Jim, Mike, Doc, and the two Bills all opened up simultaneously, laying down a wicked stream of fire on the NVA position. Frank bolted from the safety of his crater.

He had taken only a few steps toward a blown down tree when, behind him, an explosion erupted and the concussion slammed into his back. He was thrown up in the air, and his helmet was blown off. Frank saw, as if in slow motion, his helmet flying forward, landing several feet from him. He took two steps in midair before his boots hit the ground, and he continued running.

His flak jacket was riddled with shrapnel from the explosion of a Chicom hand grenade that the NVA had thrown into his shell hole. If Frank had remained in the crater, he would be dead. Luckily, Chicoms are more concussion than deadly shrapnel. And the shape of the shell hole where Frank had taken cover caused the blast to blow up and out, hitting him in the back of his flak jacket and helmet.

Bullets continued to pop, crack and rip past him as he dove over the fallen log, landing on his chest. He crawled behind a burial mound to join his buddies. "The bastards are all over the place!" Frank gasped. "Anybody hit?"

"No, by some miracle," Mike answered.

"We're in the kill zone. We gotta get out of here and back to the tree line," Jim screamed.

"Where the hell is Sims and the others?" Frank asked.

"They took cover back in the tree line behind us," Mike growled.

"Okay, let's do it this way," Jim shouted over the roar. Frank, you stay with me. We'll give Mike, Doc and the new guys covering fire, while they pull back about half way to the tree line. Mike, then you give Frank and me covering fire when we pull back." He was breathing hard and his face was covered with dirt and sweat. "We'll fire and maneuver until we get outta the cross fire."

Mike and the others crouched and got ready to run. Jim and Frank crawled up to the top of the burial mound.

As the NVA firing let up slightly, Jim yelled, "Now! Move! Move!"

Jim and Frank opened up on the NVA positions while the others sprinted, zigzagging as they ran, toward a row of burial mounds half way back to the tree line. The NVA tried to follow them with streams of fire, but the covering fire from Jim and Frank forced the enemy to take cover.

"Come on! Get back here!" Mike screamed. They had taken cover about ten meters behind Jim and Frank.

"Okay! Let's go!" Jim yelled to Frank.

Frank slammed in another fresh magazine, and he and Jim sprinted across the graveyard. The NVA opened up, but so did Mike, Doc and the FNGs. Jim and Frank dove behind the mound and landed next to Mike and Doc. They immediately turned and began firing back at the NVA. By now, the NVA were shooting at the fire team from three sides: the front, and at a slight angle on their right and left. The Marines were still in the kill zone.

Twenty meters behind them, Sims waited with the rest of the Platoon in the woods.

For now, Sergeant DI and 3rd Squad, who had been pinned down on the other side of the graveyard, were forgotten. There was no sign of LT.

"Mike, you go with Doc and move back again," Jim shouted. "Try to get as close to the tree line as ya can!"

Again, Jim and Frank provided covering fire into the woods while Mike, Doc, Big Bill and Little Bill jumped up and began moving toward the woods. But as they stood to make their break, both the Bills suddenly began to jerk, dance, stumble, and then fell.

"I'm hit! I'm hit! Oh, God, I'm hit," mumbled Big Bill. Blood poured down his face from a bullet through his cheek, and two more rounds had torn open his right arm and right leg. Little Bill was hit in both legs, and he began screaming at the top of his lungs, "Maamma! Maamma!"

The two lay in a crumpled heap just behind Frank, Jim, Mike and Doc. Doc grabbed his Unit One medical bag, turned and dove to the ground next to the two wounded Marines. Landing next to Little Bill, Doc rolled him on his back and began to work on his legs. He'd taken two rounds to his right leg, one above and one below the knee. His leg was shattered, and he was bleeding badly.

Doc then moved over to work on Big Bill. Doc took out a gauze dressing, pressed it against Big Bill's face, and then secured it in place by wrapped it around his head. Doc then cut open Big Bill's shirt and trousers, exposing two gaping gunshot wounds. Doc tied tourniquets on both the arm and the leg in an effort to stop the blood hemorrhaging from the wounds, and then used a field dressing to cover the wounds.

"We can't move them! We can't move them!" Doc screamed over his shoulder as he worked on the two wounded Marines.

Jim, Frank and Mike huddled behind a burial mound, looking back at Doc and the two wounded new guys. Doc was shooting morphine into both of them.

"Guess we oughtta stay a while," Jim said in a resigned voice. The three looked at each other, shrugged their shoulders, and nodded their heads in agreement. The safety of the tree line seemed so, so close. But they knew they would never reach it carrying their two wounded Marines.

The NVA continued concentrating heavy automatic weapons fire at their position. Jim, Frank and Mike were kneeling behind the burial mound, crouched shoulder-to-shoulder, returning fire. Mike was on Frank's left and Jim on the right. Doc continued to work on the wounded a few feet behind them. The shooting rose and fell, as the Marines and NVA fired back and forth. Bullets pounded the ground and popped and cracked through the air as the deadly exchange continued. For a moment, it looked like a standoff.

A shrill, ear-splitting scream pierced the morning light. And out of the woods came three or four NVA soldiers charging across the cemetery toward the Marine's position. Frank saw that one of the NVA had an SKS assault rifle with the fold-down bayonet extended. "Oh, shit! Here they come! Here they come!" Mike yelled.

They held their fire until the enemy soldiers were only about fifteen meters away. Then Jim, Frank, Mike and Doc rose up above the burial mound and opened fire. They swung their M-16s back and forth on "full automatic", spraying the NVA soldiers as they ran toward them. The high-pitched screams of the NVA soldiers became almost deafening as they closed in on Frank's position.

Jim, Frank, Mike and Doc were on their knees firing when Frank saw Mike suddenly shudder, drop his weapon, and fall forward. Frank dropped his empty rifle and reached for Mike. He rolled Mike over on his back and looked into his eyes. All Frank could see was Mike's expression of complete and total surprise.

"Mike! Mike! Where are you hit? Where are you hit?" Frank's voice cracked as he saw the jagged line of holes running from one side of Mike's chest to the other.

Mike blinked his eyes and the surprised look went away -- replaced by terror.

"All over. Hit all over!"

Frank held Mike's gaze as tears rolled out of the corner of Mike's eyes, washing days of dirt off his face, as gasps of air escaped from his open mouth. Mike's bullet riddled lungs could no longer hold air, and his shattered heart couldn't pump life's blood through his veins. Frank fell forward crying, holding his friend in his arms and begging him not to die.

"Noooo! God. Noooo! Not Miiiiiike!"

Frank held Mike and begged him not to die. But just then, Jim and Doc began screaming at Frank to take cover because more NVA soldiers were charging toward them. Frank quickly pulled Mike's lifeless body down behind the burial mound where his body would not be exposed to more gunfire. Frank tried to make him comfortable. He didn't want his friend to get hurt, anymore.

Frank picked up his M-16, made an animal sound, and began to methodically open fire at the charging NVA soldiers. Suddenly, Frank felt a sledgehammer smash into his right shoulder -- an AK-47 round ripped through his flak jacket, and the force of the bullet flipped him backwards on to his back. Frank gazed up at the clear blue sky, listening to the screams around him and thinking, *Oh, my God! I'm hit!*

Frank looked at his right arm and tried to lift it, but it wouldn't move. He pushed himself back up on his knees and saw that his right arm was dangling, uselessly, at his side. He could see blood streaming down his arm, soaking his jungle utility jacket. The blood trickled off his fingertips and spilled on the ground, absorbed quickly into the sand.

The initial searing pain subsided, but his body was slowly going into shock. Frank now believed they were going to be overrun by the NVA soldiers, and he and all of the Marines were going to die in this Vietnamese cemetery. At that moment, Frank suddenly resigned himself to the fact that he was going to die, and almost felt relieved – he was experiencing a strange sense of freedom, and everything around him became very clear.

Frank reached for his rifle with his left hand in what seemed like slow motion. He propped up the M-16 on the top of the burial mound, steadied the weapon as best he could with one hand, pulled the trigger and began firing. The charging NVA soldiers were now right on top of them when suddenly, Frank's M-16 stopped firing. He thought, *It's jammed! The son of a bitch's jammed!*

Frantically, Frank rolled over on his back, held the rifle between his knees and tried to clear the jammed shell with his left hand. He jerked the charging handle backward trying to eject the jammed shell. But he couldn't clear the chamber. *Oh, Jesus! Please, God, let me clear it! Let me clear it!*

Jim and Doc were both changing magazines when

the last NVA soldier ran up to within a few meters of them. The NVA soldier stood on top of the burial mound and, in a split second, he emptied a full magazine into all five of the Marines. It seemed like his firing lasted forever, and Frank kept praying, *God! Make it stop! Make it stop!*

Jim screamed as one bullet ripped into the top of his left shoulder, near the collarbone. Doc couldn't scream: one round tore through the left side of his throat, another hit him in the right forearm, and two more smashed his left leg. Jim called out to God.

Mike shuddered silently as several more rounds pounded his dead body. Frank lay on his back looking over his left shoulder at the NVA soldier when he suddenly felt a spike being driven through his left foot. Frank silently screamed, "Oh, God, not my foot! Oh, God, no!" He looked down and saw his leg bounce into the air.

The muzzle of the AK-47 was smoking as the NVA soldier knelt down and looked at the dead and wounded Marines laying in front of him. He looked very young -- probably a teenager, Frank thought. He wore a blue t-shirt under his olive green field uniform. He stared at Frank and laughed at Frank's frantic attempts to clear his jammed rifle.

No one else moved, and Frank knew he and all his buddies would soon be dead. He threw aside the useless rifle and reached for a grenade. The NVA soldier just stood there laughing as Frank desperately tried to straighten out the pin on the grenade with his teeth. As he worked with the grenade, Frank suddenly remembering his ITR Gunny telling them, *unlike the heroes in the movies, don't try to pull the pin with your teeth. All you will do is pull your teeth out.*

Frank screamed to himself, *Laugh you bastard! Go ahead and laugh! If I get the pin out, we'll all laugh in hell together! You son of a bitch!*

Frank flattened the end of the pin with his teeth and he began to viciously jerk on the O-ring to arm the grenade. He and the young NVA soldier stared at each other.

The NVA soldier quickly moved to change out his empty AK-47's banana magazine. As he inserted the new banana magazine into the rifle, Jim (who was slumped over next to Frank) finished reloading his M-16. Panic filled the NVA soldier's eyes as they both heard the unmistakable sound of a round being chambered in Jim's M-16.

Jim rolled over in the direction of the NVA soldier, pointed his M-16 at the soldier's face, and pulled the trigger -- full automatic. Jim's M-16 poured a bust of rounds into the young soldier's head and, in what seemed like slow motion, his head exploded, flying apart like a ripe melon. He flew backwards and his body landed next to another dead NVA soldier.

Jim dropped his rifle and looked over at Frank who was still jerking on the "O" ring of the grenade.

"Got that son of a bitch," Jim said.

"You ain't shitting," Frank answered, and then whispered a simple "Thanks." Still gripping the unarmed grenade, Frank silently mumbled a prayer, thanking God that he was still alive after all of that.

After the NVA's last assault on the Marine positions failed, the remaining soldiers gave up trying to over-run the Marine's position. They had paid a heavy price for their efforts and decided to go around the isolated pocket of resistance. Frank and Jim could see lines of enemy soldiers moving through the tree lines on either side of the cemetery. They were heading south to engage the rest of the Platoon.

Doc was bleeding to death, and Big Bill and Little Bill were both going into shock. With his one good hand, Frank worked on Doc. He was able to stop the bleeding in Doc's arms and legs by using two belts and straps used as makeshift tourniquets. Jim's wound didn't seem too bad; he was able to stop the bleeding on the two FNGs, and then gave them each a shot of morphine.

Frank saw that his shoulder wound was oozing blood, and he suddenly remembered something he had learned during boot camp: "arteries spurt blood, veins don't – they ooze blood." Realizing that the round hadn't hit an artery, Frank sighed in relief – and began to believe he wasn't going to bleed to death among the Vietnamese burial mounds. He also could see the hole in his left boot where the second bullet hit, but he couldn't tell the extent of the wound – only that it was bleeding too. Frank and Jim decided that they wouldn't take morphine because they both knew they had to stay conscious; someone had to defend their position if the NVA returned.

Jim and Frank gathered all remaining ammunition and grenades, organized themselves so they could defend the position if the NVA tried to overrun them again. Jim's M-16 looked like it might be in good working order, but they weren't sure. No way to know until they fired the weapon.

The plan was to hold out until a relief force could arrive. They took the eight grenades they had left, and Jim helped flatten and loosen the pins so it would be easy for Frank to pull the pins out, even if he had to do it with his sore teeth.

In less than thirty minutes, heavy firing erupted south of their position. As the morning sun rose in the sky, they lay quietly behind the cover of the burial mounds, watching and waiting. Swarms of flies began attacking the blood-soaked wounds of the Marines and the dead NVA in front of their position. The stench of those dead and dying bodies, the dried blood, and burned gunpowder, was overpowering.

They didn't talk much, and Frank took the opportunity to examine his wounds more carefully. His right arm and foot hurt like hell. He could see the gaping hole in the top of his boot where blood oozed out. He propped his foot on the crown of his helmet, hoping this would stop or slow the bleeding.

His right arm was useless. He couldn't move his hand. And when he tried to sit up, he had to hold his right arm with his left because the weight of the wounded arm sent intense shooting pains through his shattered shoulder. He couldn't see where the bullet had ripped through his flak jacket, but he could feel the hole with his left hand. He stuck his finger in the hole and found that the area around the entry wound was numb. Sharp, shattered bone scratched the end of his finger, and he could feel the wet warmth of the inside of his body. Not wanting to make his wounds any worse than they were, Frank decided just to leave them alone.

Mike's body lay under a poncho next to Frank. Flies tried to get to him, but Frank swatted them away. He stared at the body of his friend, trying to comprehend what had happened and thought: *Why'd you have to die, Mike? You were so alive this morning. And every other morning we lived together. You never thought it could happen to you, and I never thought it could happen to me. You were wrong. I don't know why you died and I'm still alive. If they hit you, and we were shoulder to shoulder, why did the bullets stop when they went through hitting you? They should have come right across and hit me, too. But they didn't. You died Mike and not me. What a goddamn surprise. I always knew it couldn't happen to me. I've always known that. Someone else always died, but never me. See. I'm still alive and you're dead. I'll miss you and I'll never forget you. You were the best buddy anyone ever had. God, I'm sorry you're dead. But, I gotta say, better you than me. I didn't want to die and I'm glad it wasn't me. I'm sorry Mike. So sorry!*

Frank was overcome with grief and guilt. His chest heaved, his throat burned, and he tried to choke back the sobs as tears ran down his face.

"Frank, don't cry for Mike," Jim whispered. "He's outta this shit and we're not."

"Why? Why did he have to die? Why are we alive and he's dead?" Frank softly mumbled.

"Because that's the way it was supposed to be," Jim answered. "That's just way it is."

Noon and the Relief Force

Throughout the morning, artillery and air strikes pounded the battlefield north of the Blue Pagoda. Shells slammed into the graveyard, while jets and gunships strafed back and forth killing the living and blasting the dead out of their graves. The surviving Marines hugged the ground and prayed while the carnage continued all around them.

Reinforcements from Charlie-4 and Cua Viet arrived, and they began to push back the NVA. Frank and Jim could see the enemy retreating through the tree lines shouting and running as the advancing ranks of Marines pushed forward.

One Marine machine gunner led the wave of grunts, tanks and amtracs as they charged past the Blue Pagoda, across the open space, and into the tree line. Five hours after the first contact with the NVA, Marines from Charlie Company and 1st Amtracs reached the 2nd Platoon.

"Take Mike, Frank, Doc and the two new guys out first," Jim said as Marines and corpsmen dropped down beside them.

The dead and wounded were wrapped in ponchos, and dragged, one by one, across the killing field and loaded into a waiting amtrac. NVA snipers fired at the Marines carrying Frank, and he prayed, *Not now God. Don't let me die, now! Not after all this! Please don't let me die now!*

Safely inside the amtrac, Frank looked around to make sure everyone was there. Mike, Doc, Big Bill, and Little Bill, all lay nearby, each covered by a poncho. He saw Jim loaded last. Then Frank passed out.

U.S.S. *Repose*

Marine helicopters flew the wounded from Charlie-4 to the aid station at Dong Ha where their wounds were cleaned and dressed. They were given morphine to ease the pain. A few hours after arriving at Dong Ha, another chopper picked them up and flew them to the nearby Navy hospital ship, U.S.S. *Repose*.

Frank was carried from the helicopter on a stretcher. And as he passed through the hatch leading to the emergency room, the ship's Captain was standing at the handrail on the deck above, looking down at the new arrivals. Frank could see an American flag flying in the breeze behind the skipper. The Captain stood at attention and saluted the wounded Marines as they were carried past him.

Frank was groggy and half-conscious as he was wheeled into surgery. He heard the doctors and nurses talking about the gunshot wound to his right shoulder. "Not much left to hold his arm to his body. The head of his Humerus is shot off, and the tendons and muscles of his rotator cuff are shot through. There's only skin and a few tendons holding his arm on. We may have to take it off." *Amputate my arm?* Frank was overcome with terror.

"Please don't take my arm! Please, Doc! Oh, God, don't let them take my arm!" he begged.

"Take it easy son," a doctor in a surgical mask said. His voice was soothing. "Just relax and breathe deeply now. We're going to put you to sleep for a while."

A mask was placed over Frank's nose and mouth, and someone behind him told him to count backwards from one hundred.   Instead of counting, he prayed out loud:

> *Our Father...Who art in heaven…Hallowed be Thy Name...Thy kingdom come...Thy will be done..."*

AFTERMATH

Go tell the Spartans, stranger passing by, that
Here, obedient to their laws, we lie.

In 450 BC, Herodotus wrote this message to the citizens of Sparta
about King Leonidas, leader of the 300 Spartan warriors who fought
and died at Thermopylae.

Marine intelligence was right. There had been a large NVA unit dug in and hidden just north of Charlie Company's TAOR. When 2nd Platoon extended the patrol route north, crossed the open area and crept into the tree line, they literally walked into the perimeter of some 200 NVA regulars.

The NVA 400-K Battalion had been headed south and planned to attack the Marine Base at Cua Viet on January 31, the beginning of the Tết Offensive -- a coordinated country-wide surprise attack by the VC and NVA against the U.S., ARVN and allied forces. As a result of the January 19 battle with 2nd Platoon and its relief force, there was no ground attack on either Charlie-4 or Cau Viet during the Tết Offensive.

By late afternoon on January 19, 1968, 2nd Platoon, Charlie Company, 1st Battalion, 3rd Marines ceased to exist as a fighting unit. Of the forty-seven men who fought in the battle at the Vietnamese cemetery on that day, three died and thirty-three were wounded. The enemy lost 23 confirmed killed, and they dragged off the battlefield an unknown number of dead and wounded.

Staff Sergeant Wright, and most of the Marines in the 3rd Squad who had been pinned down north of the cemetery survived, but two 3rd Squad Marines were killed and several others were wounded.

Lieutenant Newman was wounded and medevacked to the rear for treatment.

Sims was also wounded during the battle, and he was medevacked back to the US where he recovered. Later, he was discharged from the Marine Corps on disability.

A corporal from the machine gun team assigned to 2nd Platoon had taken command, while the badly outnumbered Marines maintained defensive positions until the relief force arrived.

Captain Olson, Charlie Company's CO, led the relief force to rescue 2nd Platoon and, as always, the Skipper led from the front. His heroism that day, rescuing his Marines, earned him the Silver Star.

The machine gunner that led the line of Marines charging across the open area was awarded the Silver Star for heroism.

Doc McKay was medevacked back to a Naval Hospital in the Midwest where he spent ten months recovering from his wounds. Doc was medically discharged from the Navy, attended college and taught history at a junior high school in Cleveland until he retired.

Jim spent three months recovering from his wound at the hospital in Da Nang before he was sent back to the bush. He finished his tour in Vietnam, and returned to the States where he was honorably discharged from the Corps. He returned to his family in Alabama.

Ken had been medevacked out before Christmas, so he missed the battle on January 19. His infected intestines were so damaged that he was medevacked back to the US Naval Hospital in Pensacola, FL where he received extensive medical treatment that finally cured his infection. When Ken was honorably discharged from the Marine Corps, he returned to his home in Pensacola, attended college, turned out to be a great student, and earned both an undergraduate and graduate degree with honors. Over the past 40+ years, Ken had a great career, and today is a successful entrepreneur and president of his own software company. Like many combat veterans, Ken "feels cheated" because he wasn't with his buddies on January 19th. Not so. God's will.

EPILOGUE

After Tet

Militarily, the three-month Tet Offensive in early 1968 was a complete loss for the Viet Cong and North Vietnamese. While the initial attack had taken the U.S. and ARVN forces by surprise, their sustained response resulted in a devastating defeat for the VC and NVA. The losses inflicted by the Americans crippled the VC and NVA, and proved to them that they could not conquer the South by force. However, at home in the United States, the U.S. military Tet victory was quickly turned into a "devastating defeat" for the U.S. Forces by the anti-war rhetoric from politicians, the press, "intellectuals", and TV pundits. They asserted that the Tet Offensive was proof that the U.S. could not win the war in Vietnam, and their antiwar drumbeat grew louder and louder with each passing day.

As the loss of support for the war increased in 1968 and into 1969, so did American casualties. In 1968, 16,899 American warriors died and many thousands more were wounded. From 1969 when another 11,780 died, to 1975 when the last American was killed, the casualties declined each year until all American forces were withdrawn.

From the Johnson administration to the Nixon administration, the defensive war of attrition continued. Seeing that the tide of public opinion was turning, Johnson implemented the Vietnamization program so the South Vietnamese Army would do more of the fighting and dying. American casualties began to decline but the Pentagon continued to track carefully the kill ratios.

Political leaders and civilians in the Pentagon were certain that the North Vietnamese and Viet Cong would tire of losing so many soldiers. Certainly, the experts and intellectuals thought, we can kill so many more of them while only losing a much smaller percentage of Americans and, logically, this will lead to victory. The "kill ratios" spewed from the computer programs demonstrated that this must surely be true.

By any measure, the Pentagon's defensive strategy was fatally flawed, and it eventually led to America's humiliating withdrawal from Vietnam and its first defeat in war. The sacrifices and struggles of countless warriors carrying out this strategy resulted in the deaths of the 58,318 warriors whose names are engraved on the Wall, as well as the estimated over 150,000 service members who were wounded and required hospitalization.

Jammed – Too Little, Too Late

In October 1968, while Frank, Mike and their fellow Marines along the DMZ were being constantly reminded to carefully clean their M-16 to avoid jamming, new information was being disclosed in Washington, D.C. about the real cause of the M-16 jamming.

The House Armed Services Committee, under Congressman Richard Ichord (D-Mo, 8th), Chairman of the *Special Subcommittee on the M-16*, issued its startling finding that the cause of the M-16 jamming was not troop failure to maintain clean weapons. Rather, it was the ball powder propellant of the ammunition being fired that caused the jamming!

The Committee concluded that the U.S. Army Ordnance Corps, who was ultimately responsible for developing and testing weapons for U.S. troops, had failed to properly field test the M-16 with the ammunition issued to the troops. For the troops in the field, no amount of "clean your weapons" would prevent magazines loaded with this ammunition to jam their M-16s.

As Frank and the Marines of 2nd Platoon, Charlie Company prepared to extend the TAOR north of C-4, they cleaned their weapons and prayed they would fire in combat. The NVA soldiers they would face were armed with the reliable Soviet AK-47 assault rifle.

Based on the findings of the Armed Services Committee, the U.S. Army Ordnance Corps immediately directed the ammunition manufactures to modify the powder propellant and casing of the bullets for the M-16. Unfortunately, the new ammunition was not available to Frank, Mike and the other members of the 2nd Platoon when they moved out on the morning of January 19, 1968. For them, it was too little, too late.

Welcome Home

For the Americans who fought in Vietnam and won countless battles, including Tet of 1968, the returning warriors were branded "losers". The Korean War was a draw, but Vietnam was viewed as the first U.S. military loss in the history of our country. There were no "welcome home" parades for veterans, only hostile shouts from the antiwar activists of "baby killers", "murders", "mercenaries", "killers", and "warmongers". It was a national disgrace.

Killed in Nam, Died at Home

Cancer

Many Vietnam Veterans suffer with delayed, and deadly, long-term wounds caused by exposure to Agent Orange. For years, the U.S. Government denied Agent Orange harmed Vietnam Vets, and it delayed providing medical care, or compensation for their deaths.

In 1991, almost fifteen years after the conclusion of the Vietnam War, Congress finally passed the Agent Orange Act. It gave the Department of Veterans Affairs ("VA") the authority to declare certain conditions "presumptive" to exposure to Agent Orange/dioxin, making these veterans who served in Vietnam eligible to receive treatment and compensation for these conditions.

The VA currently lists over 15 deadly diseases that are caused by Agent Orange. These "wounds of war" include many types of cancer, heart disease, Parkinson's, diabetes, neuropathy, etc. There is no doubt that after the sacrifices made by Vietnam Veterans, their lives in later years are being impacted and shortened because of Agent Orange.

If a Vietnam Veteran is diagnosed with any of the 15 diseases on the VA list, the cause of the illness is assumed to be Agent Orange exposure. And the Vet, whose life is being cut short, is awarded 100% VA disability. Depending on the Vet's family situation, he is paid between $3,197.16 and $3,458.06 per month for his chronic, often fatal, debilitating disease.

Suicide

The experience of close combat, the sounds and sights of life and death struggles, near death experiences, seeing the mutilation and death of fallen brothers, is seared in the hearts, minds and souls of all warriors. In the midst of the fighting, the door that separates life from death opens, the warrior peers through, but for reasons only God knows, it's not his time to pass through that threshold. But you see your dead buddies disappear on the other side. And there is never an answer to the mystery of why you lived and your brothers died. While you are grateful for survival, the end of battle brings a life of mystery and guilt.

Well-meaning physicians and psychiatrists decided to rename post battle conditions from previous wars – "shell shock", "the thousand-mile stare", and "battle fatigue" -- to a more clinical term: Post-Traumatic Stress Disorder (PTSD). But the traumatic scars of battle are hidden wounds – not disorders. They are no different from a gunshot wound that destroys bones and organs, or blasts that take off limbs. Post-traumatic stress inflicts severe wounds to the warrior's mind, heart and soul.

The rise in Vietnam, Iraqi and Afghanistan Veteran suicides is a crisis that has been studied and documented by the VA and several other organizations. Approximately 20 veterans die by their own hand each day – that is 7,300 each year! Thirty-one percent of these suicides are by veterans age 49 and younger, while sixty-nine percent are age 50 and older. Most are male combat veterans. While the government, family, friends and fellow Vets do their best to stop these tragic deaths, the decision to take one's own life ultimately rests with the individual suffering from these hidden traumatic combat scars.

When wounded warriors "return to the world", they experience the typical trials, disappointments, challenges and tragedies of "normal" life, like everyone else. But too often, warriors with these hidden wounds are also haunted by demons that visit in the middle of the night. They are plagued by a nagging, intermittent tug on the heart and soul that beckon the wounded warrior back to the open door to death.

Before thinking of suicide, pause to thank God for every day we live, remember that our brothers would want us to enjoy the lives they lost. Lock the terrible memories safely away in a box that is probably too dangerous to open. And regardless of what we experience now, nothing can compare to the trials we experienced and overcame in Vietnam. Keep the box locked – live.

War is a terrible experience for everyone who serves in a combat zone. The warriors who actually engaged in close combat with enemy soldiers are scarred for life. Many suffered physical wounds, but almost all have life-long mental and spiritual damage. The loss of combat brothers and the mystery of survival break their hearts. This is why, when you see TV interviews of veterans describing their combat experiences, it is not surprising that these remembrances are often accompanied with tears for the battles they fought and the buddies they lost.

The Cross of Gallantry is written for all Vietnam Veterans, and specifically the 3rd Marines Amphibious Force. It honors their sacrifices, suffering, wasted lives, and broken bodies, minds and souls – this was the price each Marine paid for fighting and winning battles in Vietnam.

Here's health to you and to our Corps
Which we are proud to serve....

ABOUT MIKE AND FRANK

Lawton, OK 1968

On a cold, rainy day toward the end of January 1968, Mike was buried with full military honors in a cemetery on the outskirts of Lawton, OK. His mother, uncles and friends wept as the Marine pallbearers folded the flag in silence.

The seven Marines in the honor guard fired three volleys. A Marine Corps bugler stood alone nearby and played *Taps*.

A young Marine Corps Lieutenant knelt down in front of Mike's Mother, presented her with the folded U.S. flag that was draped over Mike's casket, and quietly said, "On behalf of the President of the United States, the Commandant of the Marine Corps, and a grateful nation, please accept this flag as a symbol of our appreciation for your loved one's service to Country and Corps."

Cape Cod, MA 2017

And Frank -- Patrick M. Blake, the author -- spent a year in the Naval Hospital in Pensacola recovering from his wounds. He declined to accept the medical discharge offered by the Navy. He reenlisted in the Marine Corps on a medical waiver, but the waiver stipulated that he could not continue to serve in the infantry. He was given a desk job that he quickly came to hate. Over the next six years on active duty, he attended college at night and eventually retired on disability in 1975. Pat began a second career in the computer software industry, and today he is the president of his own life science software and consulting company.

Pat is writing a sequel to *The Cross of Gallantry*.

Semper Fi

Empty Boots...

By Richard Preston ~ 3/9/02
3rd Battalion, 4th Marines
Vietnam 1966-67

Walk a mile in another man's boots?
I don't think it's possible.
Yeah we have pounded the same ground.
... but each journey is different.
In Vietnam, each man walked his own destiny.
... Destiny maps out longevity.
Unlike men,
Boots were alike for sure.
Black leather
Green canvas...
Caked with red mud
... But the man,
The Soldier
... often lay Caked with red Blood.
The Warrior experiences War.
... War will suffocate the experience of life.
... Boots are removed.
The journey has ended for the man.
... Even so
... His boots remain,
Age has no effect.
... His journey continues in the hearts
Of the Brothers of war.
The boots are empty.
... But our hearts are full
We continue to walk in sorrow.
Alas, we could not walk in freedom
If not for the empty boots.